C000282804

THE MURDER OF THE MUDLARKS

MARTIN DAVEY

Copyright © 2022 by Martin Davey
All rights reserved.
No part of this book may be reproduced in any form or by any electronic
or mechanical means, including information storage and retrieval systems,
without written permission
from the author, except for the use of brief quotations in a book review.

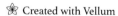 Created with Vellum

For my Family

Twenty Bridges from Tower to Kew –
    Wanted to know what the river knew,
    Twenty Bridges or twenty-two,
    For they were young, and the Thames was old
    And this is the tale that River told
    — Rudyard Kipling

CONTENTS

1

BLOOD IN THE WATER

Henry Swift Cockle was the son of His Royal Highness, the most revered and magnificent Lord of the Grey Waves, and first amongst the Mudlarks – King Walter Cockle of Albion. His had been a charmed, comfortable life up until now. He rose at whatever hour he wanted to, spent as much as he liked, and was considered to be somewhat of a waster. His hands were soft and clean, and his piercing blue eyes were bloodshot most of the time. Gaming, drinking, and wenching were his favourite pastimes. Work was what the peasants did. In short, Henry Swift Cockle was a brat, but even he, born as he was to rule and intoxicated with entitlement, did not deserve what was happening to him right now.

Henry was staggering back home when he was waylaid. At first, through eyes that were powered by brandy and rum, he thought that he had taken a bit of a tumble and that honest, caring passers-by had come to his aid. He quickly sobered up and realised that he was in danger when the four men began to beat him with their cudgels. The blows rained down, each one was well placed, on his elbows, then his knees, and finally his testicles. Henry Swift Cockle passed out, and if there had been any luck on his side, he would have stayed that way. For when he finally regained consciousness he watched as one of his attackers leaned over him and drove a large wicked-looking metal spike into his wrist.

He did not cry out or scream to the heavens for help because the pain had dissipated hours before; now all he felt was a strange sense of detachment. He was above himself; he felt as though he were floating in the air and looking down on his own battered and bloody body. The four men were busy crucifying him. They were down on the banks of the Thames under one of the bridges, in the mud, with the water rippling nearby. After a while the men left and Henry dreamed that he was piloting his boat, the good ship *Constance*, out in the channel, with his sail full of good clean air, and a white wake that stretched away to the horizon. When he looked more closely he suddenly became aware, a cruel gift indeed, and realised that he was floating away on the tide, nailed to a plank of wood, and into a darkness that he would never return from.

2

MEETING THE SNAKE

The cat's tail was swishing far too quickly. It had been a mild irritation at first, a bit of a novelty, but now it was distracting him. Flick! Flick! Flick! Back and forth like a hairy metronome. The animal was also sitting on his boardroom table! His highly polished, Scandinavian boardroom table, imported from just this side of the Arctic Circle. The website he'd bought it from hinted that it was constructed from the sinews and bark of trees that could trace their line back to Yggdrasil itself. It was very expensive and was hardly ever used as a table at all, and woe betide anyone who placed a coffee cup down on it without a coaster in place. But that was just by the by. Now, there was a cat lolling about on top of it. The cat looked as though it was about to stretch out at any second, or, horror of horrors, it might begin to wash itself.

"That would be one lick too many," thought the man.

He also wondered what was going on behind those unblinking and inquisitive eyes. Men were easy to read, they could give you their life story in a few words, but beasts, they were tricky – very tricky. He would have to focus his energies on the cat's partner instead. He cleared his throat, for dramatic effect, and drummed his fingers on the table-top. It was time to get down to the nitty gritty – this was a business meeting after all, albeit a *secret, off the books, scheduled to start promptly at midnight* sort of business meeting.

The rest of the building was empty, save for the security guards and the cleaners. Only the faint hum of an industrial strength floor polishing machine being used in the corridor outside could be heard. Or was it the cat, purring? They were supposed to sound like small refrigerators, apparently, but he'd never noticed. He didn't like animals much, and he hated snakes in particular. His first, and only experience with a reptile had been a disaster, it made him wince to think about it. But that was a long time ago – before calendars were even invented.

The digital display on the screen of his new wafer-thin mobile phone told him that it was nearly midnight. He needed his bed, so he leaned forward and rested his elbows on the table in front of him.

"Shall we begin?" said the man.

The name of the cat was Cat Tabby, and his business partner went by the name of Richard Whittington, or Dick, to his very few friends. Cat Tabby was not your run-of-the-mill cat. He could speak all the languages of the Under Folk, disappear if he chose to do so, bargain like a wizard, and was as tricky and crafty as a goblin. He was also the go-to cat for magical mediation, and a spy for the highest bidder. Dick Whittington used to be a big noise in the City. But after a few deals that weren't particularly legal and a high-profile court case, he stepped away from the City, and went back to the world he knew best, the Underworld, and his best friend – Cat Tabby. They were inseparable and as bent as a £7 note.

The man they were here to meet was a handsome chap,

with high, well-defined cheekbones and expensive skin. He was smartly dressed and wore the latest James Bond 007-inspired Omega timepiece on his wrist; in fact, it peeked out from under a Gieves and Hawkes double-cuffed shirt, like some sort of covert monitoring device, surveying the room and recording all that it saw. From their point of view, he was well dressed and quite obviously a bit of a buffoon.

"What should I call you?" asked the man with the nice watch.

"Cat Tabby is fine, and this is my associate, Mr. Whittington. You can call him Mr. Whittington. It's a pleasure to finally meet you in person. After the 75th unreturned call we were beginning to think you were avoiding us."

The cat paused and looked sideways at his associate, and Mr. Whittington shook his head. The cat looked confused for a second.

"**76** unreturned calls," said Dick Whittington.

"Right as always, Dick, my memory isn't what it used to be. Let's crack on though, I'm sure our friend here regrets every one of them."

Cat Tabby turned back to the man at the head of the table.

"We've heard a lot about your company, *First Garden Creations*, an eco-friendly land development company with a heart and an impressive bottom line, no less. We've also been impressed by what you've achieved in such a short time. You've been snaffling lots of – in our humble opinion – hard-to-acquire land, and snapping up lots of very prime real estate in our backyard – dear old London town. It has proved very easy for you, much easier than it has been for, shall we say, more experienced, and older hands. Isn't that right, Dick?"

"As usual, Cat Tabby, your paw is right on the pulse.

We'd like to know how you managed to get the Count of Chiswick to let go of those fields down by the river, and how you persuaded the Raven Coven to part with some of their woodland."

The man at the end of the table stood up, then sauntered down the room and took a seat next to Cat Tabby and Dick Whittington. He stared into their eyes, again, for dramatic effect, as if being closer would enable him to see into their souls and ascertain their thoughts and motives. Cat Tabby almost started laughing and Dick pretended to cough to disguise his amused reaction.

"So then, Mr. Whittington, and his *cat*. What can I do for you both? You seem to have done a lot of digging. Most of what you appear to know is not in the public domain so I should like to know how you came by that information."

Cat Tabby stood up on all fours and arched his back, stretching as cats are wont to do after a long slumber. His tail shot up, almost straight, and his ears flattened against his skull. Then he relaxed and sat down on his haunches, affecting the pose of an Egyptian sculpture.

"We understand there is a piece of land that you want badly, and no matter how hard you have tried, the present owner isn't interested in parting with it. We may just be in a position to help you acquire it."

"And how much is it going to cost me?"

Dick Whittington leaned forward, smiled his most trustworthy smile, and then began to weave not one but two barefaced lies together.

"First things first. We have enough land to be going on with, and we have no intention of challenging you for any of your targets. You can take our word on that. What we *do* want is for one of our competitors not to be a competitor anymore – dead is preferable, maimed horribly and unable to walk will do at a pinch. We need to remain as far away as possible from this – if our names are ever connected with it we will have to take a long holiday, if you catch my drift. We can get you the land you want if you take care of this small bit of business for us. How does that sound?"

The man blinked twice and gripped the bridge of his nose between thumb and forefinger. He was not a very good actor, and his attempt to look as though he were some sort of Captain of Industry, rushed off his feet, and with the ills and pressures of the world upon his milk bottle shaped shoulders did not fool anyone sitting at that table. He smiled, exhaled and then sat back in his chair. The chair's leather creaked ever so slightly. It was more of a sigh really, and all the while Cat Tabby and Dick Whittington scrutinised his face intently. They were very good at watching people, so good in fact that Cat Tabby could do it with his eyes closed.

"And what makes you think that I, a mere businessman, can arrange a hit or arrange for someone to fall out of a 16-storey window? My company's name is First Garden Creations, not Murder Incorporated."

Cat Tabby padded across the table and then turned so quickly that it made the man jump.

"We know who you are and what you are, my friend. We also know of a certain someone that would just love to find out *where* you are. A lady with half a face and a very big axe to grind. You know who we mean, don't you?"

The man gulped, his eyes widened, and what little colour he had in those perfect cheeks drained away faster than spilled water in the desert.

"We can see that from the look on your face that you do. Now, do we have a deal?"

Cat Tabby was enjoying this now. Could it be that their

moment had finally come? They were so close to getting back what had been stolen from them, and they wouldn't even have to do any of the dirty work, for dirty work it was. Filthy, nasty, despicable work. But oh, so worth it in the long run. The man was as white as a new sheet. His lips moved but no words crept out. Finally, after a few seconds of internal panic, he regained his composure, shot the cuffs of his lovely shirt, and ran a well-manicured hand through his Toni&Guy hair.

"If you can get me the land I want, for a price that I am willing to pay, I can make your problems drift away like the morning mist on a pond. If you cross me though, and you think that you can pass on my whereabouts to the lady in question regardless, and then steal what is mine, think carefully. I have powerful friends."

Cat Tabby glided back across the table and curled up in a ball in front of his partner.

"We understand perfectly. If you have a piece of paper and a pen, Mr. Whittington will make you aware of our terms."

The man stood up and crossed the room. On the far side was another long table. This one was short in comparison; it was only big enough to seat fifty people. On it were some notebooks, arranged artistically in the shape of a fan, and several expensive Mont Blanc pens. He picked up one of each and returned to the table. Dick took the pad and placed it on the table so that all could see, then he unscrewed the top from the pen and started to write. The man noticed that Cat Tabby's tail did not swish at all. It hung down over the edge of the table and only flicked occasionally, which struck the man as odd. If he had just agreed to favourable terms during a business negotiation, his heart would be bouncing around inside his chest and his pulse would be racing. The opposite seemed to have happened with the feline.

Dick Whittington finished writing and passed the paper across the table. The man scanned it quickly. There wasn't much to read: just a single name and a date. He nodded, then folded the paper up and placed it inside his jacket pocket. Then the two men stood up, and shook hands. Business was completed and Dick turned away and headed for the boardroom door. Cat Tabby jumped down from the boardroom table and sashayed across the thick carpet to join him there. They both turned, expecting the man to at least show them out but he had repaired to the chair at the far end of the room. From where they were standing, all they could see was his face, caught in the lamplight. Pretending not to be offended, Cat Tabby slipped between Dick's legs and left the room. Dick followed shortly afterwards. Cat Tabby was waiting for Dick by the lift doors with his head cocked to one side. A look that Dick knew only too well.

"Forget it, my friend, he's far too slow to think that fast. Insulting us is not what's on his mind right now. I think he's reliving those final days with the lady we were talking about. How he misled her, lied to her and then sold her down the river, all the while pretending to love her. When she catches up with him, whenever that may be, he'd be better off killing himself before she takes her turn."

"Well said, Dick. I can always rely on you to cheer me up. Now, press that bloody button and let's get out of here. The night is young and there are deals to be made."

Seconds later, the lift arrived. The doors opened with a whisper and they both stepped inside. On the way down to the ground floor, Dick noticed the name of the man's company engraved on the mirror behind them.

"*First Garden Creations!*" said Dick, chuckling.

"At least he has a sense of humour," said Cat Tabby.

"For how much longer though my friend, for how much longer?"

The cleaner with the heavy-duty floor polisher had been working hard. He'd made his way down to the ground floor and was trying to turn the tiles into a sheet of glass.

"Now there's a man that looks happy in his work, Dick."

"It's the simple jobs that make you the happiest, Cat."

The man in the boardroom watched the odd couple wander across the car park and then disappear into the bushes near the front gate on one of the many security cameras that he had installed to keep him safe. He thought back to the veiled threat that they had made about the woman, and he shuddered.

"If that cocksure talking cat and his stupid silent partner can enter and depart without tripping the alarms, maybe *she* can too? Note to self – get some more cameras in the morning, and some dogs – big, nasty, snarling, eat children for breakfast sort of dogs."

And with that he reached across the desk and flicked the light switch to the off position and relaxed into the quiet darkness with only the digital display of his phone for company. Pretending to be dim had got him a long way, but Lord, it was exhausting! He knew who those two chancers were and what they wanted. He may be a long way from the Garden of Eden and that treacherous serpent, but *He* was Adam, the first man, and he was not going to be blackmailed or intimidated. However, there was still a small part of him that was uneasy about the woman being so close. He'd charmed her, and then betrayed her, and you know what they say about women – *Hell Hath no Fury Like a Woman Scorned.*

STAND AWAY

DCI Judas Iscariot removed his silver coin from the pocket of his Frahm City Coat and started to rub his thumb across it. The coin, one of thirty he had received long ago for certain services rendered, felt cold against his skin. It was like touching concentrated moonlight. The action of rubbing the coin had worn the markings on both sides from the coin centuries ago, and now it was impossible to tell where it had come from or who had minted it. How many times since God had cursed him with immortality and sent him out into the world to fight evil had he stood like this? Thousands of times? Millions? More? It would not surprise him.

Rubbing the coin like this helped him to think. It centred him, and established a sense of calm, which was in short supply at this moment in time. Crime in the Underworld beneath the Underground was on the rise, and Scotland Yard's secret occult magic division, known as the Black Museum, had never been busier.

Judas looked up into the grey, drab sky. The clouds hung

there, not moving, as if they were looking down on him and judging him.

No change there, he thought to himself.

"Sir? We can take a closer look at the body now if you'd like. Bloody Nora has finished making her notes and taking her photographs."

"Bloody Nora? I wouldn't let Dr. Blake hear you call her that. She has friends in low places and there's plenty of room in the Black Museum's morgue, Sergeant Lace."

"Yes sir, apologies."

Lace was new to the Black Museum – she was a feisty, hard as nails, rabid terrier of a police officer, and Judas was glad, and lucky to have her. Bloody Nora was the Black Museum's resident medical fruitcake. Her real name was Nora Blake, and she was to be found most days at Scotland Yard (if she wanted to be found, that is) in the oldest police mortuary in the world, up to her armpits in buckets of ghoul blood, giants' gore and goblin spittle. Whatever it was, a crushed fairy, a decapitated Polish Golem, or a giant with a sucking chest wound, Bloody Nora never batted an eyelid. She could not be shocked or frightened, and she was relatively calm and steady, unless you tried to steal one of her Orange Hobnobs. To attempt this heinous act was pure folly and not recommended.

Judas lifted his left foot from the deep, dark and sticky mud, all the while hoping and praying that his Wellington boot would accompany it. Miraculously, his prayers were answered (which didn't happen very often, for obvious reasons) and he squelched over to take a better look at poor Little Henry Swift Cockle. Judas had recognised the prince as soon as he saw his face, or what was left of it. A note had been pinned to his waistcoat – with a nasty-looking knife. Again, this was uncalled for. It was theatrical and just downright unnecessary. He made a mental note of that. Most of the killers he dealt with – Jack the Ripper, John the Baptist, trolls, demons, warlocks or witches, ghouls, ghosts and the darker side of the Fae – killed in their own way, there was a style, a way of working, if you can call it that. Whoever or whatever had done this was just being cruel.

Stand away, and cast off your lines, if you do wish to follow in his wake. Signed by the Night Plunderers, the Light Horsemen, Lumpers, Game Lightermen and the Heavies.

"What do you think, Inspector?"

"I think, Sergeant Lace, that we are about to get knee deep in more than just black mud and filth. The Lumpers and the rest of them are also River Folk and well respected in the Under Folk, just like the Mudlarks. We're going to have to work fast, it looks like the tide is rising."

THE SONS OF COLQUHOUN

nother darkened room. This one not so grand. With a small, round wooden table and candles in sconces on the wall instead of designer bulbs and shades. The thick, blood-red coloured curtains have been drawn tightly, so tightly that the brass rings on the curtain rail that support them look stretched. The drapes are fastened together with a rope of gold braid; no light will escape this room tonight. A small, meagre fire burns in the grate – it gives off very little heat and the room suffers for it. Seated around the table are four men. They are the Sons of Colquhoun, and they are not to be trusted or crossed. They are descended from the original Marine Police officers that patrolled the waterways of the capital long ago. It was their job to protect the businessmen and the importers and exporters. It was their job to catch and incarcerate the criminals and the gangs that preyed on the river's trade. However, what started out as a noble endeavour soon transformed into something much darker and altogether less wholesome.

The gangs that ruled the river would never give up their

spoils. They had become fat on them, and they fought back against the Marine Police. Then the Fae arrived in London, and the world of the waterside turned upside down. Now, there were water sprites, and mermen, and all manner of creatures that could breathe under water, transporting the stolen goods from the ships' holds to the dockside. From there, 12-feet tall giants and great hulking talking beasts lifted full carts of stolen barrels away on their backs. A month's worth of work done in the space of one night. And with that, demand grew, and more shipments were taken, more wealth pilfered by the gangs. The Marine Police were vastly outnumbered and outgunned. Each time they encountered one of the gangs, catching them in the act of emptying the hold of a clipper from the East, the police officers ended up patrolling the riverbed with a heavy weight attached to their ankles.

Something needed to be done. The police needed reinforcements, not in manpower, that would not help them win the day. What they needed was the strength and the abilities to compete with the criminals. They wanted to be able to play the gangs at their own game and to match them, punch for punch, bite for bite, and spell for spell. The Marine Police needed magic. At least, that was what some of the Marine Police believed to be the case. The main body of the Force said no to magic. The Law was the Law, and it would always overpower and overcome the criminal element that preferred to flout and to break it. But there were those that saw the situation very differently; their love for the Law was pure and their desire to keep it that way was strong. At the beginning they were just two. Two brother officers assigned to the same beat, who during the dark hours they spent walking the docks and trying to keep order, discussed how they had seen one murder too many and felt impotent and unable to make the difference they so wanted to. And in those words they discovered something in each other, something that united them, and they made a pledge then and there that they would recruit others that felt as they did and fight back.

They watched and listened to their brother officers at the station, and in the taverns and the public houses they frequented once their shifts were over. Over pints and many a dram, individuals were identified, their qualities noted and analysed, and if they proved to be worth recruiting, they were. After a year there were enough soldiers to form a secret cell within the Marine Police. These men were the hardcore element. They had the zeal and the desire to cleanse the waterways – in their minds' eyes they saw a clean, safe and orderly place where women and children need not fear to tread. Everything and anything should be risked in order to make their world a better place, and that included using magic.

Changelings, fairies and sprites were targeted, bribed, threatened and cajoled to go into the streets and the alleyways that the Under Folk and the Fae had made their own. Once there, their mission was simple: find someone that would not shy away from teaching the men of the Marine Police a little magic, just enough to make it a fair fight. The Marine Police were not interested or concerned with what colour that magic might be, black magic or white, and that was their biggest mistake, and what haunts them to this day.

The Sons of Colquhoun look like men, they have the regulation two arms and two legs, a head and eyes, but inside each of them you will find nothing in the way of lungs, spleen, kidney, or heart. They are something entirely different now. Dark Magic has consumed them, eaten them away from the inside like a parasite. If you were able to cut one open, you would find only dark fire and the crackling of insanity. A long time ago they had human names to go with their human organs, but now those names are gone. They have been forgotten.

Now they are known as: Mr. Deck, Mr. Waterline, Mr. Mast and Mr. Sail.

"The Mudlark's body has been discovered at last, up the river. I am told that the Black Museum were in attendance so we must move quietly from here on in. It would be unwise to trouble that place just yet," said Mr. Deck.

"And what of the payment for the Mudlark?"

"We shall collect it this evening, Mr. Mast. Our employer has more work for us to do. I suggest we discuss the new job after we have taken payment, how does that sit with you Mr. Waterline and Mr. Sail?"

"Well enough," said both.

"Good, then we shall go and see the man tomorrow morning."

Before that, perhaps we might hear more about this man, Mr. Deck?"

Mr. Deck was the face of the Sons of Colquhoun, he met with potential employers, haggled and negotiated the terms and the fees for their services. He was the broadest and the tallest, and when the darkness descended, he was the most ferocious of the four.

"Well now, my friends, he's an odd character to be sure. Smartly dressed, young in appearance, but I feel he is ancient. He tries to hide it with his fancy wardrobe and lotions and potions, but there is no mistaking it when speaking with him face to face."

"Old like us, Mr. Deck?"

"Oh, far older, Mr. Waterline. Far, far older by my reckoning. He has power, but he hides it, and I always get the notion that he's looking over his shoulder, like there is someone coming for him."

"Where does his wealth and his power come from?"

"I don't rightly know the answer to that question, Mr. Mast. He is all for property and land at this moment in time, but he looks like someone that can get bored right quick."

"And it's our job to do his bidding, and to keep him safe from harm too, Mr. Deck."

"It certainly is, Mr. Sail, we four have never failed in any task set to us. It would be bad for business if this were to be the first instance."

"We've never gone up against the Black Museum and those angels before though. I'm not keen on poking that wasp's nest, Mr. Deck."

"All will be well, Mr. Sail. With any luck we shall be done before the Black Museum even knows that a crime has been committed."

There is a rumble of assent from around the table. White gloved hands reach into the middle of the table and are rested one on top of the other. Mr. Deck says something. The words are clipped and sound odd, but the rest of the men nod. Then they drink, smoke their pipes and complain to each other about the fire.

5

KEW AND THE SIN EATER

The Royal Botanic Gardens are situated in the leafy, green, and just too damn expensive to buy a flat, let alone a semi-detached, borough of Richmond. The gardens are affectionately known as just plain *Kew* to the great unwashed. They are a wonderful place to lose yourself, to get away from the hurly burly of the city, and to escape the rigours of modern living. Some people come here to look at the flora and fauna, others to stroll around the park in order to help their toddler to doze off. Every now and again, someone or something comes to Kew to hide.

Lilith was working in the new, and as yet unopened, Orchid Rooms. It was very hot and steamy inside; at first she'd found it hard to breathe but she had got used to it now. It was also very quiet and peaceful, which she loved most of all. It was a round room with a circular walkway around the outside and two others that crossed it like the head of a screw. In the centre of the room there were two small benches. Lilith took her lunch there each day, preferring the quiet to the packed staff canteen.

Kew was a calm place, and the rest of her colleagues

were nice, quietly spoken types; a few were mid-way through a PHD in something or other, a couple were children of the earth, happiest when communing with nature or racing their wheelbarrows around the park. She was one of the odd ones. A young chap called David who worked with the tree surgeons was another. She'd heard him talking French on his mobile – he was trying to keep his voice down and she wondered if he were in trouble and laying low. The truth was much simpler. David had spent five years in the French Foreign Legion. He'd only recently returned to England and was trying to get used to the flow and the rhythm of life in civvy street. She discovered this when taking a quick look at his personnel file one night. Getting into the main office was simple – she had just put a spell on Tim, the security guard, and waltzed right in. David intrigued her for some reason. Men weren't to be trusted on the whole; some of them were okay, but Lilith had been bitten badly once, and she wasn't about to let it happen again. She just liked to know who she was working with.

Lilith finished her sandwich and drank yet another bottle of water. For some reason she was feeling hotter than usual – either the thermostat had packed in or one of the fire doors had been wedged open again. Lily packed her lunch box away and walked over to the double doors near the entrance hall to find a bin for her plastic bottle. When she returned someone was sitting on her bench.

"Hello, Lilith, it's been a while my love, how are you?"

Lilith took a step back – an instinctive, run for the hills step backwards – but she mastered her fear and calmed her nerves. Fear was what he wanted, but she would not give it to him.

"My Lord Lucifer, Ruler of Hell and Sovereign of Sorrow,

most high amongst the Host, and truly as bright as the Morningstar! Welcome, I was not expecting you."

"Little Lilith, oh how you have grown! You look fantastic, positively blooming, if you'll excuse the geographical pun. This is an interesting place, isn't it? Full of life and hope and renewal. Not the first place I would have thought would appeal to you but much changes, does it not? Please, take a seat. I have something to talk to you about, something that may possibly be of interest to you."

Lilith sat down opposite Lucifer, who looked the same as he had ever done. He was tall, handsome and athletic. He was perfect in every way, and that was what scared everyone the most. There was nothing wrong with him. No weaknesses, no imperfections, he was the most beautiful angel ever created. It was easy to see why so many of the Host had listened to him, been beguiled by his words, agreed to commit treason with him, and then followed him into battle against the Archangel Michael, and the power and might of the Heavenly Host. *When he fell, he dragged us all down with him*, she thought to herself. Would she do it all again? Very possibly. But that was his power. He could see the weakness in others, and he used it.

"You'll never guess who I bumped into the other day, my dear. A friend of yours, a very old friend, someone that you would probably like to bump into, or drive into with a transit van perhaps. Can you guess who?"

Lilith felt her pulse quicken and she sat up. One half of her was screaming not to trust him, not to entertain his comments, not to get involved, that way only heartache and ruin lay, but the other half of her was cold and hungry; hungry for revenge.

"I have searched the world twice over for him, Lord Lucifer, I have walked across deserts and fought the wind on the top of every mountain. I would pay a pretty price for his whereabouts."

Lucifer stood up and ran one hand through his thick, dark hair. He was imposing and grand, and he was too big for the room, too big for any room. But there he stood, the King of the Dark Places, the Regent of Despair, and for a short time – ruler of her body, and her lover.

"I bet you would, Lilith. How long has it been since that lumbering fool betrayed you?"

"More days than I can count, Lord."

"Well then, let's see what we can do about that shall we? Have you ever heard of a man called Huxley Montague? He is an Eater of Sins, quite well known hereabouts. I hear he does quite well, which is a little annoying for me, but I shall get around to relieving him of what is rightfully mine at some point. He and your friend are quite close. I believe that one keeps the other busy. It's a marriage of convenience of sorts. But my thoughts wander. If you find the Sin Eater, you will surely find the man himself. And before you ask, I do not want payment, nor do I wish for you to owe me anything. If you manage to find Huxley Montague and he leads you to your prize, let me know where to find him, will you? I'm so busy these days and my to-do list is so long."

Lilith dropped to her knees in front of Lucifer and reached out to take his hand ... but he was no longer there.

6

THE RETURN OF THE GIANTS

Corineus needed to see the sky and to feel the rain and the spray from the sea on his face again. He'd been below decks for the last three days, a precaution against being spotted as he made his way home to England after his years of enforced absence. There was still a price on his head, and if it had risen with inflation then it should be an enormous sum by now. Big enough to turn friends and foes alike into informers and turncoats. Still, he was tired of being cooped up and he wanted to leave the hold, once and for all. It was big enough for him; the captain could have squeezed a hundred new combine harvesters in here, or 100,000 barrels of whatever, but the hull was closing in on him now, and he wanted to be out.

The roll of the ship was lessening – they were approaching the chops of the channel. Traffic would increase soon. Huge ships ferrying grain and ballast would be heading out, passenger ships would be loading up with stores and passengers, and there would be the smaller boats, launches and sail boats, and yachts too. He must be patient. He wanted to rip the main hatch off, clamber out onto the

deck, and roar and shout that Corineus the Giant had
returned, but that would have been folly. If he was seen, it
would all be over for him. That must not happen, not now,
not after all this time. *Patience. Patience. Patience.*

Corineus walked across the hold. It only took him five
strides to reach the other side. He touched the hull and then
returned to his bed. It had been constructed for him by the
Captain. They had used four inflatable Gemini Ribs; sleek,
black speedboats, favoured by the Coast Guard hereabouts.
The four were lashed together to create an air-filled
mattress big enough for him to lay upon. He would miss it,
but not much. Corineus laid down and closed his eyes. He
started to dream of the cove in Cornwall, and the Mermaid
and her partner, and the remains of the castle that he would
call home for the rest of his life.

The giant rolled over and winced. He was sick. No, he
was dying, there was no need to hide that from anyone,
including himself. The old wounds that he had received did
not want to heal anymore, they had given up on him, and he
did not blame them. Long ago, when Albion was still as
green as green could be he had fought with Gogmagog,
another giant, and a formidable foe. The fight had lasted for
two days and two nights. No quarter was given or asked for
and all of the Lords and Ladies of the Fae had turned out to
witness it. Corineus had won the day and cast Gogmagog
into the sea from atop the cliffs, but had received a fatal
blow in the process. His days amongst the living were going
to be few, and that is why he wanted to slip away, unde-
tected, to a place where he could die quietly, and listen to
the song of the sea.

The Captain came to wake him, and to bring the giant
some good news. They had navigated the busy river faster
than expected and were cruising towards Crossness

Pumping Station, the arranged point where the giant Corineus would transfer to a smaller boat and then make his way to the Isle of Dogs. Corineus had very little in the way of belongings, so he was packed and ready, one hand reaching for the uppermost rung of the oversized steel ladder the Captain had installed for him.

"When we reach the next marker buoy, and I am happy that we are in position, I will open the main hatch and you must climb up and make your way over to the Port side. There you must wait until we receive three flashes from their torch. Then it is safe to proceed, and you can hang over the railings and drop down into their hold. It will be a much tighter squeeze for you, but the journey is short, and then it is luxury, open air sailing. Now, Corineus, you must not be seen or else we are all dead."

Corineus felt something stirring inside him and realised that he was feeling a mixture of guilt, at having put so many people in harm's way, and of gratitude. He loved his friends dearly; it was a shame that he would not be seeing many of them ever again. The Captain climbed quickly up the ladder on the starboard side of the ship and disappeared through a hatch. The engine was humming to itself, making soft revolutions of the screws, and the ship drifted on. Then, he heard the electrical motor that pulled the doors of the great hatch open begin to stir.

At first, nothing happened. Nothing, no movement, and he began to panic. He imagined that the hatch doors had been damaged somehow, and that he was going to have to stay down here in the gloom until they could prise them open again or cut them with a blowtorch. His hand tightened on the rung, and he heard the metal protest. Then, a small hairline crack of light appeared above him, and he urged the little motor on. It was the first hint of daylight he had seen in many weeks. It widened and widened, and on any other day, the grey sky would have meant little. It was drab and pale, the sort of sky that brought on bad moods and depression, but today it was brilliant and bright, a welcome sight after the darkness and confines of the hold.

As soon as the hatch was fully open, Corineus climbed up cautiously. When he reached the top rung he waited, as he had been told to do. Seagulls were already swooping low over the ship; scavengers, all chancing their wing, hoping to find food or spoiled goods in the hold. The Captain's head appeared directly above him; he looked pleased with himself.

"How about that, my friend, am I not the King of the Sea? We could not be any closer. Be swift now, my friend, away with you over the side, and say hello to the Mermaid for me. Good luck, mighty Corineus."

Corineus swung himself up and onto the deck. He waved at his friend and then as quickly as he was able, dropped from the deck of the ship and landed on a pilot's barge. The barge's hold was open and the pilot, holding a lamp, was pointing downwards into the square black hole, where a space had been made for a giant to hide.

CAT TABBY WAS SITTING on the dashboard of the car. He was cold, and had asked Dick Whittington to put the windscreen blower on. He liked the hot air on his stomach, it made him feel like purring. Dick was sitting behind the wheel with a strained look on his face. They had been for a drive and ended up in Canary Wharf. They hadn't intended to, but here they were, looking out over the river, and thinking so hard that it was giving them both their own special, bespoke mother-of-all headaches.

"Where are we going to get enough cash to put up for that stretch of London across the way? We're stretched thin, Cat, stretched tighter than a Hollywood A-lister's skin, and my nose is so far out of joint after seeing you know who, that it hurts."

Cat Tabby shifted slightly.

"Can you turn the heat down a smidgen please, Dick? That infernal cold is in retreat finally. Have you ever known it to be this harsh in February?"

"How's that?" Dick asked, as he turned the dial down.

"Much better thanks. Now, with regard to the bunce, the pennies and the pounds, as you say, we are in a tight spot, everything we have is down and in use, there is nothing in the bank, so we have to be clever, my friend. We need to think outside the box."

Dick shuffled. His long legs were feeling cramped, so he reached down between them and pulled on the release catch on his seat, easing it back. Cat Tabby must have been feeling the same, and hopped from the dashboard onto the passenger seat.

"If the man at First Garden comes through for us, and there's no reason to think that he won't, a certain group of ladies will disappear from the property market. Overnight, I hope. Then, we shall step in and offer our services."

"And what of the Black Museum, Cat? I'm sure he'll have something to say about who gets what and when."

"He may do, Dick, but with all the trouble we'll be lining up for him, he might not have the time. Now, think Dick, think hard."

CORINEUS MADE himself as comfortable as he was able. This hold was a much tighter squeeze, but he need only suffer it for a short while, and there was at least a window for him to look out from and it helped him pass the time. On the right, he could see the tall buildings of the money men. Beyond them, the City, and the home of his great enemy, Gogmagog. The pilot appeared as they were approaching the rendezvous. He pointed to the tallest mast in the marina. Flying from it was a green flag that wouldn't have looked out of place on Nelson's frigate. It was incredibly long and even the slight breeze was making it dance.

"It's illegal to fly anything that long when moored, but with any luck, they shall be pulling it down very shortly because their guest has come aboard," said the pilot. Corineus smiled at the sight of it and crossed all of his fingers.

"Not long now, Corineus, but this is the really dangerous part. When we pass that red light over there, you must slip overboard and then wade across to that jetty, where the tall-masted yacht lays. You'll only be out in the open for a second or two, so make haste, but don't make too much of a din, softly now."

The pilot disappeared; his place was behind the wheel in the wheelhouse. Corineus clambered forward, and pulled himself up and out of the hold. Once on the deck he crouched down as low as possible and stared intently back towards the wheelhouse.

CAT TABBY WAS HAVING a bout of the fidgets. He often felt like this when thinking hard.

"Let's stretch our legs, Dick. Walk down to the marina, take our minds off things for a second or two. You never know, we might find some inspiration down that way, we might even get struck down by a sudden and yet not unwelcome flash of an idea!"

A SMALL CIRCLE of light appeared inside the wheelhouse. It was the pilot's torch. It winked twice in quick succession and then disappeared. They were on station and soon he would have to disembark. Corineus wanted to signal his acknowledgement, that he understood, and was ready, and there was a part of him that wanted to say thank you, but he knew that the pilot would already be looking ahead, scanning the surface of the river, watching for changes in the tide, and staying out of the way of inexperienced sailors. When Corineus was sure that the deck would not be skipping or bucking against the waves and tripping him up, he moved to the starboard side, and then in one fluid movement, slipped over the side of the barge and into the river.

He kept one hand on the edge of the deck, gripping it tightly, allowing the steady push of the boat to take him the last few feet of his long journey. The bottom half of his great frame was below the waterline. The water was very cold, but he had no time to worry about that, because within seconds of his entering the 'Oggin', he felt the barge list slightly. His bulk was beginning to act as a sea anchor and was pulling the craft off its course. There was nothing that Corineus could do though, and he trusted the pilot to know his business, which he did. Corineus heard the engines begin to roar and groan, and then the barge was forced to get its nose back in the water and shortly it was back on course once again. The slight course correction had wasted a few minutes of their time but not enough to make it a concern.

It did, however, allow Corineus a few moments to reflect on his current, precarious situation, and to rue the day that he had declined to put on a pair of oilskins before leaving the container ship. He had lost all feeling from the knees down and his lips were starting to go numb. If his teeth could have chattered they would have told him what a great lump he was for not planning ahead, but mercifully they were silent. The ache in his side was all too present though. In the beginning it had been but a mild inconvenience; now it was savage and undeniable. The barge edged closer to the marina and the ship with the long green flag, and when he was close enough, he released the barge and tried to kick out with his legs. They had not forsaken him completely, thankfully, and with a couple of uncoordinated heaves, he would be able to reach the slipway just inside the marina, from there, he would be able to wade across to the shallow moorings, and slip aboard.

DICK WHITTINGTON SAT down on the jetty and dangled his legs over the side. Cat Tabby joined him shortly afterwards. A selection of delicious aromas had carried across the marina to him from the restaurants nearby, and it made his stomach rumble. It was while he was removing a small splinter from his paw that he felt Dick stiffen. His friend pointed silently towards a beautiful yacht moored at one of the jetties. Cat Tabby stared intently, and he quickly saw what had caught Dick's eye. At first it was just a great shape, rounded and huge, but soon, as their eyes became more accustomed to the strange combination of neon bulbs and moon reflections on the water, they could both see that it was no dinghy, boat, or harbour master's launch. Then the shape reached up with one long arm, pulled itself aboard the yacht and disappeared below decks.

"Well, well, well," said Cat Tabby.

"Is that who I think it is?" asked Dick.

"Your eyes do not deceive you, my good friend. That is indeed the one and only Corineus of Troy. And, as we all know, he is the only living thing to stand toe to toe with the mightiest and nastiest piece of work that ever walked the streets of London, and put him on his back.

"We were at that fight if you recall, Cat Tabby. I made a small fortune, and you lost your shirt! Your face was a picture that night! If I remember rightly, Corineus, who I had put my bet on, knocked your Gogmagog out in the 58th round. That was some fight, wasn't it? Blood everywhere, ribs stoved in, cuts and bite marks all over them both and half the ring threatening to give up the ghost too!"

"Yes, Dick, it was. I don't recall how much the final purse was for the winner, but you would have had to have been a giant yourself to carry it away on your own. Some fortunes were made that night, and I have just had a thought that could go some way to making ours, Dick. We know someone, don't we, that would pay a fair price to learn of the giant Corineus' whereabouts? A fair price indeed. Wait a minute! What was the last bounty on him?"

Dick Whittington didn't wait to answer, he just stood up and turned quickly, and seconds later they were back in the car. Cat Tabby didn't ask for the heating to be turned back on; the cold was the last thing on his mind.

"Right then, Cat Tabby, we have two calls to make. One is to the Harbour Master's office – we need to know when that ship is sailing – and the second call is to the Guildhall Under. We can claim that reward and all our prayers will be answered."

Cat Tabby was pacing back and forth, his tail twitching and jittering. The seed of a great and intricate plan was forming in his mind.

"Let's not be too hasty now, Dick. We shall go and see the Harbour Master, and then we shall go and see his Lordship Gogmagog, but not just to claim the reward. Something has occurred to me that could make us ten times the sum of the reward. Imagine now, Dick, the return bout between Gogmagog and Corineus! The return fight, the final battle, the whole Underworld would pay to see that! Just think about it for a second. We can propose that we act for Gogmagog in this. We become the promoters. We take care of the betting side of things and take a cut of that purse too. Gogmagog will agree to our terms, or we don't tell him where Corineus is. He won't dare call our bluff or raise a hand to us because he wants Corineus so badly. It's a fortune in waiting, Dick. What do you say?"

"As always, my cunning feline friend, you have imagined a way to maximise our potential. Let's get going, our luck has changed my friend, truly!"

"Just so, Dick. When you call the Harbour Master, you must ask him about the yacht called Zennor. Find out what you can about it, where it has been, where it is heading, and where the owner lives."

Dick put his seatbelt on and turned the car's ignition.

"Zennor you say? I think that might be Cornish."

7

THE SIN EATER

uxley Montague, resplendent in his new Gieves & Hawkes cashmere overcoat, triple-buttoned and with a very subtle dusky pink bar under the collar, was on his way to his last appointment. To the passer-by he looked smart, very possibly even dapper, but if they could have seen inside his mind and felt the weariness of his limbs, they would have known that he was dog-tired. Earlier that day, in the morning to be precise, directly after a rushed coffee and a Danish that could have easily doubled for a discus, he had attended a dying Harpy in Tottenham. She was slipping away quickly; her sisters said it was because of a broken heart. Huxley doubted that because they are devious and spiteful creatures on the whole, but a job was a job – and the Harpies paid well. The act of eating the Harpy's sins had taken its toll on him immediately; she had been a terrifically mean creature, and he had needed to rest almost straightaway.

Then, he had schlepped over to East London, and done the same for a Gorgon. She was drifting away to the distant lands after being cursed by a sorcerer in nearby

Streatham; the cause of the curse was not spoken about and the act of eating her sins had been made even harder because he had to use a mirror to look into her eyes. The family of the Gorgon were incredibly sad, as you'd expect, and heartbroken obviously, but they were stoic and spiritual, and very, very generous. At the end of the service they had asked him to remain in the cellar, where the act of cleansing had been performed, and presented him, from behind a screen, with a magical flower – that would never die, it would remind him of the wonderful service that he had provided for their beautiful daughter – *apparently*.

The bloom was beautiful to behold and incredibly fragrant, but it was of no use to Huxley, and had gone in the nearest bin he could find. As he walked away from the house of the Harpies, he had time to reflect. The newly eaten sins were crashing around inside him. He could hear their voices tuning in and out like a broken radio. It hurt, but as Huxley knew full well, the pain would pass quickly. That was his gift – he took the pain of others, and the sins they carried through life and then disposed of them. He would have preferred the gift of second sight or the ability to fly, but that was life: you get what you get, and you get on with it.

Back in the world of the now, the darkness was gently kissing the automatic sensors on the top of the lampposts. Montague checked his watch, a lovely little Breitling that had come his way via the horny hand of a naughty little Goblin he did business with occasionally, and lengthened his stride. He detested tardy timekeeping in others, and wanted to arrive at least five minutes early for the last job of the day. It was only as he was reaching the bottom of Thurleigh Road, with the corner of Wandsworth Common in sight, that he realised that he had company. The invisible kind, and that wasn't good.

Sin Eaters were always being sought out. But, normally, they were approached from the front, and in daylight. There were always strange beings and creatures that wanted their slates wiped clean before they took the long, long, lonely walk into the darkness. Some of them didn't want the rest of their tribe, or coven, to know, and sent secret messages, or employed a loyal envoy to make their pitch. At first, Montague thought that he was being followed by one of the latter, but still, the shadow that was trailing him had declined to reveal itself, and he was getting very nervous. Huxley was not a warrior, and he did not have a trusty henchman that took midnight showers in 'O positive' blood and liked to sit before a raging fire with a blanket across his knees whilst crocheting with his victims' entrails by his side.

He tried to saunter down the road and pretend that he was unafraid and ready to do battle at the drop of a hat. He was attempting to project strength – but doing it badly. Huxley's mind was racing and his imagination was doing its best to catch up. He was beginning to see monsters everywhere, and the voices of the sins were starting to get on his wick.

"Please shut up!" he shouted, and stopped walking so abruptly that it caused a dog walker nearby to pull up and shorten the leash on her dog. What protection she thought she was going to get from a dachshund was anyone's guess.

"I can't hear myself think with you lot shouting and creating in there. I'm being followed, now be quiet, or else."

Huxley realised that he had started talking to himself yet again – out loud. He waited for the sins to quieten and for the dog walker to take her rabid beast on its way. Then he composed himself, shot the cuffs of his Paul Smith shirt and stepped out. As he walked, he practised the deep breathing exercises his father had taught him many years before. The knack was to listen to the beating of your own heart and to get in time with it. Normally, it would take a few minutes at best, but something felt very wrong. He could feel a presence nearby, but it was just out of reach, on the periphery of his vision and his senses. Whatever it was, it was close. He was in the eye of his own storm, and it was about to crash in on him. Something rustled in the hedge nearby, a twig snapped, and the world went quiet.

"Run, you Muppet!" shouted one of the Sins.

"Quickly now, or she'll snaffle you up and chew you to pieces!" said another.

So, he ran, and he didn't look back or stop until he had reached the house where his next patient was waiting for him.

"Pull yourself together, you blabbering fool!"

Huxley tried giving himself a proper talking to.

"The famous Sin Eater, Huxley Montague, afraid of his own shadow and quivering at the thought of an invisible foe? Ridiculous!"

"I think you're very brave, Huxley," said another of the Sins.

"This answering back and getting involved in my conversations has got to stop! You Sins need to calm down and to know your place. You're only along for the ride until I can get shot of you, so pipe down!"

"Charming," said yet another of the Sins, but then they did what Huxley had asked them to do and stayed silent.

Huxley took a deep breath, flicked a tiny piece of lint from his lapel, and knocked on the door to Number 18, Thurleigh Road. If you knock at the door to a dark house, you must expect an echo and a semi-long wait for the inhabitants to crawl up from the depths of an imagined cellar. Number 18 was not your usual dark house though; this was the official residence of the All-Knowing Mother of the Wandering Witches of Wandsworth. The matriarch of the coven was dying, and at 599 years of age, it was widely accepted that she'd had a good run. Having lived that long it was not unexpected that she had a few things to get off her chest. Huxley prepared himself to take on her sins.

A light went on behind the glazed glass panels in the door, then a shape started to grow within it. Whoever had drawn the short straw and was on door-keeping duties was very slow. Huxley took another quick look behind him to make sure there was no shadow under the tree opposite or the steamy breath of an unseen assailant issuing forth from the nearest bush. The coast was still clear. Huxley turned back to the door to find it had already been opened and a young lady was standing there – inspecting him. She was about five feet tall, blonde haired, with rosy cheeks, and not at all what he had expected.

"You must be Mr. Huxley Montague? she asked.

"That would be correct, Miss ... ?"

"Clarity Silverwood."

"Miss Silverwood. Good evening, and as you correctly surmised, I am indeed, Huxley Montague. Please, take my card, and may I come in?"

The young lady cocked her head to one side. She looked him in the eye, and her mouth turned down at the edges. Huxley realised that he had made a serious faux-pas.

"Please forgive me, Lady Silverwood of the Wandering Witches, I beg the key and the word to pass over the threshold and into your halls. I leave all hatred and malice behind, keeping only the tools of my trade to hand. Misuse of them will seal my fate. On the gloved hand and the three circles of the Coven, I do swear."

Clarity Silverwood's confused expression disappeared instantly, and she stood to one side and bade Huxley enter.

"I was really hoping that you'd forget the words of the greeting so that I could practice one of my spells on you, but you redeemed yourself. You have a lovely voice, Huxley, anyone ever tell you that?"

Huxley just smiled, and stepped inside. Clarity closed the door behind him, and he heard her turn the key in the lock.

"Did you bring a friend, Huxley?"

Huxley spun around quickly.

"What did you see?"

"Oh, not much really. There was a form across the road, hiding behind one of the oaks. It felt odd; not evil but then again, not quite right either."

Huxley moved past her and tried to peer through the glazed panel in the front door, but it was no use. Satan himself could have been standing there with a couple of Jehovah's Witnesses and he wouldn't have been able to see them clearly. Clarity wandered down the hall and then stopped at the foot of the stairs and waited for him to finish his spying. Huxley turned away from the door and joined her at the foot of the stairs.

"I'm awfully sorry about my entrance, Clarity. It has been a long day. A very tiring day, and I am loathe to say it, but my attention was somewhere else."

Clarity stopped abruptly in front of him and turned.

"What was it that lured your attention away then, Mr. Handsome Huxley Montague?"

Huxley didn't want to admit that he had been frightened, so he said the first thing that came to mind.

"It's been ages since a door has been opened by such a lovely young woman. I was distracted momentarily, my apologies."

"Apologies for being attracted to me, or apologies for muffing your lines?"

"I would say a little of both, forgive me."

The young witch giggled. It was a nice, playful and innocent sound, and it caught him unawares. He wanted to laugh but fortunately he managed to suppress that thought and did his best to appear suitably stern and officious. Clarity Silverwood smiled a big toothy grin, then turned and disappeared into the darkness. Huxley tried his best to follow the sound of her feet scuffing through the deep shag pile of the carpet underfoot. They walked for what seemed like an unusually long time down a corridor that defied all architectural logic, until he saw the outline of a door ahead. It was open and the light from within had spilled out and stained the carpet with a sharp-edged yellow rectangle. Clarity motioned for him to go in, and before he could ask her out on a date or for her phone number, she was gone.

Huxley stepped inside and was surprised to find that the room was completely empty. No bed with an ailing body atop it, nor were there any wailing and sobbing family members, sneezing and wiping their noses on the bed sheets when they thought no one was looking. Instead there were only a few hairballs skimming the bare floorboards and a single fly that had worn itself out flying in circles, waiting for the bulb in the ceiling to burst into life. On the far side of the room was another door; it was closed and didn't look like opening any time soon. Huxley wandered around the empty room, and waited for whatever it was that was going to happen – *to happen.*

He didn't have long to wait because just as he was

making the decision to turn around and leave, the door on the opposite side of the room opened, and Wulfric, the Warden of the Church Roads, stepped in.

"Are you the Sin Eater?" said the man in the pork pie hat and sharp suit.

"Huxley Montague, at your service, sir."

"It's a pleasure, could you follow me please? The lady is waiting in a grove nearby."

The Warden turned around, stepped back through the door and Huxley followed him, and onto the Church Roads.

As Warden of the Church Roads, Wulfric was a powerful and well-respected man in the realms of the Under Folk. It was his job to ensure that the Roads were used correctly, and that those who travelled along these invisible, Ley Line powered thoroughfares did so safely. Huxley realised that the All-Knowing Mother was not dying *in the house*, it was more likely that she was being tended to in some secret forest setting that was accessible only from the Church Roads. Huxley was well acquainted with the Church Roads and their mysteries, having travelled far and wide upon them as a child with his now, long-forgotten family. The ancient Druids had created them so that the magical beings and the Fae, mythical beasts and legendary creatures could wander unmolested through Albion, and beyond. The Church Roads were like well-lit tunnels, with what looked like tracing paper for walls. From inside, one could still see the world outside, but only as a grey, blurred version, inhabited by shapes that resembled buses and cars.

Wulfric stopped suddenly and pointed towards a grey rectangular shape that hovered against the wall.

"This is your stop, Master Montague. Fare well, and good luck."

"Thank you, sir," said Huxley, as he walked through the floating square and stepped into a beautiful forest glade.

Huge oak trees with gnarly, notched trunks stood in a rough circle in front of him. Their branches had meshed themselves together to create a green and brown roof over-head. Leaves and plants that he could not identify grew in great clumps everywhere, and small birds flitted through the air. Sunlight forced its way through the branches of the trees and created diagonal beams of warm light that looked like javelins waiting for their throwers to reclaim them, and on the far side of the clearing there was a huge four-poster bed within its own canopy of bleached-white linen. Huxley couldn't see anyone in the bed through the bed curtains, and nor could he see any family or friends nearby. Only the sound of the leaves stirring kept the silence at bay.

Huxley took a breath, steadied himself and walked over to the bed. As there was no one here to make the introduc-tions, he lifted one of the curtains and peeked inside. An elderly woman, very elderly indeed, was laying on the bed. She wore a white robe and held a small branch in each hand. She looked as though she were already dead, or very close to it. Huxley cleared his throat. There was no reaction, so he decided to lay one of his hands on top of hers, to see if she were still warm. Her eyes opened the moment his hand made contact with her parchment-dry skin. At first he thought that it was a good thing, maybe she wasn't as near to death as she was thought to be? Had she woken from some deep and troubled sleep? Had a mysterious illness passed? It was none of the above, unfortunately. A green spot appeared on her white robe, then another, and then another. It looked like green rain to Huxley, so he looked up and got the fright of his life. Hovering in the air above the bed was a score of ladies that looked just like the one on the bed. All of them were crying and wailing, and from their eyes ran green tears the colour of fresh grass and young leaves. Within seconds the old witch on the bed was soaked, and so was the sleeve of Huxley's new coat.

Huxley sighed and shook his head. Then he drew himself up to his full height and began the ceremony of the eating of sins. The old witch had led her coven well. She had strived for peace and done very little in the way of sinning, so Huxley did not have as much to do as he had initially thought. When it was over, and the green rain had stopped falling, the old lady disappeared, along with her bed and its white curtains. On the floor where it had stood was a small leather bag; inside was his payment. Huxley picked it up, turned around and left the glade. The Church Roads weren't that busy; only a caravan full of performers for a country fayre passed him by. For a group of entertainers they certainly didn't look all that happy! He wondered what they might have thought of him had they known what he did for a living. Probably the opposite. Other than that it was peaceful and quiet. Huxley walked on, knowing that soon, an opening would appear.

When at last one did present itself, he stepped through it and found to his surprise that he hadn't travelled all that far out of his way. In fact, he was still very close to the house of the Wandering Witches. On the one hand, it was great because he didn't have to work out where he was, on the other it was really bad, because that awful feeling of being stalked had returned ten-fold. Huxley set off quickly in the direction of the river. It was a fair way off but all he needed to do was to reach it unscathed and then enlist the help of one of the Lighterman ghosts. He stuck to the well-lit streets now, and avoided taking any short-cuts across a park or down a canal path. When he reached Battersea, the streets were full of night-time revellers. It was busy but he didn't feel entirely safe even now. The *thing* was still there, hanging back, waiting for a quieter stretch of road perhaps? Huxley pushed on through Battersea, and when he saw the lights of the Albert Bridge in the near distance, he almost broke into a run, but stayed calm.

Nearly there, Huxley, he said to himself for the 500th time that night.

But this was the dangerous bit; the embankment either side of the bridge was busy with night joggers wearing their Lycra and high-powered chest-mounted torches, and dog-walkers pretending to have run out of poo-bags as their pooch strained to get rid of the chicken they had stolen from the dining table that afternoon. If something wanted to get him, now would be the time because Huxley Montague would have to stand in the open and wait for a Lighterman to pick him up.

Lilith had followed the Sin Eater halfway across town already. It could have been halfway across the fields of Hell on her knees for all she cared, she just wanted this man, Huxley Montague, to lead her to Adam, and then she would have her revenge. She continued to watch him, but she wouldn't let this drag on forever. If he didn't make a move soon she would simply abduct him, give him a good working over and then torture the truth from him – it wouldn't take long. He didn't look all that formidable. She decided to get a bit closer.

Huxley was trying to keep one eye on the water and one on the embankment behind him. He thought he'd caught some movement over by the gates to the park, but it could have been anything; someone from the pub across the road taking a wild wee against the railings, or maybe it was just a branch moving in a tree that made a shadow on the pathway below? He felt exposed standing there with his back to the water.

Where the Hell are the Lightermen? he wondered out loud.

They worked this stretch of the river. Normally, you couldn't move for an oar prodding you in the back and one of the ferryman ghosts asking you if you wanted to hop on board, but the river was strangely quiet. Huxley heard, or thought he heard the slap of an oar on the water and spun round quickly. But it wasn't a Lighterman. When he turned back to look at the embankment his heart nearly jumped out of his chest. The shape by the gates of the park had detached itself from the railings and slipped across the road, and was moving towards him, quickly and quietly.

"Across the river, up or down, I'll row you anywhere for half a crown."

The voice of the Lighterman came out of the darkness. It was a pleasant sing-song voice, deep, rolling and friendly, and at that moment, it sounded very much like an angel singing sweetly to Huxley Montague. Huxley spun on his heels and vaulted over the iron railings and landed with a subdued crunch onto the shingle of one of the River Thames' mud banks. The Lighterman rowed in and Huxley jumped onboard.

"North across the water, please, then down and down for the Tower."

"Down for the Tower it is, good sir, sit yourself down and I'll fly, but row as to keep you dry."

The Lighterman pushed off and heaved on his oars, and within seconds they were clear of the embankment. Huxley felt the chill of the wind and pulled his coat tightly around him, but he never took his eyes off the place where he had just been standing, and he wasn't surprised when the shape appeared there. The shape of a man, or woman perhaps?

Small wispy clouds of its breath appeared to one side of its head at regular intervals, proving that the thing was alive, whatever it was. Huxley was relieved that it had not all been some figment of his imagination, something *was* following him, it had been all day, so it wasn't some sort of chance encounter, this was serious. But who'd want to follow him? He was just a Sin Eater. A well-known one of course, but only in his world. Huxley racked his brain for anything that he might have done recently that could have caused offence. Had he made a mistake? Could this be another one of those religious sects like the White Tree Council? Or, a lone wolf operator, believing that sins belonged in someone else's possession entirely? Huxley watched the dark figure for a few more seconds and then turned away.

The Lighterman's name was Salty Peter. He'd been ferrying folk from one side of the Thames to the other for hundreds of years. Like all Lightermen, he pretended to have been rowing on these waters for much longer. Huxley sat back and listened to Salty Peter chunter on. The sound of his voice stopped Huxley from thinking about his stalker – at least for now.

Lilith saw the ferryman row away into the night and cursed herself for being so slow. In a fit of pique she slammed her fist down on the metal railings and bent them out of shape entirely. She had wasted a whole day following this man Huxley Montague and she was still no closer to her prize. He'd slipped away after he'd gone into the last house, reappearing again, a few roads over, because she had been clumsy and had let herself be known to the man.

"Stupid. Stupid. Stupid!"

Lilith was very angry, and the young man who approached her, sensing her angst and mistaking her mood as an opportunity to persuade her to come for a drink, got his sums wrong, and a broken arm for his troubles. Lilith left him whimpering on the ground. She mounted the steps that took her up onto the pavement and then walked across the Albert Bridge and headed for the King's Road. She would find a black cab there, and take it west towards her beloved Kew. She would return the following evening and search out the Lighterman that had taken her quarry from her and find out where this Huxley Montague lived. It would be a shame to kill him; he was clearly not a fighter, she could see that straightaway, and as the cab weaved its way through London's streets, she wondered what Adam, the First Man, and the biggest bastard to walk in the garden was doing with someone like Montague. Time would tell.

8

THE MUD KING

Judas pushed yet another blue pin into the map of Greater London that hung on the wall and reflected on the fact that the first map he'd used to record the odd sightings and the crimes of an occult nature, had been hand-drawn, and the city itself and been half as big. He walked to the window and looked out onto the city. The angels were flitting about as usual, getting on with the day-to-day, plying their various trades and generally being annoyingly good natured and affable. The sight of the winged ones reminded Judas of his old sergeant and the ghost-boy they had found together in the tunnels under the island of Jersey. Joachim had been a member of the Hitler Youth, born to an SS Officer and his French wife, and murdered by the Nazi Occult magic division, the Black Sun. He had helped Judas and the Black Museum to destroy the Black Sun, and after the battle, the Archangel Michael had awarded the boy a place in the ranks of the Host. Williams, his portly sergeant, a man of the valleys and a good detective had been murdered by John the Baptist in a bloody skirmish. He too had been allowed to join the Host. They were probably flying into battle with that zealot Michael in some far flung realm, battling against demons and the like.

"Good luck to you both," said Judas to his reflection in the window.

Any further reminiscing was cut short by the desk phone. It rang and Judas made a mental note to turn the ringer down. He had a sneaking feeling that some of the ghosts inside the Black Museum had found a way to keep turning it up, just to get on his nerves. They were like that.

Sergeant Henshaw was the straight and steady ruler of the front desk on the ground floor. It was his job to sort the wheat from the weasels, and those in need from the ones that had made them bleed. He didn't know exactly what went on inside the Black Museum, but he knew enough, and Judas liked him.

"DCI Iscariot?"

"Go ahead, Sergeant Henshaw."

"I have a gentleman down here, says that you know him, and you know what he wants to speak with you about."

"What does he look like?"

"Taller than average, ruddy complexion, possibly works on the river, got that sailor look about him. Has rings on his fingers, most of them at least, made of twine and string I think."

"Tell him I will be down straight away please, Sergeant Henshaw."

"Will do, sir, and just so that I might know him again, do you have a name for the gentleman?"

"The man in front of you is none other than the King of the Mudlarks. The string rings on his fingers tell you how many battles he's won, other clan leaders he's killed, that sort of thing."

"Right you are, sir, never a dull day with you about."

Judas slipped on his coat and locked the office door. Sergeant Lace was tying up some loose ends from an older case. The murder of the Gilded Goat, one of the Under Folk's more colourful characters had yet to be solved. The killer had got away with it so far, but they would face justice soon enough. The front desk was crowded as usual, and Judas had to wait before he could catch Sergeant Henshaw's eye.

"The gentleman, the King I should say, begged your pardon and said he would wait for you by the statue of the flying men by the river. I presumed you'd know where that was, sir?"

"Thank you, Sergeant."

Judas jogged down the steps of Scotland Yard and made his way to the RAF monument. Great Britain owed a lot to these men and women. Judas had done a fair bit of flying, albeit on the back of an angel or carried beneath one in a travelling bag, and he knew the fear that those born without wings had to master before they felt at home up there in the clouds. The Mud King was standing in front of the sculpture. He was rubbing his hand across the stone as if listening to the stories of those heroes through touch.

"My Lord King, fare thee well?"

The King turned to face Judas. Sergeant Henshaw had described him to a tee. But standing in his presence Judas felt the power of the water and the waves again. A fresh breeze seemed to come off him. He was evidently a very capable man, not to be trifled with or made sport of.

"Marshall of the Museum, greetings. I hope that I find you in good spirits?"

"Tolerably well, my Lord. I take it that you have come to see what progress I have made regarding the sad and untimely demise of young Master Cockle."

The King winced as Judas spoke. It passed quickly though and his keen green eyes refocused and locked onto Judas's own.

"It still pains me to hear of his passing, Marshall. The way of it and the cruelty haunt me daily. What news?"

Judas stepped aside to allow some pedestrians to pass. Once they were out of earshot, he continued.

"I will not look you in the eye and tell you any falsehoods, my Lord, you know me well enough to know that I will not lie or attempt to fob you off with mistruths. Our investigations are ongoing, as we like to say. There are strange inconsistencies regarding the note that the killers left behind, and the nature of the slaying. It seems odd to me that any of the River Folk would commit such a crime. I believe that there may be another hand guiding this sad affair, attempting to pit you against your friends, to what end I know not. But I will find out, my Lord, as the Marshall of the Black Museum, you have my word on that."

The Mud King held his gaze. Judas noticed that his fingers twitched like a child counting on them; every now and again his thumb would double tap on the knuckle of one finger. Judas made a mental note to find out what this was. The Mud King noticed that Judas was trying *not to notice* his fingers and smiled.

"Forgive me, I remember things better when I do this. It can be annoying to others."

"Not at all, my Lord, I have a coin that I rub when my mind is jumbled. I have been told that I am annoying with – and without – it."

"What can I and my people do to help you, Marshall? Our network of spies and informants is vast, and our intelligence gathering has no equal, surely we can be of use to you?"

Judas extended a hand and motioned to the steps that lead down from the embankment to the pencil-thin shoreline. The king nodded and then turned away from Judas. The river's edge was a better place to talk – more secure.

"My Lord, if you come by any information, no matter how trivial, I would be glad of it. But may I ask a favour of you? Can you suggest anyone of your kin, someone capable, quick-witted, and not afraid to venture into harm's way, to be our go-between? I am not always at the Museum, and it would be good to get any news as soon as possible."

"I have the perfect person for you. She's brave, staunch, bright as a pin, and willing to do anything for her brother. She will not let you, or me, down. You have my word on that."

"There is one other thing, my Lord King. I may need to convince some of your people to speak to me, and give me aid. Could you spread the word and let it be known?"

The King nodded and said quietly:

"I don't think that will be an issue, your word will suffice, you can count on that."

Judas and the Mud King shook hands. Judas motioned towards the stairs up to the embankment, but the King declined. A boat had suddenly appeared at the water's edge, and a wooden ramp was already being lowered into the water. Judas watched the King sail away; he was heading upriver, towards the chops of the channel. It was only when he was back inside the lift that was taking him up to the 7th floor and the Black Museum that he noticed the string ring tied around his little finger. It was a single strand, almost white in colour, and secured to his finger with a delicate little knot.

"Well, that's a good trick, I must learn that one," he said to himself just before the doors opened onto the 7th with a

little huff, almost as if they disliked being there. Judas
stepped out of the lift, heard the doors close behind him
and spent a few minutes inspecting the ring more closely.
He rubbed at the small knot with his thumb and smiled.
The King would be true to his word and make it known that
Judas and the Black Museum were to be helped. This ring, a
present from the King himself, was visible proof that he had
the King's protection. Judas walked down the corridor and
decided to pop his head into the Key Room of the Black
Museum. He hadn't spoken to any of the inmates recently.
There may be some of the ghosts and the spirits locked
inside that had knowledge of these: Light Horsemen,
Lumpers, Heavy Horse, Night Plunderers and Game
Lightermen.

With names like that, someone should remember them
thought Judas.

9

GOGMAGOG

The *Guildhall Under* was manic. Creatures of all shapes, sizes and descriptions were streaming in through its enormous wooden doors, and then disappearing down its badly lit corridors. Some of them were clutching sheafs of paper and folders, which they would wave and slam onto desks in an office somewhere. Deeds, contracts, pleas, legal contests and the deadly summons would be produced over the course of the working day. Many of these spirits and sprites, witches, warlocks, trolls and terrors came readied with heads full of grievances – or boxes – lots of differently sized boxes. What was inside one of those boxes could vary greatly. It was best not to know – or to pry. Lives had been shortened for less. Lifting a carboard flap could cost you a hand, or worse.

Eastern European security Golems stood guard at regular intervals with orders to punch first and ask questions later if a dispute were to break out. Weasel Boys ran the corridors, delivering notes and bills of trade, and here and there you'd find a Fortune Teller, resplendent in a Romany-style shawl and with gold coins sewn into their headbands. Their job was to provide advice, and give directions to particular offices or floors with the flip of a greasy playing card. Cat Tabby and Dick didn't need to cross their palms with anything though, because they both knew the Guildhall Under like the back of their hands and paws, and were sitting in the waiting room outside the office of the giant they had come to see minutes after entering the Guildhall.

Cat Tabby was excited. He was purring even more loudly than usual – and *fidgeting*. He was kneading the leather of the seat outside Gogmagog's office with his paws as though he were kneading bread. Though what shape the bread would be in after the pounding it was getting was anyone's guess. He kept on pushing and pushing the fabric under his small pads; his nerves were jangling, and his mind's eye was almost bloodshot because it was so focused on the thought of the big prize. Inside that furry little cranium a big brain was calculating some wild odds, and working out the most obscure of angles. Cats may have nine lives, and if that is entirely true, then they may have nine minds, and nine times the power to see the future.

Cat Tabby was, in common parlance, *crunching the numbers*. He and his lifelong friend, Dick Whittington, had just seen the long-forgotten and rumoured to be dead giant – Corineus –slip aboard a luxury yacht in the Docklands Basin. No one had seen Corineus for centuries, but there he was, large as life, paddling, head just above the grey surface of the Thames like an enormous shaggy dog. But why was he hiding, why was he trying to go *unnoticed*? Giants aren't very good at skulking, or cut out for spying or secret missions, for obvious reasons.

As soon as Cat Tabby had seen Corineus, and was absolutely sure it was him, his devious little mind started seeing giant-sized amounts of money. He knew there was another giant in town, one that would move heaven and a lot of earth to catch up with Corineus, and it wasn't just to shake his hand or buy him a cream tea at Fortnum & Mason. Gogmagog and Corineus were sworn enemies, and would fight on sight. This was Cat Tabby's big plan. To bring the two giants together, and to profit from their violence.

It would be the fight of all fights, a bareknuckle, shake the foundations rumble to the death punch-up, and Cat Tabby and Dick would become the fight's promoters. They could organise the fight, sell tickets, sell the experience of the big fight to the vast numbers of the Under Folk. Cat Tabby and Dick Whittington could make some serious money. With the takings from the fight they would have a significant stake, enough to buy a seat at the big table. No, if all went as planned, they could *buy* the bloody table.

Most of the giants you find in story books are big, stupid and hairy, and spend all their time smashing things with clubs, or guarding magical eggs. In reality, giants lived in villages with the little people. They weren't evil or belligerent; more often than not, they were a useful addition to a small village. Imagine a giant that was also a shepherd – no wolves would carry off a lamb whilst it was on guard; or a giant that helped with the farming – it could divert a stream to help irrigate a dry field, or uproot trees to create more land for the village to farm. Giants were a boon and a blessing to a village. They had Old Earth knowledge, and secrets that they had learned from the First Folk, and they shared them without request for payment or favour. The old giants used to be generous and fair. Cat Tabby's tail twitched; he was hoping that his proposal would persuade Gogmagog to return to those old ways.

The door to Gogmagog's office opened suddenly, and a

huge goose waddled out and straight across the room to where Cat Tabby and Dick were sitting. When Dick stood up, his eyes were level with the bird's. Dick was 6 feet 2 inches – in his socks.

"What do you two little *rogues* want with the Big G?" said the goose.

"Well met, Master Gander. I hope we find you well and unruffled?"

"As I live and breathe, Cat Tabby, are you still setting yourself up as a bit of a wit? Surely, this handsome man standing next to you must have told you that you are not cut out for it?"

"Master Gander, I meant no offence. How is business?"

The goose stifled a honk, and turned around and started padding across the waiting room and through the open door to the office.

"We haven't got all day!" honked the goose from inside.

Cat Tabby and Dick Whittington took a deep breath and marched in, trying not to look like excited used-car salesmen. The office was dark. A small, single oil lamp stood on top of the desk on the opposite side of the room. Sitting behind the desk, like a mountain, was Gogmagog. He was taller than a London bus, and almost as wide. His hair was jet-black but there was some silver at the temples now. His chest was wide and flat – he was still fit, fighting fit, and his eyes were keen and as black as a beggar's tongue. Gogmagog was dressed in a well-fitting dark-blue suit. The tailor that made it for the giant must have used a circus tent to draw the pattern on, and there was no doubt that the wool from a sizeable flock of sheep – or two – had been used to make the jacket alone. He was not what you'd expect a giant to look like at all.

Mr. Gander waddled around the desk, honked twice and

then started to whisper in the giant's ear. Cat Tabby couldn't quite make out what the bird was saying, even with his radar ears. The whispering stopped suddenly, and Mr. Gander returned.

"You've got three minutes," he said.

"Gogmagog, sir, you may remember my partner and I ... we helped you out with some business concerning the Order of the Serpentine ... some information you required, we were the only creatures able to get it for you."

"I remember. Mr. Whittington and his talking fur ball isn't it? What do you want?"

Gogmagog's voice sounded like anchor chains being pulled up and onboard a cruise liner. The sounds hit hard, like metal on metal, thumping and heavy.

"We have a proposition for you, sir. Something that we feel will make all parties happy."

Mr. Gander let out a little sarcastic honk.

"Now now, Mr. Gander, let's hear the odd couple out shall we?" said Gogmagog.

Cat Tabby felt like asking the giant and his talking goose just who made the oddest couple, but he held his tongue.

"Sir, what is your heart's desire, what one thing would make you leap from behind that desk and dance a jig?"

"You don't have anything that big or that precious Cat Tabby, we know that your business dealings haven't been coming off since that affair with the Women of the Chapel. The word is that you are on your uppers."

Mr. Gander was enjoying his moment of perceived superiority. Gogmagog remained silent.

"Is there a person that you would like to see once again, sir? A member of your own kind perhaps?"

Gogmagog sat forward quickly. Cat Tabby and Dick Whittington felt a wall of air push past them. The eyes of the giant were fixed on Cat Tabby and the feline felt the fear.

"You have news of him? You have spoken with the one who has seen his final resting place?"

Cat Tabby swallowed hard. He knew that the next sentence or two would either add some noughts to their pay cheque or see them floating down the Thames face first.

"If I were to tell you that the giant in question is not dead at all, looking in rude health if I may make so bold, would that be of interest to you?"

Gogmagog stood up and his chair shot across the room and thumped into the wall behind him. It sounded like a barn falling down. Cat Tabby and Dick took two steps back and made sure that they knew where the door was; a quick retreat might be on the cards. The giant towered over them; the puny oil lamp was courageous, but it could not illuminate the whole room and Gogmagog's head was in darkness.

"If this is some sort of attempt to con me, you treacherous little runt, I swear by all that is sacred to me, that you will die a most horrific death. The manner in which you will go screaming into the fire will go down in history for its sheer brutality and sadistic nature, you understand me?"

"Gogmagog, last of the truly great giants of Albion and Lord of the Guildhall Under, we have seen Corineus, with our own eyes, we know where he is, and we know how long he will be there for. We also know where he is heading."

"Mr. Gander! Seal the door!" roared the giant.

Cat Tabby and Dick panicked and made for the door, but it slammed shut on them. Unseen hands or magic were at play, and they were trapped. Gogmagog flicked the desk out of the way. Piles of paper fell from it and took their time in finding a resting place on the floor. Mr. Gander honked nervously. Cat Tabby leaned against his friend's legs and shivered.

"Where did you see him?" roared the giant.

"Now now, Gogmagog, if you harm Cat or me, you will never see him. Threaten one and you threaten both. We are joined with our own magic, hurt one and hurt both." Dick's voice was confident, and Cat Tabby drew some strength from it.

"We came here as soon as we were able, Gogmagog. We have a proposal, one that could give you what you want and what we want."

Gogmagog took a step forward and looked down at the cat and its human partner.

"Speak!"

Cat Tabby cocked his head towards a leather sofa on the other side of the room.

"May we sit? A beverage would be most agreeable too."

"Mr. Gander! See to it."

The goose honked and padded away to find refreshments. Cat Tabby and Dick Whittington shuffled across to the sofa and sat down, keeping all four eyes on the massive hulk of Gogmagog, watching and hoping that they hadn't bitten off more than they could chew. Gogmagog retrieved his chair from behind his desk and guided it across the room, positioning it directly in front of the sofa, and between his guests and the door. Mr. Gander re-entered the room, and a dwarf carrying a silver tray with two glasses and a decanter of something red trotted in behind the bird. Once the tray had been placed on the table and a generous measure of the wine had been poured and offered, the dwarf bowed to the giant and then made his exit.

"Well then?"

"Gogmagog, sir, we would like to organise your meeting

with Corineus, at a place of our choosing. A battle to the
death. An evening of settling scores if you will. A fight that
would define the age."

Gogmagog took a deep breath.

"My feud with that stunted little gobshite is not something for a carnival! Nor is it a cash cow for you. Do you not
realise where you are and who you are talking to? I could rip
you apart and use whatever is left to pot a house plant. Now,
give him up to me!"

Cat Tabby was about to ask for a bowl to lap from. He
was sure that the dwarf had many qualities, but intelligence
was not one of them. He had not realised that Cat could not
hold a glass. In the end he decided to say nothing.

"Before we came here, we made sure to note down
where Corineus is going. He may already be on his way, or
leaving soon. Where he is heading, only we two and
Corineus know. Killing us will not bring him to you, killing
us will not lead you to him either. We might not be able to
hold out for long if you torture us, but it might just be long
enough for him to escape."

Gogmagog sat back in his chair and placed his hands on
the armrests. Only the sound of Mr. Gander's webbed feet
lifting and lowering on the stone floor punctuated the
silence.

"What's to stop him from escaping anyway? How do you
intend to subdue him and keep his whereabouts secret? So
many questions, little people, I hope for your sake that you
have answers." Gogmagog's voice was deep and there was
violence behind it.

"If you agree to our terms and allow us to handle the
fight, we will offer you 25% of the gate receipts. We will then
set the fight at a venue or a place to suit you, somewhere
favourable, although, of course, we are not suggesting that

you need any advantage. We can also guarantee that the fight will happen because we know of a place, somewhere impregnable, and guarded by forces so strong that it cannot be breached. Once Corineus is there, his escape is impossible." Cat Tabby finished his pitch and leaped onto the floor from the sofa.

"Where is this place?"

"If we told you that, Gogmagog, we would have fewer cards to play."

Gogmagog's huge hands formed into fists.

"So be it. Tell me where and when, and do not try to cross me, you know what will happen if you do. Mr. Gander, see these two to the door. This meeting is at an end."

Mr. Gander honked with what sounded like relief, and then waddled for the door. Cat Tabby and Dick Whittington got in step behind him and left the office as quickly as they could. The meeting had been fraught, but as they walked down the corridor towards the large wooden doors, they allowed themselves a small smile. It was only when they were in their car, threading their way through the rush-hour traffic that Dick finally spoke.

"Are you suggesting that we stash Corineus inside the Black Museum?"

"I had to think fast, Dick! We were this close to sharing a pot with a rose plant just then. It was the only place I knew that Gogmagog could not get into. He'll work it out for himself shortly, but by then, the fight should be on, and he knows that he can't get inside the Black Museum."

But, Cat! How are we going to convince Judas to grab him and stash him inside?"

"That's the easy bit, Dick. We convince Corineus that Gogmagog knows where he is and is coming to kill him. We tell him that the Black Museum is the only place that Gogmagog cannot get into, spirit him over there and tell him to convince Judas to give him a bunk for the night because failure to do so will mean that two giants are going to smash their way through London, and thousands of normal folk will be killed in the carnage. Judas won't allow that to happen."

Dick allowed himself another small smile.

"That sounds like a plan my furry little friend. Let's find ourselves a venue for the dust-up, somewhere big, somewhere that we can squeeze all the Under Folk into."

Just then, the gloom lifted, the sun came out and the traffic parted to allow Cat Tabby and Dick Whittington to get on their way. A fair day or a false dawn? They'd find out in the next forty-eight hours.

10

CONSTANCE

M r. Mast did not like lifts. He did not like the metal boxes at all. He favoured the open spaces of the world, and he loved the river most of all. The others – Waterline, Deck and Sail –did not mind lifts and so he was walking up the stairs to the top floor on his own. A big number, painted in bright orange, marked the floors; he had only one more to climb. His brothers were waiting for him just outside the door to the office of the man they called their benefactor. Mast did not like the man any more than he liked the lift, but he paid well and had the same goals as the Sons of Colquhoun – the destruction of the gangs and the illegal trade that poisoned the Thames.

Mr. Waterline knocked on the door and before his hand dropped back down to his waist the door clicked open, and they walked in. As usual, the man called Adam was sitting at the head of his long table. Four glasses stood in the centre, keeping a bottle of expensive looking wine company. The Sons took their seats and Mr. Sail poured the wine. It was better than good, and they drained their glasses.

"I'm glad you enjoyed it. One of my very best, for my best team. There are more bottles on the side behind you, please help yourselves," said Adam.

Mr. Waterline retrieved four more bottles and shared them out. There was only one corkscrew, and the minutes passed in silence until all of the bottles were opened and glasses were refilled.

"I take it that your mission was completed without issue?"

"It was," said Mr. Waterline.

"So now, payment is due," said Mr. Deck.

Adam reached into a drawer underneath the table and plucked a padded envelope from inside it. It was A3 in size and stuffed to the gills. He slid it down the table and it came to rest in front of Mr. Deck.

"You can count it if you like, I shan't be offended if you do," said Adam.

Mr. Deck looked around the table. His brothers nodded and he removed the envelope from the table and let it lean up against his shin.

"Thank you for that show of trust. I have been made aware of your success and as a result I should like to commission you for another piece of business. If you have the time and the inclination?"

Adam was ladling it on a bit thick, but he realised after their first meeting that these men were stranded in the now, whilst yearning for the past. The way they spoke and dressed harked back to the days when the river was awash with the Jolly Jack Tars of the Royal Navy, and the barges and flat-bottomed boats of the estuaries. He had worked them out two minutes after they had entered the room. They wanted to bring justice and a sharp knife to the River

Thames. They were awkward around other people, but they were killers and absolutely fearless.

"What sort of business?" It was the first time that Mr. Sail had spoken. His was the softest voice of the lot but he was the nastiest by far; violence and anger emanated from him like the heat from a farrier's forge.

"More of the same, really. In fact, I need you to rattle your stick inside the Mudlarks' hive a little more vigorously. They have reacted to your first act, but I think we can hurry them on a bit. Crime is still at epidemic proportions and trade in contraband and stolen goods is rising. We must disable these gangs if we wish to see peace along the riverbanks."

"The Cockle boy was hard to kill, he lasted much longer than we allowed for. We shall need to know more about the next target so that we can plan ahead. There is talk that the Black Museum has been alerted. We do not wish to cross paths with the Master of the Museum, if it can be helped," said Mr. Waterline.

Adam sat up and straightened his tie.

"The next target is another Cockle. This time I want you to kill Constance Cockle."

Mr. Deck placed his glass back down on the table. Adam did not like the look on his face.

"We are not child killers. What is this Constance to you, and how will murdering her bring about peace?"

"It's Mr. Deck, isn't it?"

Adam hadn't prepared himself properly before arranging the meeting and now he was flailing.

"I abhor the death of any innocent, believe me, but Constance Cockle holds a very important position within her family. I have it on good authority that she handles the flow of information and the passing on of secrets for them.

To look at her, you would think she was just a slip of a girl, but mark my words, gentlemen, she has sent many of my agents to the seabed."

"A girl?" How sure are you of her guilt?" Mr. Deck had already poured himself another glass of wine.

"As sure as I need to be."

He lifted his hands from the tabletop and studied them theatrically.

"There is no innocent blood on these hands. You have my word. If you want me to place one of them on a bible, please, ask away."

Mr. Waterline tapped his glass on the table three times and there was silence.

"The same fee as before then?"

"Because of the delicate nature of the assignment, the individual's age and sex, and the appearance of the Black Museum, I would be happy to increase the amount by 50%."

"We will complete the task," said Mr. Waterline.

"Fantastic! The details are over there. Please help your-self to another bottle of rouge if you like. Take the whole case, and let me know using the same channels as before when the assignment is completed. I shall wish you a good night then, gentlemen." Adam was keen to get rid of the Sons of Colquhoun.

"Until next time then." Mr. Deck picked up the box. There was a faint chiming from inside as the bottles settled, and then one by one they trooped out and were gone.

Adam looked at the wall of security monitors in the anteroom adjoining the boardroom. Three had taken the lift, and one was taking the stairs. He watched them until they had left the building – something about them made him very uneasy. If he had heard what the Sons were saying to each other about the job and their employer, he would have been scared, not just uneasy.

"There is something not quite right about him, Mr. Deck, I can feel it."

"We have no choice but to use him as he is using us, Mr. Sail. He claims to want the same things we do, but we are all of us not so green as to think that that is all he wants. There is more at stake here, I believe that. Let us carry on as we are, there is a possibility that when we turn the next corner, something better may come our way. Until then, let us take the fool's gold, and if he turns backstabber on us, then we shall deal with him."

11

THE GOAT AND THE MAN

J udas stood on the roof of Scotland Yard, nudging some of the grey gravel that was supposed to deter the pigeons from making their nests with the toe of one of his Kickers' brogues. The wind whipped at his coat and Judas shoved his hands into his pockets to keep warm. Rain had been forecast but thankfully it had passed the Met by. Judas was waiting for his friend, Angel Dave. The little angel (he was only 7 feet tall) helped out whenever Judas needed a spare pair of eyes and wings. He could be trusted and had proved his worth on a number of occasions; most recently Judas had asked him to fly across the Irish Sea to liberate a spear from the Dublin Museum. The weapon had enabled Judas to kill the Captain of the Night. Now he hoped that Angel Dave would be able to find out some information for him about Charles Murrell, also known as the Cunning Man.

Judas looked up into the sky and tracked one of the smaller passenger planes that ping-ponged in and out of London City Airport. As the plane began its steep descent, Judas's eye was drawn away to the hundreds of angels. They were flying back and forth, running errands and earning a crust. Some days, Judas envied them. They could pass between worlds, fly off at the drop of a feather whenever they felt like it, and they were content. They were happy in London, and the other places they had chosen to settle, they had great power and great strength, and they could have ripped the world of man to pieces if they had truly wanted to. But they chose to serve and to teach instead. Judas was glad that they did. He had his own angel minder; God liked to keep an eye on him. The Archangel Michael was a royal pain in the proverbial, but he was invaluable when the chips were down and danger was everywhere.

Judas started to fasten the buttons of his Frahm City coat. The cold was winning, and a bank of dark clouds was rolling his way. It looked like the rain was coming around for another pass and he intended to be inside in the warm and dry. He was going to give it another ten minutes and then if Angel Dave didn't show, he would give the traffic boys a ring and tell them to enforce one or two of his unpaid parking tickets. That would teach him to turn up on time. But Judas didn't need to make that call because Angel Dave suddenly swooped down out of the grey sky and landed like a hawk in front of him.

"My nose is running and my hands are freezing, did you lose your way, or your watch?" asked Judas.

"A million apologies, Judas, forgive my tardy timekeeping, please." Angel Dave looked flustered.

"Something up my friend?"

Angel Dave pulled in his wings and then rolled his shoulders so they folded away behind his back, compact and neat.

"There's something up with the Angels of the North, Judas, messages have been flying around, pardon the pun,

and most of the old Host have gone up there. Looks bad if
you ask me. It's not often that the really powerful angels get
together. But, as you know, I'm just a lowly foot soldier, I just
run errands and go where I'm told. That's why I was late.
Sorry."

Judas ran his fingers through his thick, dark, curly hair.
He had enough on his plate just now, and if there was something happening with the angels as well, he'd need to pull in
some favours and get some help.

"Come on down to the museum then, Angel Dave. I will
brew up some coffee and tell you want I need, but, if you're
needed elsewhere, let me know now and I can make a few
calls."

Judas opened the door that led down to the lift that
would take them straight to the 7th floor. Angel Dave just
stepped off the roof and disappeared. He would fly down to
the 7th, and hang in the air until Judas opened the specially
designed window to let him in.

Judas made a pot of coffee. His latest indulgence was a
Le Creuset cafetiere – he'd grown tired of the plastic tasting
variety of instant coffee that the Met supplied and had
become a bit of a coffee snob. He'd tried to convert Sergeant
Lace, but she always made a face when she saw him making
a pot. She was a tea person and liked her tea as dark as his
coffee. Lace was away from the Black Museum looking into
the River Gangs. Judas poured the Ethiopian blend into a
warmed mug and offered it to Angel Dave.

"Smells good," said the angel.

"Not bad is it? Now, down to police work and why I
called you. A short while ago the Gilded Goat was killed. I
was supposed to be looking out for him, but someone got to
him. I know who the murderer is, but he's gone to ground,
and I just don't have the manpower to search for him right

now. I need you to track him down for me. Just find him, let me know where he is and I'll do the rest, okay?"

Angel Dave sipped at his coffee.

"The Gilded Goat? Wasn't he a fence of some sort, stolen goods and money changing?"

"That's him. Not a bad sort, didn't have a bad bone in his body and was taken advantage of by a nasty piece of work called Charles Murrell," said Judas.

"I know of *him*," said Angel Dave.

Judas placed his mug down on his desk and walked over to the map of Greater London on the wall. He took a red pen from a pot on the nearest filing cabinet and drew a rectangle.

"This is where Mr. Murrell was last seen, him and his *bodyguard*, someone that I want you to steer well clear of, understand? The last thing I need right now is another situation. These streets have a high concentration of Under Folk places. Start here, see what you can dig up and then if you draw a blank, extend the search area by a street or two. Let me know when you do though. You okay with that?"

Angel Dave just smiled, finished his coffee, and placed his mug back on the draining board next to the sink in the tiny kitchen.

"Leave it with me, Judas, I won't let you down, trust me. Do you have anything that I can read about this chap Murrell? Be nice to know what he's about."

This time it was Judas that was smiling.

"A case file you mean? You'll be signing up and carrying a truncheon next. It's on the desk over there, the one marked 'Cunning Man'. Have a read, but leave it here when you've finished. I have a date with Jack the Ripper now. Keep me informed. You can leave a message here, ask for Sergeant Lace or Sergeant Henshaw, and if you have to join the rest of

the angels for whatever this situation is with the Angels of
the North, try and let me know."

"Will do, sir!" Angel Dave performed a salute, as sarcas-
tically as he could.

Judas smiled. Angel Dave was as fearless as a lion, and
possessed a sense of humour that even the hardest of hearts
warmed to. It was impossible not to like him. Judas left him
to his new *case files*, and picked up the desk phone. He
pressed the quick dial button for the front desk and waited
for Sergeant Henshaw to pick up.

"Have they arrived?" asked Judas.

Henshaw's voice was steady and clear.

"Yes, sir, the lady with the silk scarf arrived first, and
then the others turned up at regular intervals. Shall I send
them up?"

"Please do, thank you, Sergeant."

Judas replace the handset on the cradle of the desk
phone, counted to eleven to allow for the lift and then left
the office. He walked down the corridor and waited outside
the door to the Black Museum. Seconds later he heard the
faint chime of the lift's floor indicator, and then footsteps.
They were light steps, soft, the sort of footsteps you'd
imagine following a coffin. He waited for his guests to join
him, then he took the black swipe card from his pocket and
used it to open the door to the Black Museum. Once inside,
only the tick of the fluorescent bulb in the corner could be
heard. Then, thousands of voices started talking, all at the
same time. They were having conversations with each other,
snarling and sniping, cursing and chattering. Deep voices,
hard voices, women's voices and the timid voices of children.
Judas could pick out snatches of their conversations: some
were heavily accented East End barrow boys, words from

the gutter, and others were from the opera house, in equal measure.

"You was the one that peached!" said one.

"How much you going to give me for that there knife?" asked another.

"Poison is a woman's weapon you know," a young lady murmured.

"And you shall be put to death, and God have mercy on your black soul," said an elderly judge, passing sentence on some unfortunate soul.

The exhibits ranted and railed at each other, but Judas tuned them out. His guests were surprised at first but quickly settled. They had all come to meet with Jack the Ripper, and they all needed to be focused because that vicious bastard was as crooked and as evil as they came. Judas crossed the room. His guests followed and then he used the swipe card once again to enter the Key Room. He quickly located the white glove on the long table, and picked it up and held it out in front of him.

"We all need to hold it," Judas explained.

The others reached out and grasped the white glove.

"And that includes you, Simon. Ladies, may I introduce you to Simon the Zealot. An old acquaintance and now the steward of the Black Museum."

They heard his footsteps first and then gradually, the shape of Simon the Zealot emerged from the darkness at the far end of the room.

"Ladies, hello and welcome to my new domain," said Simon.

He was dressed smartly in a grey two-piece suit; his short hair had been styled into the latest version of a skin fade. Simon was like Judas; he aged very slowly and dressed very young. Simon drew closer and then reached out and laid his hand on top of Judas's hand. At first nothing appeared to happen, but then, just at the edge of their vision, a small grey circle formed, the colour of dirty ice. It grew and folded over onto itself, then it stretched, and became a silver tunnel that angled downwards. The room was silent at first, then there was a sound like a giant piece of Velcro being ripped apart.

Seconds later, Judas was back in Victorian London and standing on Whitechapel's busy streets. Grey shadows of men and women passed him by, like floating smudges. Great cart horses pulled their heavy loads alongside him, and from nearby, he heard the bells of the ships and the barges at anchor, and the whistles of the sailors and the squeaking of the wharf-side rats. This was Jack the Ripper's prison cell; he was imprisoned here. But this was much, much more than just a mere room of concrete and bricks with a steel door and bars at the window. The black-hearted fiend could move freely here, but he could not interact with the shadows around him. He could not taste the food, or drink the wine, nor could he sample the carnal pleasures of a world he knew so well. To someone like Jack the Ripper, who lived to kill and menace, temptation was everywhere, and yet it was out of his reach. His knives were still sharp, but they would never taste blood or part soft white flesh ever again. His privilege and wealth meant nothing now. It was a life of continuous torture. Death would have been a blessing, but then that was what the Black Museum was for, after all.

Judas didn't have to wait long for Jack to appear. He heard the ferule of his cane first, tap, tap, tapping upon the wet cobblestones, and then he saw him: the familiar top hat, the long cloak, and the bulky Gladstone bag swinging by his side.

"A good morrow to you, Judas, I hope I find you well?" said the 'Ripper'.

Jack's voice was breathy. His well-educated vowels and cultured accent created words that slipped out of his mouth like dark, wet, slimy eels from a ripped net.

"So, here we are again then, Ripper. I seem to spend more time with you than any of the other 'residents'. Something I promised myself that I would sort out as soon as I could. I told you that I would not let the corruption of the angel go unpunished."

"Oh, my dear Judas, you have it quite wrong you know, it was the angel that sought me out, it was the winged warder and his spy that talked me into showing them the ways out. I was but a mere pawn in their power play."

"Jack, have you ever said a word that wasn't a lie?"

"I have often been misrepresented, Judas, as you were, I suppose. Is God still punishing you my love, still throwing you under the bus for sending his boy up the mount?"

"Let's get back to the matter in hand, shall we? You have the blood of an angel on your hands – you didn't wield the sword that cleaved him in two, but you were responsible for poisoning his heart. For that you must pay, Jack."

"And just how are you going to make my incarceration any worse?" asked Jack.

"With great ease," said Judas.

Judas stared at the *Ripper* through the mist. Ever since he'd taken over as the custodian of the Black Museum, Jack the Ripper had always been the worst of the inmates, and inside a prison that housed the worst serial killers, rapists, thugs, house breakers and footpads that ever walked London's dark streets, that was no mean feat. Jack was always toying with him, or his officers, and forever trying to taunt, hurt and torment anyone that he came into contact with. In the beginning Judas thought it was boredom, but he soon realised that Jack wasn't bored at all, he just wanted to punish the world. It was what made his heart pump, and his penis harden no doubt. But now, after the death of the angel, one that was sent to guard him, Jack the Ripper needed to be punished and reminded that he was not above the law, in either world. Judas reached inside his pocket and pulled out a white glove.

"This is a rather expensive, handmade, gentleman's opera glove. It has been stitched and worked on by a craftsman, who judging by the quality of the sewing, takes great pride in his work. There are two silver buttons at the wrist, and a very stylish looking little monogram embroidered alongside them. It's a very nice thing. Some of the other inmates have ugly little keys. A dull rusty blade, a broken bottle, a hat-pin that is bent out of shape. There is even the head of a dead rat! But none are so fine as this, Jack."

The smile on Jack's face began to fade, and small furrows appeared on his forehead.

"Silence? This is indeed a rare moment of paradise on earth. Jack the Ripper is lost for words. Hallelujah. Bring on the heavenly choir and cast the petals of the everlasting flowers into the air."

"Now then, Master Judas, Warden of the Black Museum, defender of the innocent, and so on and so forth. Perhaps we might talk of my incarceration? Maybe there is some small task that you need me to take on? Is there nothing that a man of my abilities might be able to do for you and the establishment?"

Judas waved the white glove in the air like some Victorian dandy, and he was pleased to see that Jack's eyes followed it, never leaving it, like a hungry dog following a grilled sausage.

"The sovereign has dropped hasn't it, Jack? You have finally realised what I am about to do, haven't you? If I burn this glove, any connection you have to the Black Museum, and by association, the world outside, will be severed instantly. I will no longer need to visit you, there will be no more requests from the Black Museum for your assistance in any of our cases, your use will be at an end, and you will drift away into the void of the Time Fields."

"Detective Inspector, please, let's not be too hasty. I can be of use, I know things, secret things. The walls whisper to me and I whisper back, fledgling killers pray to me, and many copy my acts. Even now there are those in the real world that desire nothing more in life than to become my heir. I can stop them; I could save the lives of many innocents."

Judas sighed and took a Zippo lighter from his other pocket. Jack the Ripper gasped and stumbled backwards, his leather bag falling from his grip and his top hat toppling into the gutter.

"Jack, at last, your moment is over, for that is all it was – a dark, ugly, fleeting moment. Your existence has been but a single second of wasted time, counted away by the clock of the universe. You are but a solitary grain of sand dropping from the neck of a giant sandglass that will pass away into any one of a million dark voids."

Judas flicked at the top of his lighter with his thumb and the metal case snapped open. A small flame appeared – it danced from side to side at first, but then it steadied. It was only slight, but here in this blurry nightmare version of London, it could have been the glow from a coastal watch-tower. Jack the Ripper saw it and tried to stand up, but lost his footing, stumbled and went back down on one knee.

Judas looked down on him and saw the panic in the Ripper's face.

"I would give anything to hold this flame to your glove, Jack, but that honour has never been mine."

"No! It is ours!"

The voices of the women that had accompanied Judas to Whitechapel cut through the night like one of Jack the Ripper's knives and even Judas shuddered at their coldness and severity. Jack the Ripper trembled as the women came forward.

Judas waited for *her* to take the glove, and then the lighter. In story books this was the moment when the pursuer, having run his enemy to ground, chopped the remaining strand from the rope that held the bridge across the causeway, or kicked the last rafter that held the roof in place above the inferno below. Judas remained exactly where he was. He was not going to miss this for the world.

Jack the Ripper watched as the remaining Women of the Chapel emerged from the white curtain of mist in front of him. At first, he didn't even recognise them, and then, like a slow sunrise, it dawned on him. Here were his trophy victims, back from the grave, back from the surgeon's table, back to haunt him. They looked whole and hearty, not like he remembered. He liked to think of them with their throats cut and their female organs removed and thrown to one side. In his mind that was what these poisoned and poxy prostitutes deserved.

They wore clothes that he was unfamiliar with, tight-fitting clothes. He could see their bosoms – they dressed like they were ready to perform at some filthy burlesque or advertise their wares at a seedy knocking shop. But the thing he hated most of all was their confidence and their attitude. They looked strong and focused. The women he had stalked and then butchered had been drudges, weak women, scared women, easy to hurt women, but these women were different – they were strong, and he feared them.

The lady wearing the silk scarf was the first to speak.

"And so, we have come to the end. Not our end, but *yours*. A long time ago, after I had been saved and made whole again, there was only one thing I wanted. It consumed me and turned my heart to ashes. Every waking hour I spent dreaming and scheming of ways to take my revenge on you. But you were gone. You were resigned to history and as such you were far away from me, *from us*. Then the Master of the Black Museum showed us this new world."

The lady wearing the silk scarf waved her hand around in the air.

"This other place, where your spirit, your entity lived on. A place of existence, the last you would ever know. And he promised us something, something that would end our pain and allow us to heal and to move on."

Jack the Ripper stood up. He pretended to smooth the silk of his cloak, to rearrange it, but it was obvious that he was looking for his Gladstone bag, and his sharp, deadly Crimean field surgeons' knives. It was an impulse move; there was nothing that he could have done with them even if they were in his hands right now. He was at their mercy.

"We were poor women, destitute, fit only for an early grave that we could not afford to pay for. We were nothing to you, but to each other we were everything! We could not buy a decent life; we tried, we even sank so low as to offer up our bodies, for rich men and poor to abuse and soil. We only wanted to see the bottom rung of society's ladder, we would have been happy there, but then you came and stole that away."

Judas was becoming concerned that Jack the Ripper might bolt but he saw that the other women had moved to surround him silently.

"Enough now!" roared the woman with the silk scarf.

Judas watched as she raised the white glove so the Ripper could see it clearly, then she held the lighter underneath it. At first it singed the fabric, then it took hold, and then the small orange line crept up and started to consume the white glove. Judas heard Jack the Ripper start to scream. He was shouting something about the King, and then it was something about a Brotherhood, then all they heard were screams and echoes.

The essence of Jack the Ripper was destroyed at that moment, and soon his jail would vanish. They watched in silence as the shapes of the people faded, buildings disappeared, and the sounds of the time were turned down and then off. Soon, only Judas, Simon the Zealot, and the Women of the Chapel remained. A grey fade stretched away in all directions. Gone were the streets and the landmarks; emptiness remained. The lady in the silk scarf dropped the small scrap of silk, all that remained of the glove. One of the silver buttons fell, unnoticed by all except Simon. It made a light sound as it landed, and Simon coughed to disguise it. Then the women embraced each other, but there were no tears, and as they huddled together Simon plucked the silver button from the floor and placed it inside his jacket pocket.

Judas took the silver coin from his own pocket and started to run his thumb across its surface. Around and around it went – the coin was incredibly smooth now, almost wafer thin. Judas made a mental note to take another from his hoard.

Had the years passed so swiftly since he'd taken the last one out?

Judas closed his eyes and dreamed of redemption, just one of the other impossible things that he coveted.

"Thank you. We all thank you. Each and every one of us. Here is your lighter, Master of the Black Museum. As a flame, it has no equal, along with our regard and appreciation of you, DCI Judas Iscariot. The Women of the Chapel are eternally grateful to you. If you could only know the magnitude of the service you have done for us. The night will not have fewer demons for our kind, but we will do our utmost to show our sisters that we are all strong and that we can win in the end."

Judas returned the silver coin to his pocket. He looked at their faces. Everyone was smiling, including Simon, which was odd, but maybe he was changing too?

"We won't be travelling back to the Black Museum the same way we got here, I'm afraid."

Judas reached inside the inner pocket of his coat and removed what looked like a highwayman's mask.

"Gather round, ladies, I hope you all like horses!"

12

THE WORD ON THE WATER

T he ghost of the Lighterman hadn't stopped talking since Lilith had stepped aboard. She had disguised herself as best as she was able to in a cloak with a large hood, but soon realised that she needn't have bothered because all the Lighterman was interested in was himself and what was happening on the Thames.

"Soon, mark my words, they'll dredge up so much silt that the riverbed will crack and then them that lives under the river will have a look out, mark my words they will."

This chirpy line of conversation switched effortlessly to the sighting of swimming giants, to the werewolves in the Paddington Basin, and on to the rumblings coming out of the City about the collapse of some building or other.

"Apparently, so I'm told, the foundations were exposed. There was rubble everywhere and the Ley Line express runs through there, could have been messy! Do you ever take the train?"

On and on it went until Lilith could take no more and decided to attempt to steer the conversation her way.

"A good friend of mine, a Sin Eater, said he was on the

River the other night and dropped one of his 'Thought Boxes' by accident, in a Lighterman's skiff. It's very valuable to him, not worth a scrap to anyone else really, but I think he's the sentimental sort and I hear he's thinking of paying whoever finds it a reward."

The Lighterman didn't even miss a beat.

"I had one of those Sin Eaters in my boat the other night, talking to himself all the way across he was. I can't bear them that talk all the time, can you? Kept looking over his shoulder at the riverbank for some reason. Funny sort. He wanted me to row down the river towards Tower Bridge and then asked me to drop him off just by the warship. Paid well, talked a lot, didn't leave anything in my boat though."

Lilith smiled under her cowl.

"The grey warship? The big steel boat? HMS Dublin, or something?"

"HMS Belfast," said the Lighterman.

"Could you drop me off there, please? I don't think I've ever stood on her deck."

"A pleasure fair lady. *Row dry and row quick, we'll cover the water in half a tic,*" sang the Lighterman as he pulled hard on his right oar and made for the shoreline.

When Lilith was on dry ground again she wandered around affecting to take in the sights. Finding the Sin Eater was proving to be very difficult, but thanks to the Lighterman, she now had something to work with. And once she had the Sin Eater, then she would have Adam.

13

THE NIGHT PLUNDERERS

Sergeant Lace pinned the last chip to the bottom of the polystyrene tray with a small wooden fork. Only the last few scrapings of batter from her sausage remained. She wetted the tip of a finger, ran it round the bottom of the tray and devoured them. There was nothing like sausage and chips from a mobile snack wagon. Only a Cornish pastie could come close. Lace was sitting on a low wall, a hundred metres away from London River House on Royal Pier Road in Gravesend. She had a cold bum but a warm and happy stomach. She checked her watch again and then stood up and brushed the salt and what was left of the chip crumbs from her jeans. As she walked towards London River House she thought about the strange series of events that had led to her joining the Black Museum and working for DCI Judas Iscariot. She smiled. Her only regret was that she hadn't done it sooner.

The location she had been given by Gilbert Lines, a young man convicted of theft from one of the Queen's dock-yards and summarily hanged by the neck until dead, who was now doing time in the Black Museum, was just up ahead and on her left. *The Hall of the Night Plunderers* didn't appear on any map, no cartographer had ever inked it or scratched its name on any paper, and the Google Earth satellite would have to get up a lot earlier in the morning if it wanted to sneak up on it. It was perched at the river's edge, and if you didn't know the right number of times to strike the small iron bell that hung from a rotten looking piece of old timber nearby, you'd never get inside.

Lace found the bell exactly where the ghost of Gilbert Lines had said it would be. She reached out for the slimy bit of rope that hung from it, and sounded the bell: four times, rest for a beat, three times, rest for two beats, and then five quick strikes. The sound of the old bell was true, and Lace was pleased with the chimes. They hung low over the water, lasting for far longer than she expected. The minutes passed by; Lace began to wonder if Lines had given her a bum steer, or she'd rung the bell six times when she should have only struck it five?

She was about to ring the bell again when she heard the sound of a large wooden door creaking open to her left. A rectangle of warm orange light appeared, not quite over the water but then again, not directly above the shingle of the shoreline. It hovered in the air. A few years ago, Lace would have stood there and reasoned it out. Was it a reflection, some sort of trick perhaps? But now, after working at the Black Museum, she took things as she found them, however odd they might be. She walked across the wet sand, her footsteps crunching loudly, and then she stepped into the glow.

"David Blaine, eat your heart out!" Lace exclaimed.

The hall was huge, not particularly high, but very long and wide. Great stacks of wooden chests were piled along the walls, along with bales of colourful materials. On closer inspection she realised that this is what a cargo hold must look like. It was full to the rafters with contraband. It was also full of pipe smoke; almost everyone she could see, and that included children, was busy puffing on pipes of all shapes and sizes. Lace guessed that whatever they were filling their pipes with wasn't paid for either. If asked, they would probably tell her that it had all fallen off the back of a barge, or something.

"Would it be possible to speak to the head man or woman?" Lace enquired.

All talking ceased and every eyeball turned her way. A tall woman with full sleeve tattoos on both arms smiled at her and then spat an enormous tobacco quid down onto the wooden planking at her feet.

"That would be me, and I'm guessing that you are the lass from the Black Museum?"

Lace hadn't been called a lass, a slip of a girl or a pretty young thing since she was knee-high to a panda car, and she bristled. But then she relaxed; most of the people she met these days lived in some sort of time warp – they had one foot in the past and the other firmly in the here and the now. More often than not, although the language was out of date, the meaning was very much more civilised.

"I am Sergeant Lace. My boss, DCI Judas Iscariot sends his greetings and his apologies that he cannot be here in person right now, and hopes that he can make your acquaintance at the next earliest opportunity."

The woman with the tattoos crossed the room and when she was near enough she extended her hand and Lace took it in her own. They shook, and then the woman with the tattoos led her over to a table on the far side of the room. It was quickly vacated by the men and women drinking around it. Lace sat down with her back to the wall and flicked what she hoped was a leftover chunk of half-eaten bread from the tabletop. The other woman sat down opposite her and introduced herself.

"Mary Tar, Captain of the Night Plunderers."

"Pleased to meet you. Do I call you Mary, or Captain Tar?"

Mary laughed; it was a deep, happy laugh from the bottom of the rib cage. Lace liked her immediately.

"Mary is fine. How should I address you?"

"Lace is good. I'm not that keen on my first name. Lace sounds a bit more ... petite."

"Well then, Lace. Can I offer you a drink?"

"Yes you can, as long as it isn't some super-strength rum."

"Rum? We lift all manner of goods from the River, Lace. We have some rather spectacular champagne chilling in a net under the water, or there is Bavarian beer, some sort of lager made by monks in Austria – or would you prefer an exotic-flavoured Russian vodka? Apparently, elderflower vodka is all the rage in the City."

"It is this month, along with cheap cocaine and networking weekenders in Bristol. I like my vodka plain and strong."

"Well said."

Mary looked over her shoulder at one of the children standing nearby. No words were exchanged but the boy ran off, reappearing moments later with a chilled bottle of very expensive vodka on it and two crystal shot glasses. Mary poured and she and Lace drained them quickly. They chatted and skirted around the main issue until they were half a bottle in, then Lace, feeling that she knew Mary, the Captain of the Night Plunderers a little bit better, decided to fire her first salvo.

"We're looking into the murder of one of the River People. A very important member of the River People," said Lace.

Mary Tar responded quickly.

"Aren't all folks of the River important? The life of any one of mine, young or old, useful or useless, is dear to me."

Lace poured them both another drink.

"You're absolutely right. I apologise, that was clumsy of me. We're investigating the murder of a young chap called Cockle. He is one of the Mudlarks."

The noise inside the Hall of the Night Plunderers abruptly stopped and Mary Tar, whose glass was very near her mouth, replaced it on the table and sat forward, locking eyes with Lace.

"Maybe we should go somewhere else to talk. There is a room across the way there. We will not be disturbed, and we can talk freely."

Then, she turned around to her people and shouted at them.

"We've just landed more cargo in one week than ever before! We're having a party aren't we? If any of you would prefer to be back out there on the water, hustling for news or clambering over some wet and rusty deck, you have my blessing. Now, are we working or partying?"

The noise level shot up immediately. Drinks were replenished, fresh smoke was inhaled and gradually the sounds of merrymaking returned. Captain Mary Tar, head of the Night Plunderers, pushed her chair back and stood up. It was clear to Lace that she was a formidable woman. Her words carried weight and there was no shortage of alpha males in the room – big burly men, hard men that looked like they knew the right end of a blade. Lace followed her as she walked to the far end of the hall. There,

Mary Tar turned to the right and Lace saw that the hall had a lot in common with the Key Room back at the Black Museum. Behind another stack of bales, liberated from the hold of some other vessel no doubt was an open door, through which Lace could see that the hall had another wing. She followed Tar through the door and into another hall, equal in size to the first.

"Just like the Key Room," said Lace.

"Sorry?" said Tar.

"We have a room back at the Black Museum that defies all logic in terms of space and size, like this one. You can't see it from the outside but once you're inside, it stretches on forever."

"Interesting. We, the Night Plunderers that is, have a number of holds like this one. They are handy for storing goods and other things."

Lace looked around. There were giant shelves running all the way down the walls. Stacked on them were new cars, performance sports models; wooden pallets sagging under the weight of blocks of £50 notes wrapped in cellophane; oil drums; and clothes rails full of mink coats that made them look like static bisons. Lace tried to take a visual inventory; the policewoman in her couldn't help it.

"I hope that you have import licences for all this."

"Of course, they're all stacked in a neat pile just behind the unicorn saddles," said Mary Tar.

"Just what I thought, good to know," said Lace.

'We deal in most things, Sergeant, but we don't get involved in anything heavy like drugs or people. All of the River People signed an agreement long ago. We try to stay as clean as we can. Any interference from the Black Museum and your master is kept to a bare minimum, it keeps every-thing running smoothly. By the way, ask him if he needs any more of those coats he likes so much, we've just come into a few. Tell him he can come down and take a look when he wants, just give me a heads-up so I can change into something more ... suitable."

Mary Tar stopped outside a steel door, reached into her pocket for a large brass key, and unlocked it. Lace followed her inside. She was expecting a storeroom or something like an overflow cupboard, packed with boxes liberally sprinkled with dust. She was surprised to find herself inside a rather pleasant room, however. A large, polished wooden table squatted in the centre of the room on top of a beautiful Persian rug. The walls were lined with bookshelves crammed with books; first editions by the look of them. There were only two chairs in the room, so this was obviously the place where decisions were made, and judgements handed down.

Mary Tar took one and motioned for Lace to take the other.

"We decided on a round table, like King Arthur's, just so that no one gets any ideas above their station. Most of the time it's just me and one other. If it's a big meeting, we move some more chairs in. So, Sergeant Lace of the Black Museum at Scotland Yard, there has been a murder?"

"I'm afraid so. A couple of days ago we were called to the scene, just down the river from here as it happens. A young man called Henry Swift Cockle, a member of the Mudlark family it appears, was killed quite horrifically, and a note was 'attached' to the body with a large, rather nasty knife," said Lace.

"And what was written on the note, Sergeant?"

Lace removed her notebook from the inside pocket of her leather jacket, flipped to the relevant page and started to read.

"Stand away, and cast off your lines, if you do wish to follow in his wake. Signed by the Night Plunderers, the Light Horsemen, Lumpers, Game Lightermen and the Heavies."

Mary Tar's jaw dropped, and her eyes opened widely. The look on her face was of surprise at first but it quickly turned to anger. She jumped up and began to pace the room. Lace watched her closely.

"Mean anything to you, Captain?"

"Of course it *means* something to me, Lace. It means that Henry Swift Cockle, son of the King of the Mudlarks has been slain, and the blame for it has been shared around, with some of it laid squarely on my shoulders! The Mudlarks are the oldest and most powerful family on the River. They have fingers in every pie; they control the flow of contraband, and they know people in high and low places, lots of places. Why was our name on that note? We haven't fallen out with anyone, there are no feuds in play. Why us?"

Lace flipped her notebook over and replaced it inside her jacket pocket. She was good at reading people and the look on Mary Tar's face was not manufactured. She was shocked and then she was frightened and now she was bloody angry.

"Hellfire and drudgery! Henry Swift Cockle! Murdered? This is going to sting and there will be plenty of blood in the water unless this thing is sorted out, Sergeant. You can take it from me that no Night Plunderer has anything to do with this, upon my soul and honour as a captain. Have you spoken with the other captains? The Horsemen, the Heavies, the Lumpers?"

"Not yet, you were first on the list. The Chief wants me to have a chat with everyone first and then report back."

Mary Tar was pacing now, and she had started to twist a lock of her hair. She was agitated and Lace recognised a coping mechanism when she saw one. She herself had a tendency to rub her leg when she was thinking hard.

"What do you plan to do, Captain?"

Mary Tar stopped pacing and looked down at Lace.

"Well, for starters, I'm going to have a word with that lot in there and get some tongues wagging. Then I'm going to send an envoy to the Mudlarks to tell them that we had nothing to do with any of this madness."

"How can you be so sure that none of your people are involved, before talking to them?"

Mary Tar swelled at the accusation, but her logic managed to wrestle her indignation to the floor before she reacted.

"It's like this, Sergeant. The agreement has been in place for centuries. There's never been anything like it before, it just isn't natural! And for all of us to be implicated? Are you telling me that all of the captains have had a sit down, including me, and then agreed to kill the son of the King, then all put our hands up for it? Makes no sense, Sergeant. We all get along – I mean, we're not bosom buddies and we don't go on holiday together or anything – but we do respect each other, and we know that we have it good. Why jeopardise all that? Why make waves?"

Lace believed her. She had a good nose for treachery.

"Okay then. I should be getting back."

Mary Tar guided Lace back through the hall to the large set of double doors she had stepped through earlier that evening. A lot of the Plunderers had taken their captain at her word and were very merry. Someone was squeezing something close to a tune out of an accordion and there was dancing on the tables, along with a fair bit of falling off tables as well. The air was even thicker with smoke than before, and the floor was sticky with puddles of beer. When they reached the doors, Captain Mary Tar held out her hand again and Lace shook it, turned around and walked out of the Hall of the Night Plunderers.

"Don't forget to tell Judas that he's welcome down here, *very welcome,* if you catch my drift," said Mary.

"I'll be sure to. Thanks for your time, and the drinks."

Lace made off in the direction of her car – she'd parked it up the road from London River House. The short walk and a blast of fresh air would do her good. When she reached the unmarked silver Ford Mondeo she was relieved to find it in one piece and not resting on bricks. She got in and turned the heater on. The radio came on automatically and she listened to Talk Sport for a while. It wouldn't have been her first choice of radio station – the detective that had used the car previously must have liked it – but she found the voice soothing and although the presenter was talking about the Champions League, something she had absolutely no interest in whatsoever, she left it on.

"One down, only another four to go," she said to herself.

Then she flicked the indicator, pulled away from the kerb, and drove back to the Yard, leaving the Hall of the Night Plunderers and the delights of downtown Dagenham behind. She didn't fancy being in the shoes of anyone in that hall right now. If Mary Tar was true to her word an inquisition would be in full force, and thumbscrews and the cat-o-nine-tails would be tightening and whipping around, loosening tongues – and bowels. Fortunately, the traffic was practically non-existent, and she made good time. Over the course of the short journey she learned a lot about the new offside VAR system from the pundits on the radio, and how absolutely useless it was.

The duty constable on the gate tried to appear interested in her warrant card when she pressed it up against the inside of the car's windscreen, but he barely looked at it. She could have shown him a supermarket loyalty card for all the scrutiny he made of her ID. She parked the car in one of the spaces reserved for the Black Museum and took the stairs to the 7th floor. One of the many things she liked about working for DCI Judas Iscariot was his lack of interest in filing and the writing of reports. She popped her head into the office thinking that it would be deserted but to her surprise, she found Angel Dave slumped at her desk, asleep. Spread all over the desk in front of him were open case files. Lace coughed loudly in his ear and was rewarded when he sat up quickly and sent the papers flying.

"And just what are you doing, Angel Dave? A little light reading is it? These files are off limit to civilians you know?"

The angel composed himself after the shock and set about retrieving the papers he'd just spilled all over the floor.

"I have been seconded to the Black Museum I'll have you know," the angel replied, a little sheepishly.

"Oooooh. We have a 'Special Constable' on the books. Hold my coat, aren't we the progressive force now?" Lace smiled at the angel to show him that she was only kidding.

"What does he have you working on?"

Angel Dave, a little embarrassed at being caught off guard, flexed his wings a bit and drew himself up to his full height. He was only a small angel compared to the majority of his kin, but he still filled the space in the office well.

"I'm just doing a bit of homework on the case of the Gilded Goat. The gaffer wants me to find someone he thinks is connected with his death."

Lace had got to know the Gilded Goat quite well during a previous case – he had been mild-mannered and gentle, she had liked him, and she was sad that he had been murdered. He was one of the better bad guys.

"Good luck with it, let me know if I can help."

Angel Dave nodded, then continued to pick up the files that he had dropped on the floor. Lace turned around and walked over to the only other free terminal in the office. She sat down and as she waited for the terminal to boot up she chuckled at the angel's use of the term *gaffer*. When the screen in front of her had finally stopped flickering and displaying virus warning messages, she transferred her notes from her notebook to the relevant file. When she was done she looked up and found that Angel Dave had left. She powered the terminal down and followed suit. Tomorrow was another day, and she had more River People to interview.

MARY TAR WAS TIRED. Tonight was supposed to be about kicking back and having a good time. Instead, she was banging heads together and threatening violence and much, much worse on her people. Civil war amongst the River People was something that kept all of the captains awake at night. It would be catastrophic for business, and if one clan had decided to attempt a land grab or make a move into another's territory there would be blood. There were old allegiances, of course; the better captains had spent many years forging them, marrying off their sons and daughters in the old way to stave off any future unpleasantness. And there were the under the table deals and alliances. It was expected – everyone skimmed the cream from the top if they could, a shipment went missing every now and again – but the goods flowed, and lines were never crossed.

"Until now!" she said to the empty room.

There was a small pool of blood on the polished floor at her feet. It ruined the symmetry of the office. During one of the evening's interrogations, one of the men had grown surly and angry at her line of questioning and slammed his fist down on the table, sending a few tankards crashing to the floor. Thinking that their captain was in danger, one of her minders, a thick-set loader with hands like sandbags had rushed across the room and issued a small correction. The other man woke seconds later to find that he was now the proud owner of a broken nose. He sobered quickly, pulled himself up and sat back down.

"Your pardon, it was the beer talking, apologies, my captain," he'd said.

Mary had shaken her head instead.

"It is I that should be apologising to you. There has been enough questioning and prying. If I can't trust one of you then who can I trust?"

"We are all loyal to you, you can depend on that," he'd said, making her feel even worse.

The man's nose had begun to swell, and his voice had started to sound more nasal as his blood blocked his airwaves.

"Away with you now, get someone to look at that nose."

He had stood up too quickly and nearly fallen over again, but strong arms caught him and helped him from the room. Now, Mary Tar sat in silence and tried to collect her thoughts. She could hear the rush of the River Thames through the wooden walls of the hall, and she imagined that beyond these walls she could hear the faint but inevitable beat of war approaching, or something like it – something terrible. Someone was trying to destroy the peace and it was her duty to find that person and put a stop to it.

14

WORDS FROM INSIDE

The bright morning sunlight was trying to force its way in, but the thick curtains were standing firm and no ray was allowed to pass. It was like sitting inside a pint of lager. Everything in the flat had an orange tinge to it, even the snake plant and the huge flatscreen television carefully positioned on the wall between a clock and a poster of a wooden jetty.

The skies above Battersea were clear. It had all the makings of a lovely day, as long as you were not being pursued by some strange character that clearly wanted to see you harmed. The Sin Eater had slept well for a change, and he'd eaten plenty of decent food, most of it green and mostly fresh. Everything was not all unicorns and roses though, because the voices of the sins that he'd consumed were getting restless again. One of them had gone so far as to tell him that he was being a coward and he should throw open the curtains and ride out and challenge whoever it was that was following him to single combat – to the death.

He decided that the voice was going a little bit over the top, but they did have a point. The Sin Eater had made another decision too: he was going to stop being afraid. He would throw those drapes wide open, but he would not ride out – mainly because he was on the 5th floor of a block of apartments that looked over the Thames. After allowing the sunlight to finally enter, he rummaged around in his well-stocked cupboards for some muesli and a pot of natural yoghurt. To this he added some pure honey and he made himself a pot of coffee. The news on his laptop was greyish; neither too bad nor too positive. He surfed for a while over breakfast and then showered and changed.

It was while he was getting dressed that one of the more vocal voices inside him decided to ruin his day.

"If whatever it is that's following *us* is still out there, which it probably is, then we're not going to be too safe, are we? And if you don't send us on our way before it kills **you** then **we'll** be stuck in this world, and we'll turn into dark spirits, the left-behinds, won't we?"

The Sin Eater finished tying his shoelaces and then stood up and looked in the mirror. The voice continued.

"And we'll never see the City of the Heavens, or find peace, and then you'll have failed in your duty and you'll go to Hell, and the Morningstar will punish you for depriving him of souls. I wouldn't want to be in your shoes then," said the annoying but well-informed voice inside.

"Well, I had better not let that happen then. I wouldn't want you to suffer. After all, you're only being saved from the pit because I stepped in. Now shut up and let me think," said the Sin Eater.

"Charming," said the petulant voice of a sin.

The Sin Eater brushed his teeth and stared at himself in the mirror. He was looking much better than he had done over the past two weeks. The suitcases under his eyes had reduced in size to man-bags and he looked more alert than usual, surely a good sign. He picked up his door keys from a small blue bowl by the front door and slid one of the keys into the lock. He was about to turn the handle and step out to meet his foes when he suddenly realised that he hadn't made a plan, and that he was just going through the motions. So, he returned the keys to the bowl and then, defeated before he had even engaged the enemy, rested his forehead against the door and thumped the Formica, three times in quick succession.

"If I might make a suggestion," said the annoying voice.

"If you really must, and I mean *really* must because what you are about to say is going to change our situation for the better. Otherwise, please do me a favour and keep quiet."

The voice inside waited for a beat and then started to outline a plan for its host.

"I have heard of a place called the Black Museum, and its master, a very powerful warrior, is sworn to protect the Under Folk. If we can get to this place, and you throw yourself on his mercy then there might be a chance for us to find sanctuary. It's a thought."

The Sin Eater reached for his keys once again then spoke quickly and quietly.

"So where do I find this champion of the Under Folk?"

"He is to be found at a place called Scotland Yard," said the voice, smugly.

"That's just across the river. We might just make it alive, hopefully."

The Sin Eater turned the key in the lock, took a deep breath and opened it a fraction. He could see down the hall in both directions. There was no shadow lurking there, so he stepped out and locked the door behind him. He made his way to the lift, pressed the button to call it, then just before it arrived, he took the stairs instead. When he reached the bottom he waited and watched the entrance to his apartment block through a thin strip of glass in the door. No one came in, and again, he could see no unusual shadows or feel anything untoward, so the Sin Eater pushed the door open and calmly made his way onto the Embankment.

He walked with purpose, and resisted the urge to tell the voices of the sins inside to pipe down; he found their chatter comforting now. After a short, brisk walk he crossed over the Thames using the nearest bridge. His neck was beginning to hurt from scouring shop windows for the reflections of imagined enemies. None materialised. Scotland Yard was now only a few hundred metres away. This was the bit – that last bit, the *finishing line in sight* bit, the *just when you thought you'd made it* bit when some awful catastrophe befalls you. But the sun was shining on the Sin Eater today and he reached his destination unmolested and still breathing.

He walked into a large room with a long desk that ran all the way down one side. Standing behind the desk were a number of policemen and women – they were like a dark-blue rock in the middle of the ocean, with wave upon wave of problems, issues, and complaints crashing up against them relentlessly. The Sin Eater did not know what to do or who to talk to regarding the Black Museum, so he waited until a space appeared and then launched himself forward. The senior policeman, easily identifiable as such by his grey hair and lined face, looked down from his lofty perch. He was wearing three silver stripes on his arm and a curious look on his face.

"Good morning, sir, my name is Sergeant Henshaw, and how may I help you?"

The kind and accommodating nature of the man showed the Sin Eater that he had made the right decision, and he wasted no time in telling him about his concerns and who he wanted to converse with.

"I wish to speak with the champion of the Black Museum. I'm in grave danger and being followed by a suspicious and clearly deranged shadowy form. I am also carrying large amounts of evil sins that need to be released. If I am taken by said shadowy pursuer and killed, the sins will be taken to Hell, and I will be damned as well," said the Sin Eater.

The policeman did not bat an eyelid, nor did he question the man in front of him or signal to one of his younger and more physical constables to escort the man from the premises. He shook his head and let out a small sigh.

"Oh no, here we go again," said Sergeant Henshaw, and reached for the phone.

Judas had arrived early that morning. He had received a text from Lace the night before regarding Angel Dave and his new perceived status within the force, and he wanted to reassure her that the watching role he had assigned to Angel Dave was the only role he was going to get. He also wanted to see if the angel had found anything of interest in the files. After a coffee and a quick skim of the international news websites he sat back in his chair, listened to its familiar creak and took out his silver coin and began to rub the tip of his thumb across it. Something had happened in the Black Museum after they had removed Jack the Ripper. Something that didn't feel right to him. The Women of the Chapel had all left the Yard in good spirits, and he should have been over the moon too, but he had a *feeling*. It was niggling at him – he'd missed something. And why did Simon the Zealot seem so chipper afterwards? It was never a good sign when 'the Zealot' smiled.

The shrill sound of the desk phone broke his chain of

thought. It was the front desk, which could mean anything. He picked up the receiver smartly and held it to his ear.

"DCI Judas Iscariot?"

"Speaking."

"It's Henshaw, sir, down on the stockade."

"How goes the defence of the realm, Sergeant?"

"Not too bad, sir. I think I may have one of yours down here, reckons he's being pursued by dark forces. Apparently, he has a gut full of sins that he's recently eaten, which are now in peril, sir."

"He's one of mine all right. Please send him up, Sergeant, and thanks."

"No problem, sir, I'll stick him in the lift now. Will you be greeting the gentleman?"

"Leave it with me, Sergeant, I'll meet him at the door."

"Very good, sir."

Henshaw was a good man; he had made his way up through the ranks and Judas remembered his first day at the Yard. He'd been young then, dark haired, athletic, a real credit to the Met. His arrest record was exemplary, and he was respected by the rank and file. He'd come to Judas's attention when word had reached him that Henshaw had rejected an offer to join the Brotherhood, better known as the Freemasons. When he refused to don the apron and take his place on the 'Square' his meteoric rise faltered then came to a halt. He was obviously a man of honour and scruples. Judas made sure that he was looked after. Too many good coppers found themselves back on the beat or directing traffic for not becoming a Freemason. The Met didn't need another secret organisation; there were enough of those as it was.

Judas heard the chime of the lift arriving and made his way out of the office and down the corridor. A man stepped out of the lift. He looked both ways twice, and then put his back to the wall. You didn't need to be a detective to see that this one was petrified.

"I understand you are looking for me?"

"Are you the champion of the Under Folk?"

"I am one of them, what seems to be the problem, Mr ... ?"

"Montague. Huxley Montague. I am in need of your help."

"DCI Judas Iscariot at your service, also known as the Champion of the Under Folk and Warden of the Black Museum. Why don't we step inside the office and you can tell me what this is all about, Huxley."

Judas led the way down the corridor and Huxley Montague followed him, talking to himself in urgent whispers. When they reached the office door, the Sin Eater stopped dead in his tracks.

"What is it, Huxley?"

"There are voices inside that room, evil voices, cruel voices. I will not enter that place!"

"That's the Black Museum, and you're quite right, you won't be entering that place. We're going in here."

Huxley Montague peeled himself from the wall of the corridor and stepped through the open door and into the office. He took a seat when offered and started to relax. Judas thought that he had a nervous tick to begin with, but soon realised that Huxley Montague was listening to a lot of conversations and trying desperately not to get involved in any. He was well dressed, smart, and obviously not short of a bob or two.

"Huxley, can you tell me what brings you here? How can I help? Just speak freely, you're in no danger from me."

Huxley Montague took a breath and started to tell his tale.

"Do you know of the Sin Eaters, Inspector? It matters little if you do not. We are an old people, from the eastern part of what is now called Europe, and we are burdened with taking the sins from those who have renounced evil when they pass across into the other world. I take those sins away and consume them, and then, when I need to, I release them by performing a ritual. The sins are then freed and travel to the City of the Heavens, where they are made whole again and find peace."

"I have known a few Sin Eaters in my time, on the whole they have been decent enough," said Judas.

"Well, Inspector, it's like this. I have been pursued many times by groups from this level and below. People and demons have the same idea about the sins; either they want to steal them and make a gift of them to their King, or they want to destroy them because they believe them to be against the nature of things."

"Which ones are chasing you this time, Huxley? The demons or the people?"

"It's neither, Inspector. It doesn't feel like the evil or the misguided, but it wants me, or it wants the sins I hold now, desperately."

"Why not release the sins then?"

"When I perform the ritual I am vulnerable, Inspector. I have to remain completely still for at least forty-eight hours. It's not a quick thing, I'm afraid."

"And where do you need to be in order to complete the ritual?"

"My *place of offering* is a small church on the edge of the water in Battersea. Only there can I feel safe. But this dark shadow has followed me to this place already and it knows that I must return there. I can hold the sins inside me for a while longer, but if they are not sent on their way soon I may not be able to release them at all."

Judas continued to question Huxley Montague, slowly and patiently, teasing out a word here or a truth there, until he felt he knew the Sin Eater's story as well as he could. He'd need to find a place to keep him safe, the question was, where? The Black Museum was off the list, the sins would be in open conflict with the spirits of the Museum. A holding cell downstairs would offer him no protection really. Lace was off on her travels checking in with the River People, and Angel Dave was keeping an eye out for the Cunning Man. Judas reached down and pulled the bottom drawer in his desk open, retrieving a small battered green notebook.

"Why don't you take a seat over there by the window, Huxley, while I make a few calls. Relax if you can, this may take some time. I'll wake you if you fall asleep."

Huxley Montague stood and made his way over to the reclining chair by the angel window. Judas watched him settle himself and within seconds, Huxley Montague's head began to nod, and the faint sound of snoring carried across the room.

Judas started to turn the pages of the notebook – inside it were the names of people that had helped or been helped by the Black Museum in the past. He was looking for someone to act as a babysitter to the Sin Eater – someone staunch, fearless and able to defend themselves if need be. He was very near the last page when he saw the name of a person that he hadn't thought about in decades: Robert Junior, late of Her Majesty's Royal Marines. A hard man with a soft heart. If he were still alive, he'd be the perfect man for the job. Judas picked up his mobile phone and keyed Robert's number in. He answered straight away.

"Inspector! This is a pleasant surprise! What can I do for you?"

"You're a good man, Robert. Can you keep an eye on someone for me? Might get messy, hopefully not, but it's best to be clear up front."

"Are we talking normal messy or magical messy?"

"The latter I'm afraid, you still comfortable with that?"

"Of course I am, let me know where and when, and I'll be there."

"Stay by your phone, I'll get back to you within the hour."

Judas hung up and replaced the phone on the desk in front of him. Then he sat back down again and searched in his pockets for his silver coin. Mr. Huxley Montague was being pursued by someone or something that needed the sins he'd eaten, for what purpose was a mystery right now. Charles Murrell, the so-called Charming Man, was still roaming free. The Gilded Goat's murder had not been closed, and he was no closer to finding out who was responsible for taking the life of Henry Swift Cockle. All he needed right now was for the Archangel Michael to show up with a bee in his bonnet about something that Judas had done, or not done, and for the First of the Fallen to make an appearance too, for a full house. Judas thought that he had compiled a complete mental list but then he remembered Simon the Zealot, and groaned.

Huxley was still slumbering in his chair by the window. When Judas approached, he woke with a start and stood up quickly. His clothes were dishevelled, and his hair was awry and messy. He looked well slept though, even though it had only been an hour since Judas told him to get some shut eye. He looked calmer.

"Get your coat, Mr. Montague, I'm taking you to one of our safe houses. It's not far and I'll be taking you there myself so please don't worry. I would offer to keep you here but your reaction to the Black Museum might make that hard for you, so, I have arranged for you to spend a little bit of time with one of *our people.*"

"Thank you, Inspector. Please lead on."

Judas and Huxley Montague left the Black Museum together. Judas didn't fancy taking the tube; once down there in the bowels of the city, there wasn't much room for manoeuvre if you were attacked. He did know some people down there, living in the old and disused stations, and some who lived even further down than them. Now was not the time to take any chances though. His travelling companion was far too unsettled for that, so they took the bus instead.

Robert Junior lived in Archway in North London. His two-bed flat was situated on the ground floor of a red brick building not far from the Archway tube station. The street outside was pleasant enough. Clean too, there was clearly a lot of civic pride. The Neighbourhood Watch stickers on the lampposts and the green signs shouting in a very polite manner that this was a green area were in abundance. Judas was not surprised to see the front door to Robert's flat open before his finger pressed on the doorbell. Robert was not a curtain twitcher, but he had certainly timed all the routes that Judas may have taken and was ready and prepared. They stepped inside without talking. Robert was a cheerful and pleasant host, but he did not like to exchange pleasantries on the doorstep and before closing the door completely he took a quick look outside, checking for watchers or cars that shouldn't be there. Old habits died hard.

"Inspector, welcome. And who might you be, sir?"

Huxley was wary but Robert's open face showed no threat or suspicion, and he raised his hand and they shook.

"Huxley Montague, Sin Eater, and you are?"

"I am your babysitter, Mr. Montague – Robert Junior. If you want to take a look around the place feel free. Your bedroom is the one on the right, the bathroom is one door on, and my room is at the back. The kitchen is opposite my room, it's open plan and you'll find the fridge and the cupboards fully stocked. If there's anything that you don't eat or something you need, just let me know. Please, make yourself at home. There are clean clothes still in their packaging on your bed and some washing stuff on the bedside cupboard. I'll talk to you about our exit strategy in detail once you're settled. You're safe here, Mr. Montague."

Huxley wanted to say thank you again but was lost for words. A lot of kindness had come his way in such a short time, and he felt a bit overwhelmed. Instead, he just smiled and took himself away to explore the flat, and to brush his teeth; his breath must be heavy with coffee by now. When Judas and Robert heard his bedroom door shut, they sat down and talked.

"He's a Sin Eater, Robert, harmless really, but someone is after him and I can't leave him at the Museum. All I need is a few days to find out who his shadow is and if there is anything I can do to help him. That okay?"

"Absolutely, Inspector. Anything I need to know about this shadow? Not going to materialise in the bath when I'm shaving or fly through the window?"

"No idea as yet, Robert, just be prepared and keep him safe, all the usual protocols are in place if things get out of hand. You won't have to answer any questions from my lot, okay?"

"All clear, leave him with me and let me know when you need him back or dropped off anywhere."

"Good man. How are you by the way?"

"Right as rain thanks, the dreams don't swing by as often as they did. Mary and the little one are gone. They're safe now and away from all of this rubbish, thanks to you, so I just try to take each day as it comes."

"The next time I speak to *HE* of the flaming sword and the bad manners, I'll ask after them for you."

"I'd like that very much, Inspector, but I won't expect anything. I know asking an Archangel for a favour is a task in itself, but if you can I would be very grateful."

"I'll do my best. I had better get going now, you know how to get hold of me if it's really urgent?"

"I do."

Judas shook hands with Robert then slipped out into the night. A cat passed by but did not look up at him. Judas studied it carefully and watched it trot around the corner, just to be on the safe side. In his experience cats were slippery, fickle, and deceitful – or at least the one he knew best was. The journey back to the Black Museum on the Underground, normally so disagreeable, was in fact quite enjoyable because it was uneventful, and when he walked into the Yard the reassuring face of Sergeant Henshaw was there to greet him. The day had been long but at least there had been no real disasters to deal with. There was always tomorrow.

15

ZENNOR

The Zennor was a super yacht, not a gaudy mega yacht of the sort preferred and never sailed by Oligarchs. It was also, by definition, an expedition super yacht on the grounds that it had a deeper hull, it was designed and built for longer journeys at sea and the extra space was for extra provisions – or giants. Corineus was comfortable and on the verge of being happy because he was one step closer to reaching his destination. He was sitting upright with his back resting against a pile of mattresses, bought for him by his friend who was also the captain. The high-powered hose, used normally for the cleaning of the hull and the upper decks had been turned into a shower so that he could clean himself. The long passage below decks on the last leg of his journey had offered few opportunities to bathe. Now, at least, he felt more like himself and the heavy yoke of tension that he had been carrying had been cast off. He had dreamed of the quiet stretch of coastline where the mermaid swam for a long time. The cave in the cliff that looked down on to the golden sand of the beach had been transformed into a warm and comfortable living space for him. Only a few people knew he was dying – his fight with Gogmagog had left him with scars on the inside as well as on the outside.

He had gone into self-imposed exile after the fight. He was sure that Gogmagog was not dead – the blow that felled him was not a lethal one, it was the fall from the cliff that won the fight. Gogmagog would return, and he would seek out Corineus again and again until he was victorious. Corineus knew this and that is why he had slipped away. He left behind a legend and a crazed giant that would never be taken seriously, at least not in his own mind. If Gogmagog knew that Corineus was near, he would waste no time in challenging him once again.

The Captain of the Zennor was a man called Mathey Trewells, a proud Cornish man that had slept with a mermaid long ago and had been blessed with a long life and rude health. Corineus counted him as a friend, and he could trust him. He had shoulder-length white hair, the sort that a student from Central Saint Martins fashion school would die for. He was tall, had green eyes and was lithe and strong. Corineus heard him climbing down the ladder and then swinging the bulkhead levers open. Seconds later, his head appeared around the door.

"Up I see, and looking a fair bit better than when you came aboard. Your face has lost that white pallor and some of your colour is returning. Have you eaten?"

"I have, Mathey, there was almost too much for me, but I soldiered on and finished it. It was a tough task, but I did it for you and the Zennor."

Mathey Trewells stepped inside and pushed the door gently closed. He picked up an old packing case and placed it in front of the giant. Corineus reached over, picked up one of the many blankets and cushions that had been packed for him and laid it over the case so that his friend could be comfortable.

"I have some news for you, Corineus. It might be something, but then it could be nothing at all, and I want to tell you so you are at ease."

The giant sat upright, and the yacht creaked at the sudden restowing of weight.

"Is it him?" said Corineus.

"No my friend, at least I think not. Another yacht came in during the night and was to be moored just up the way from us, but it foundered for some unknown reason and now it blocks our passage to the main river. There are folk scampering all over her at the moment but she's listing badly, and you can see more of her hull than is healthy. She'll need looking at below decks just to make sure that she hasn't been pierced below the waterline. It's a strange thing to happen though, Corineus. I've never heard of a ship that big sinking so fast, and inside a marina too. As I said, it may just be bad luck on their part and on ours."

"Could I swim over under the cover of darkness and lift it out of the way?"

"I believe you could my friend but that would bring more undue attention than we need. '*Miracle of sinking yacht that rights itself and then moors itself*'? We'd have half the authorities down on this place checking the seabed and searching for saboteurs. No, best you stay hidden for now. Let me check it out and see what the Harbour Master says. We don't want to miss our tide if at all possible."

Corineus sat back again and smiled at Mathey.

I am in good hands and need not worry thought the giant.

Mathey stood up, crossed the hold and lifted a tarpaulin. Underneath were wooden barrels stacked five high, and burned into the wood were words that made the giant smile.

"Ale, Irish Ale! You are the most perfect host and the best of friends," said Corineus.

Mathey rolled one across the deck to his friend who wasted no time in cracking it open and drinking off the contents in one go.

"I shall be more respectful with the next barrel, Mathey," said Corineus.

"This is all for you, but don't finish it all off today, it was hard to come by."

Mathey left Corineus to his ale, climbed back up the ladder and made his way through the ship to the wheel-house. He'd had it retro-fitted with a wooden steering wheel the size of a circular dining table, and removed most of the technology that modern-day sailors seemed to need before they would cast off a single line. He picked up his binoculars and trained them on the yacht ahead. She hadn't moved and the few men that had been scrambling over her had turned into an army. Lines had been cast off from every deck and then made fast to both sides of the deep water dock. There was no way anything bigger than a skiff was sailing around her right now.

Something was eating away at Mathey Trewells; the back of his right hand was itching, a sure sign that something was not right. He wished that his wife were here – she could have swum underneath the yacht, ascertained what was wrong in a trice and then they'd make a plan. But she wasn't.

"More's the pity," said Mathey to himself.

Mathey left the Zennor and made his way up to the Harbour Master's office. He wasn't the only Captain there; it reassured him that his were not the only plans that had been thwarted. The Master looked ruffled, and his neck was red. Mathey thought about making a comment about it, asking him whether the current situation was making him feel a bit hot under the collar, but decided not to. When his turn came, Mathey spoke quietly and calmly.

"It's a piece of work isn't it, Master? How on earth does a yacht that size come to grief in a shallow channel like that. Never seen the like before, I bet you haven't either."

"Captain Trewells," said the Harbour Master. "In all my years afloat, I've not seen or heard of a situation like this. The Captain of the White Lady, out of Nassau, was as fine as could be – no problems, no issues, nothing – and then all of a sudden he says there was an almighty thump, like hitting a reef in the dark he says, and now he has a cracked keel and four feet of water in the forward hold. He's trying to get her towed over to the dry dock so he can get a look at her."

Mathey pretended to look at one of the charts stapled to the wall of the office, and then scratched his head.

"I don't suppose he'll have his Lady out of the water before Tuesday will he?"

The Harbour Master's eyebrows lifted and then he shook his head.

"I don't see why not, Captain Trewells. It would be dark forces and all the bad luck in the world if it weren't the case. No, I think you'll get your tide."

"Thank you, Master. Before I go you shall come across and see us off in the old way! Eight removes and as much as you are able to drink, salutes to the Queen, the whole thing."

"I should like that very much, just let me know and I shall be there."

As Mathey walked back down the jetty toward the Zennor, some of the words that had passed between them kept coming back to him.

"Dark forces and all the bad luck in the world."

It would be cruel on the giant if he had been discovered already.

He jumped aboard the Zennor, pulled up the little gangway behind him and disappeared below decks. He wanted to check his charts in his own cabin and make some emergency plans.

Standing at the edge of the jetty nearby was a man. He was watching the White Lady closely. At his feet was a cat. Both man and feline seemed to be in very good spirits – very good spirits indeed.

16

THE FLAG CALLS

Sergeant Lace was tired. Judas could see the big, dark circles under her eyes. They looked like tractor tyres but he was too much of a gentleman to say as much. Simon the Zealot, the new custodian of the Black Museum on the other hand was chipper and full of beans. So much so that he had taken to playing classical music in the outer rooms of the Black Museum. It could be heard from outside in the corridor. Judas wondered what the inmates were thinking, but not for long. The search for the Cunning Man – the suspected murderer of the Gilded Goat – was ongoing; Lace was questioning all of the River Gangs; and he was keeping a Sin Eater in a safe house run by an ex-Royal Marine because person or persons unknown were after the sins he'd eaten. There was never a dull day in the Black Museum.

Lace was the first to speak.

"Sir? There's an awful lot of leg work tracking down these River Gangs and finding a good time to speak with them."

"And there's the unholy amount of drinking involved,

let's not forget that, Sergeant Lace," said Judas, mischievously.

"And there's that, sir, but honestly, I'm drawing a blank with a few of them, word seems to have gone out about the murder of the Mudlark and now everyone is shutting up shop."

Judas stood up and looked at Lace. She was exhausted.

"There is someone in the Black Museum that can help us. He knows the river and he knows the gangs. Let's try him, it might make things a bit easier for us."

Lace followed Judas into the Black Museum. Simon the Zealot was absent and Judas made a mental note to speak to him, and find out what he had been doing lately. They passed through the anteroom and into the Key Room. Judas wandered down one side of the long table. It took him a few minutes to find what he was looking for. It was a medium-sized brush, its bristles clogged with a black sticky substance – tar. Judas picked it up and motioned for Lace to join him.

"Where are we off to this time, sir?"

"The Desolate Point, Sergeant. The last resting place for one Captain Kidd, the pirate."

"Clarke Gable?" said Lace.

"Errol Flynn, and I think you're confusing Captain Kidd with Captain Blood, the pirate," said Judas, then realised that Sergeant Lace was making light of the situation.

"Shame, I liked Clark Gable."

"Very good, Lace, very funny. Let's go."

Judas felt the now very familiar pull of the Time Fields – there was a brief sensation of movement and then of weight-lessness. It passed swiftly and then the light changed. The flickering neon of the cheap light bulbs in the Museum was replaced by a thick mist, silver-grey in colour, that moved across their field of vision as if on well-oiled casters. Judas walked straight ahead, and Lace followed. She was wondering just how he was navigating his way through the mist when she stubbed her toe on a small stone marker on the ground. It hurt very much, and she winced. She looked more closely at the stone and saw that it was surrounded by brown grass and strands of dead seaweed.

The pain passed and she continued on her way. She could still see the dark shape of the inspector in the mist ahead and she ran to catch up with him. They had only been walking for a few minutes when the creak of the gibbets signalled that they were getting closer. They followed the sounds and soon the gibbets came into view. There were ten in total but only one was occupied. They could see much more now because the mist had thinned. They were closer to the river and short sharp gusts of wind from the sea pushed at the mist wall, keeping it away from the shingle beach. As they drew closer they heard the sole occupant of the gibbets singing. The voice was breathy and low and the words were muffled and hard to decipher. Judas picked up a stone and skimmed it across the surface of the water, and waited.

The song finished and the singer stood. Captain Kidd was a rock star pirate – loved and hated in equal measure – but he was a personality and that was why his corpse had been painted with tar. Pirates, after they were hung, were always painted with tar so that the body lasted longer and remained a symbol of the sheer barbarity that would be visited upon a soul should they veer off the straight and narrow. Kidd's corpse had been double wrapped and his limbs were hard to define. His head was just a blob, but his eyes were clear, and his mouth was still functioning.

"Inspector! How wonderful! How are you, sir? You look

very prosperous might I say. Dandy even. And you have brought a friend to parley with me! As always, you are a kind jailer. What might your name be then, young man?"

Lace wore her hair short, and her usual outfit of leather bomber jacket, jeans and boots were practical, and very on trend. She was about to fire something back at the pirate but then realised that ladies of his day would have appeared and dressed quite differently.

"Sergeant Lace, captain."

"Well met then, Sergeant Lace of the Black Museum," said Kidd.

Judas stepped forward and looked up at the remains of the pirate.

"Captain, may I ask a question of you?"

"Normal rules apply?" asked Kidd.

"If you like," Judas replied.

"What is it that you would like to know, Inspector?"

"The captains of the River People have gone to ground; we need to question them."

"About what?" said the pirate.

"There has been a murder."

"Someone important?"

"The son of the Mudlark King."

Captain Kidd shuffled in his gibbet. His mouth worked and made soft, gurgling sounds. Judas picked up another stone and skimmed it, then another. Eventually, the Captain stopped gurgling and silence returned to the beach.

"What you say is true then, Inspector. I have spoken with the Dead of the Sea. A Mudlark, murdered? I see why you are so keen to get them all together. There will be blood in the water and the docks will serve as battlefields. Unless, that is, you find who is responsible."

"I don't suppose you could have another *gurgle* with the spirits and tell me who did it could you?" said Judas.

Kidd's gibbet creaked as the tar-encrusted captain readjusted his position.

"I wish I could, Inspector, but the culprit or culprits are shielded it seems. Strange. Whoever or whatever is responsible may not be of our kind – and possibly more like you."

Judas looked at Lace, whose eyes were mirrors of confusion.

"Can you elaborate on that, Captain?"

"Unfortunately not, all I can say is that the killer, or killers, are not of the Under Folk."

Judas shook his head; another lone wolf assassin was all he needed right now.

'Can you help us with the other thing?"

"All the River Gangs must flock to the King of the River's banner. None are allowed to abstain; all must attend with half a day. It is their law."

Lace was distracted by the state of her toe; it was swelling inside her sock, and she wanted to get back to the station and to the First Aid tin.

"Where can we find this flag, Captain, and where will the River Gangs flock to?"

The Captain started to sing again but this time his voice was strong and true.

"Brave Walworth, Knight, Lord Mayor that slew
Rebellious Tyler in his alarmes;
The king therefore did give him lieu
The dagger to the city armes."

"And just what does that mean?" Lace enquired.

"Sergeant Lace. The flag can be found in a vault deep inside the bowels of the Mansion House, and where else should it be flown but from London Bridge?"

"Thank you, Captain," said Judas.

"A pleasure, Inspector. Now, what of my payment?" The captain shuffled once more, and the gibbet complained about it with a high-pitched squeak.

"Of course, what would you like?"

There was a soft gurgle from inside the captain's cage.

"I should very much like to hear Sergeant Lace sing a song of her choosing."

Lace looked up smartly then turned to face Judas.

"Me? Sing?"

Judas smiled and walked to the water's edge with a handful of smooth stones. He limbered up with a few shoddy bungs then turned back to Lace.

"That's the cost of the information, Lace. Sing sweetly now, or he'll expect another!"

Judas turned back to the river and continued to skim. Under a gibbet holding the remains of a pirate captain painted with black sticky tar, Sergeant Lace of the Black Museum started to belt out 'Wonderful World' by Louis Armstrong at the top of her voice. Judas winced once or twice, but Lace held it together and finished on a high note, and thankfully for all, the captain did not ask for another.

When they were back in the office Lace removed her boot and sock, and gasped when she saw that her big toe had turned blue and yellow. It was ugly and very sore, but not as painful as having to sing a song to a gooey pirate.

THE MANAGER at the Mansion House proved to be a difficult man to deal with, especially, Lace thought, because she was a woman. Eventually, after a lot of card-showing and threats of obstructing a police officer in the course of her duties, he gave in and showed her the way to the vaults where the flag could be found. She thought he was going to have a heart attack when she rolled it up and stuffed it inside the carrier bag she had brought with her, but she sidestepped him and got clear before he could cause a scene.

From Mansion House to Tower Bridge took only a matter of minutes; the traffic gods were watching over her today. The top floor of Tower Bridge can be rented out for business meetings or parties. The Masonic Brotherhood are said to have their own suite. The only way to get inside is with a funny handshake, but that's just a rumour. Lace flashed her badge again and was allowed to explore without a chaperone. One of the security guards kept looking at her plastic bag. If it had been a 'bag for life' he wouldn't have batted an eyelid. She found the window she was looking for, and opened it quickly. If the people downstairs had known this was what she was planning she'd never have made it past the turbine room. Lace climbed up onto the windowsill and then edged out and onto the ledge.

Way below, traffic on both road and river was shuttling back and forth. From her position, even the larger boats and the river taxis looked tiny; they could have been toys in a bath. Lace grabbed her carrier bag and held it close to her chest. She could just imagine the look Judas would give her if she were unable to complete the task because she'd let the flag fly out of her hands at this precise moment. The flag would end up in Richmond, or Heathrow. Fortunately for Lace, there were to be no hair-raising climbs or death-defying leaps. The ledge she was on led directly to a small walkway and at the end of it was a flagpole. Once there, all she needed to do was run the flag up and the River Gangs would come running. Or at least that was what Captain Kidd said.

17

THE THIEF–TAKER

Gogmagog did not trust Cat Tabby. In fact, he disliked him and felt itchy and unclean after speaking with him. And just what that idiot Whittington was doing hanging around with the little furry menace was beyond him. They were inseparable, joined at the hip, always in the wrong place at the right time. He reached over and removed a six-inch steel nail from the dish on his desk, and started to pick his teeth with it. He was just fishing out a long, thin stringy bit of beef from the area around his back molar when his peace and moment of pleasure were destroyed by the honking of his personal assistant, Master Gander. The goose barged his way into the office through the polished oak door, and waddled across the carpet.

"He's here, sir. Very interested in working for you, as usual. Slightly higher fee than usual this time. I have not said a word about the job, not a sausage. But, apparently, due to the unforeseen economic climate, prices are up across the board."

Gogmagog spat the piece of offal he'd just liberated from

his mouth into his wastebasket. The nail followed it and made a pinging sound as it bounced out and onto the flagstone tiles of the office floor.

"I don't care about the bloody money, Gander! I want that so-called giant standing in a fighting ring with blood pumping out of the new holes I've just put in him with my spear tip. Don't talk to me about money and economics, just bring in this Thief Taker, and do it quickly."

Master Gander let out a little embarrassed honk and made his way, *quickly*, back to the office where a certain gentleman was waiting for his audience with the King of the Giants. Gander had taken notice of his master's current mood and did not mince his words.

"He's a little tetchy this morning. Don't mention your fee, I will negotiate that on your part. You will get what you want and then some if you can find the person he's looking for."

The gentleman Gander was speaking to was leaning, casually, against the wall. Tall, pale complexion, white scar across the bridge of his nose, jet-black hair that he wore long, the tips just brushing the shoulder, and one vivid green eye. The son of the Thief Taker General was an imposing figure, and it was said that his one green eye was where his power resided. He could see things that others couldn't. Which, as a catcher of thieves and witches, stood him in good stead. He was a calm man, on the whole, but if his temper was raised, he could change in the blink of an eye and his ability with the sword was well known. All in all, the perfect chap to find a giant for you.

"Would you step this way please?" said Master Gander, with a dramatic sweep of his wing.

The Thief Taker eased himself away from the wall and glided past the giant goose. He walked slowly, as if he were approaching a vacant pew in an empty church. The goose trotted past him and took up his station at the side of the giant's desk, ready to make the introductions.

"My Lord Gogmagog, here is the man you instructed me to find."

Gogmagog leaned forward across his desk and brought his massive hands together, forming a steeple with them. The giant had the high ground, as always, and he looked down on the man in front of him.

Not much to look at, not nearly the man his father was thought Gogmagog.

"No indeed," said the Thief Taker.

Gogmagog flinched, dismantled the steeple he had made, and sat back in his creaky chair. Master Gander winced.

"So, that is the trick of it, is it *son of the* Thief Taker General? You can see far, and you can hear unspoken words? Well, no matter, you will know what is in my mind before the hour is at an end. I require your services to complete two tasks for me. One: I want you to find a giant called Corineus. Two: I want you to keep an eye on Cat Tabby for me. I think that following the feline might enable you to complete the first task much more quickly, but work as you see fit."

The Thief Taker nodded.

"Corineus? I thought he was dead long ago."

"He's been seen, here, in London! He's alive, thank the stars – but not for too much longer," growled the giant.

"I see. And where does Cat Tabby fit in? I presume that his sidekick Mr. Whittington is still in the picture?"

"It matters not what the cat or his companion do or do not do. If they know where Corineus is, use whatever means you feel necessary to make them part with that information."

"And what of the Black Museum?" the Thief Taker asked.

"The Cursed One? I wouldn't worry too much about him. If he becomes involved or the Black Museum start poking their noses about, I will see that they get their noses *cut off*!"

The Thief Taker motioned towards one of the leather armchairs with his hand.

"Please do," said the giant.

The Thief Taker sat down and made himself as comfortable as he could. A trained eye would have seen that the man's overcoat was heavier to one side, and when he sat back he had to adjust his position to accommodate his stash.

"What do you know so far then? Do you have anything that I can use to get started?"

They talked for the best part of an hour. The Thief Taker probed and pushed the giant for any background material that he could use but Gogmagog would not speak about Corineus with anything other than disgust. When he tried to pry into the arrangement between the giant and Cat Tabby, the giant grew surly, and his chair creaked even more. Master Gander grew nervous and looked as though he might lay an egg, if that were possible. Unfortunately, the questioning went on for one question longer than it should have and Gogmagog grew visibly angry, then he leaned back into the light and rapped his knuckles on the desk. The sound was like mortars landing. Thump, thump, thump, thump! It was his private signal for a meeting to end. Master Gander jumped and produced a high-pitched honk in reply, turning on a sixpence and padding away on his big, flapping webbed feet.

"I can fill you in on what we have in the outer office, if you'll follow me?" he said as he passed the Thief Taker.

"Until the next time then, Lord Gogmagog."

The Thief Taker looked up at the giant and tried to make out what was going on inside that huge head, but the giant had pulled the portcullis down on his thoughts; the Thief Taker realised then that he had made a mistake and showed his hand far too early.

When he returned to Master Gander's office, he found the giant goose sitting behind an unusual desk of his own. It was like a large wooden horseshoe. The goose sat in the middle and from there he could move his paperwork around with his white wings. He had a speaking device designed so that a creature without visible ears, a huge beak, and no recognised way of picking anything up and holding it to its face might communicate with the world outside. It looked clumsy and difficult to operate but use makes master, and the goose flapped a wing to close it down.

"You know that the Mundane Folk have these things called headsets now? You place it on your head, and it connects to a mobile speaking unit," said the Thief Taker, mischievously.

Master Gander ruffled his white feathers and the reverberations of his body continued up to his thick neck and made his head wobble a bit.

"I have heard of them, thank you. This device can perform a number of actions that a commonplace phone cannot, but that is neither here nor there. Why did you ask Lord Gogmagog so many unrelated questions? You must have heard of his temper and his desire to locate the false giant, Corineus. You were close to danger in there and yet you continued. Why?"

The Thief Taker leaned back against the wall once

again. The weapon he carried in the folds of his coat had proved uncomfortable when he had decided to take a seat, so he stood.

"I need all the information I can get; experience has taught me that. Please explain this to your Lord and Master. He will understand and forget the perceived slight if I can locate the other giant before Cat Tabby. Now, to my payment, what is the reward for finding him? And what additional payment can I expect if I have to remove the cat from the caper?"

Master Gander leaned to one side and extended a wing. Then he swept a large envelope towards the front of his desk. The Thief Taker reached over and took it.

"It will surely be enough, Thief Taker. If you require more, you know how to contact me. Now, if that's everything?"

The Thief Taker did not open the envelope to check the amount; that would have been rude and unprofessional. He did, however, quicken his pace and once he was outside the Guildhall Under, found a quiet spot away from prying eyes and ripped the letter open. The figure was adequate. No, it was more than that, it was very generous. The cash would certainly pay a few overdue bills, that was for sure, but he owed the 'Cursed One' a debt, and this would wipe his slate clean. Furthermore, he liked Judas, and enjoyed working for him when the situation arose. Gogmagog was a bully and a nasty piece of work. The Thief Taker set off for Scotland Yard, stopping occasionally to make sure that he was not being followed.

18

THE GREEN PATH

Lilith reached out for the small, delicate leaf. Her fingertips brushed it briefly, and to her horror, it turned yellow then brown, curled up at the edges and dropped from the healthy plant to the soil below. She recoiled from the plant, fearing to touch it again lest she destroy it entirely. She quickly put on her green, well-worn gardening gloves and stepped away from the display. Her anger and frustration at not finding Huxley yet was beginning to show and she did not want to touch anyone or anything by accident and see it suffer the same fate as the plant.

It was time for her break. Most of the other gardeners and botanists had joined to wish a fellow worker a happy birthday. Usually, she would have attended, but now was not the right time for singing songs and pretending to be happy, so she slipped away to the great tree on the boundary and hid behind its trunk. The branches moved gracefully above her. They hushed and sighed and she thought perhaps they were trying to make her happy. For a moment at least they succeeded, but the face of the man Adam returned to turn her thoughts ugly once again.

She had loved him in her own way. They had lain together and he had whispered to her of the future and the intertwining of their lives. She had been at her happiest then, but one morning she woke to find him gone. The garden was in uproar. Plants cried out in pain, the rivers dried and died and the birds fell from the sky; one by one at first and then in their hundreds. The sprites and the spirits disappeared before her eyes and the creatures of the earth rolled up into balls and hugged themselves, hoping that by doing so the pain in their guts would lessen. Sadly, it didn't, and they too died where they lay.

He had stolen away in the night, taking with him the heart of the garden. It was the one power that gave life and nurtured it inside the walls of the green place. At first she told herself it was all some awful mistake. Had he been tending to the heart when evil had struck? Was there something else in the garden now? Was he trapped under a heavy bough or lying wounded in a ditch somewhere? She gave him excuse after excuse but inside she knew he had run away and murdered them all as they slept.

She was the only living thing that survived. What was once a place of great beauty was now just a barren wasteland. Nothing grew there, apart from her anger. That required no water or sunlight to grow huge and monstrous, and in time she forgot about greenery and life and replaced them with anger and spite. But now, he was close at hand. All she needed was the location of this Huxley Montague, then she would have Adam and she would take him back to the garden and make him replant every seed he had destroyed. Then when the garden was growing again, she would rip his head clean off.

"Mistress..." said a very soft voice.

Lilith started and looked around her, searching for the owner of the voice.

"Mistress, I am just here at your feet."

Lilith looked down and saw the dryad.

"Stay clear of me little one, just until I can put these on."

She reached inside her jacket pocket and put her gloves back on again. Then when she was absolutely sure that she could do no damage to the dryad, she sat down beside it, and bowed from the waist.

"The blessings of the seasons be upon you," she said.

"And to you mistress, fourfold and a day," the dryad replied.

"I have not spoken to one of your kind for a long time, too long in fact. What can I do for you, little one?"

The dryad took the form of a human woman from the waist up. She wore no clothes, and her hair was long and green. Her arms were like the stalks you find on a dandelion and her eyes were the colour of bluebells.

"I think there is something that we can do for you, my lady. We heard that you were searching for a man, an Eater of Sins. Well, we have found such a one. He sits in the garden behind a red bricked house and talks with another man of the sins he has eaten and the dark shadow that stalks him. The sins chatter and rage constantly, so we know his name."

"Is it Montague? Huxley Montague?"

"It is, mistress."

Lilith clapped her hands together and rocked back and forth. A smile, so long absent from her face, returned, and she giggled.

"Where can I find him little one?"

"We do not have the address as the Mundane Folk

would say it, but we can guide you to the door of this place."
The dryad tossed her hair to one side and folded her tiny
arms across her chest. She looked very pleased with herself.

"And what would you have as payment for this information?" Lilith was no fool, and understood the way of the
Under Folk.

"This, we will give to you freely, mistress, without spell
or deception. We want the death of the one who stole the
heart of the garden just as much as you do. It is a crime
beyond punishment, but we believe that you will think of
something. The directions to this place are as follows."

Lilith listened to every word, etching them into her
memory. She asked the dryad to repeat the directions over
and over again until she knew them by heart. The dryad left
and Lilith stayed under the branches of the tree. Sunlight
found its way down to her and it warmed her, making her
feel sleepy and content. Now was not the time for sleeping
though. Something was growing inside her and she felt the
need to retrieve her weapons and then sharpen them until
they were sore.

Lilith followed the dryad's instructions to the letter. The
last thing she wanted was to arrive at the wrong door with
an axe in her hand and a snarl on her face. The dryad's
directions were long-winded but hopefully, incredibly accu-
rate. From Kew she had to go to Chiswick House and
Gardens, then on to Ravenscourt Park. Holland Park was
next, Alexandra Park after that, Kentish Town City Farm,
Hampstead Heath, Girdlestone Park, Archway Park, and
then finally, Waterlow Park. The house where she would
find the Sin Eater was across the road. The door was sky
blue as the dryad had said, and there was a sticker with
some meerkats on it adorning the lamppost right outside.
She sat down with a book that one of the Kew people had

given her and a cold coffee in a cup that told her it had been a car tyre in a previous life. The book was something about a library where dreams enlightened you – or frightened you, she hadn't really got into it yet. It also said that *'Recycling was Rewarding'*. Only time would tell, thought Lilith.

19

THE CRYING OF THE RIVER

C onstance put the flat of her hand into her mouth and bit down on it as hard as she could. The pain was sharp and fierce, but she did not shy away from it. Instead, she used it. Constance was exhausted but knew she must not sleep. If she closed her eyes now, she would never open them again. Her hiding place was an old burned-out Ford Escort languishing in one of the scrap yards in Millwall. It was cold in the rusting shell and the stench of dog urine filled her nostrils, but she was glad of the cold and the smell because they kept her safe. If she were tracked to the yard then found here, it would be by luck and not by skill.

A bird settled on the roof of the car, and she heard its tiny feet patter across it. It seemed to be quite happy up there, foraging, until something scared it and it took to the air. Then she heard something that made the breath in her throat freeze. Glass was being crunched underfoot nearby. Her pursuers were near. They had some superhuman skill it seemed; she'd doubled-back many times, stopped regularly and checked and re-checked to see if she were being followed. She'd employed all of the tricks she'd learned from her brother, but they had found her. Constance hugged her knees to her chest and gripped her small knife so tightly that her knuckles went white.

Someone was out there, she'd been found. Well, let them come, she'd mark one of them for life before they took her.

Constance didn't want to die here amongst the steel and old oil. She wanted to see her family and the water again, she wanted to feel her father's great arms around her, and more than anything, she wanted to avenge her brother and see his killers swing. But there was only one way that was going to happen, and she'd have to move fast.

Mr. Deck could see Mr. Mast. He could also hear him, and he was angry about that. Silence was their weapon and when used properly, it could cut such a sweet line through the dark of the night. Mr. Mast was making far too much noise, but then Mr. Deck noticed that Mr. Mast was limping and favouring one side. He was clearly wounded and when he leaned against an old Bedford lorry riding on bricks his assumption was confirmed. Mr. Deck did not call out to his brother. He watched and waited instead. Mr. Mast was looking the other way when the girl clambered out of one of the wrecks and slipped away, but Mr. Deck was not.

He saw the girl ahead; she was making her way to the corrugated iron wall at the back of the yard. Over and beyond it was the beginning of the warehouses, and beyond them were the docks. She was heading for the water and safety. Something would have to be done about that. He stooped and picked up a discarded wing mirror, then took aim and hurled it high over the girl's head. It landed with an ominous clang.

Constance stopped dead in her tracks. There was someone ahead of her, waiting for her. She cursed under her breath and veered off to the right. There was another way out of the yard; it would take her away from the river but if that was her course, so be it, she would make it. Mr. Deck saw the girl move and slipped through the yard, stepping over the puddles of rusty water, and darting between the piles of dead cars. By his reckoning they were running along parallel paths and he must change hers so that it intersected with his own.

"She's over here!" shouted Mr. Deck.

Constance heard the cry. It felt too close, and she stopped to try to work out where it was coming from. She was panting, and it sounded incredibly loud in her ears. There was no movement from up ahead. The path left would take her to the wall but there was someone there, or at least she thought so. Constance ducked inside an old Volkswagen Camper Van, and crouched down behind the last remaining seat. It was the smart move; if you panicked and ran headlong in one direction for long enough you would run into trouble. If she could locate her pursuers then she would be able to select a route out. Constance stuffed the cuff of her sweater into her mouth and breathed in deeply. The last thing she wanted was for her breath to steam on the air and give her away.

Mr. Deck could not see or hear the girl now. He swore under his breath and clenched his fists tightly. She was smart and fearless. It would be a shame to crucify her like they had done her brother. He heard a splash nearby. Mr. Mast had heard his cry and was lumbering in this direction. He was making a lot of noise, which was what Mr. Deck was counting on.

Constance saw the man coming and breathed a sigh of relief when he passed her hiding place and continued on. When she was sure that he was gone she crept out of the

VW and made her way towards the gates on the other side of the yard. They were never locked and regardless, she was still small enough to slip through the gap if they were. Suddenly, one of the motion-activated lights to the left of the gate snapped on and she froze. Luckily, she had not committed to running across the clearing that led to the gate yet and she was still in the shadows. The man she had seen only seconds ago stumbled out of the darkness. He looked unsteady on his feet, like one of the old drinkers after two too many ales. He took another shaky step forward and then came to a swaying halt directly beneath the light; she could see him clearly now.

He had impossibly white skin, as though he had lived in darkness all his days. His hair was blond – very, very blond – and he was wearing a suit and white shirt. There was a dark stain covering most of the front of the shirt and she realised, with some satisfaction, that it was blood. The man stumbled and pitched forward. His face slammed into the ground and Constance knew that he was dead by the way he fell. She wanted to run now, but something told her that this could be a trap. The man did not stir and the light above the gate, sensing no further movement, eventually switched itself off. Constance stepped to one side and disappeared behind a row of metal barrels. She used them as a screen, so as not to bring the light to life again and so that she could sneak over to the fence by the gate. From there, she would be able to clamber on top of the last barrel, roll herself over the top of the wire, and drop down onto the road.

Mr. Deck saw his brother fall. His first instinct was to rush to his aid, but he could tell from his hiding place that it was too late for that.

"The river flows both ways," said Mr. Deck softly.

He waited, quietly, standing still, blending into the

ragged shadows thrown by the misshapen steel and the metal carnage around him. He didn't have long to wait though. The girl scampered towards him, unaware of his presence. He'd used his brother to push her to the gate, exactly where he wanted her. She was practically standing in front of him when she realised he was there. She tried to scream but he was too fast.

Constance tried to struggle but the man's hands were like iron, and she felt one of her arms start to go numb under his vice-like grip. But all was not lost. She turned the knife around in her hand so that she was holding it like a dagger and shoved it backwards as hard as she could. She heard the man gasp, but he did not let her go. Instead, he lifted her from the ground and then hit her across the face with the back of his hand. The motion-sensitive light came on but all she saw was darkness.

MR. SAIL, Mr. Deck and Mr. Waterline stood over the body of their dead brother. In the half-light of the boat shed he looked grey. His eyes had rolled into the back of his head and now only showed white. The once-white shirt he wore was now black. The blood from his wound had stained it completely, so much so that the dark tie he usually wore appeared to have disappeared. Mr. Deck clasped his hands together and then cleared his throat.

"The river flows both ways
It brings and also takes away
Mariner, captain, sailor, and slave
Must all return to it
One day."

The remaining Sons of Colquhoun then joined hands and formed a ring around the corpse. There was still much of their dark ritual to perform and the candle on the table was nearly a stub by the time they were close to finishing it. Outside on the river a barge passed by and its horn sounded, as if to signal to the rest of London that it could breathe once again. Mr. Mast's mouth was open and that was where the water came from first. It surged up and out of him, trickling from his ears and nose. The water was dark and brackish; occasionally a piece of seaweed or some other flotsam came out. Then his physical form started to soften, and his face began to cave in. His hair vanished, then his skin and finally the bones. The fluid seeped through the gaps in the floorboards and returned to the river below the boat shed. All that was left was his clothes. Mr. Sail gathered them up and threw them into the grate. Then he poured some of the oil from the lamp onto them and set them on fire.

Mr. Deck sighed and crossed the shed. A door was ajar and beyond it was a wooden cross. Nailed to the cross was the lifeless body of Constance. A great deal of vengeful torture had been done to her, but the Sons did not seem to notice. Mr. Waterline removed a sheet of waxed sail cloth from his pocket, then picked up a large metal spike and a wooden mallet. Once the message had been attached to her poor, broken little body they opened the cargo doors and dropped the cross into the water below. It floated away and was instantly devoured by the hungry mist; the tide would know where to take her.

Mr. Deck closed the cargo doors and pulled up a chair. The girl had stabbed him. It was a fierce blow and could have been fatal, but his life had been saved by his belt-buckle. The point of her dagger had hit its metal clasp, and been deflected. An inch either side and he would be joining with the River, just like Mr. Mast. The Sons of Colquhoun blew the candles out and poured water on the red ashes in the grate, then they stepped out and melted away into what was left of the night. They had only walked for a few minutes when they heard the first of the ship's horns.

At first there was a healthy gap between the sounds, then the number of ship's horns grew. It sounded as if every single boat on the River wanted to join in. But this was no song of celebration. This was the sound of pain, despair and sadness. The Sons turned away and hurried on. Each one was thinking the same thing, but none was brave enough to speak. Each retired to his own room, and in the darkness their dreams came to them and told them that they were cursed because they had wounded the River.

20

DEAD RIVER DEAD SKY

CI Judas Iscariot saw the small groups of people gazing up into the sky and didn't really give it much thought until the person in front of him stopped suddenly and he walked straight into him. After the customary bout of over-apologising had passed, Judas carried on, but it had only been about ten metres before he crashed into someone else. This time, he looked up and saw what everyone else had seen. Absolutely nothing. Or rather, no angels. The sky above London should be full of the winged blighters but it was empty, and that started to worry Judas.

There was a new sergeant on the front desk, a young Asian woman called Patel. She was cracking the whip over the duty constables and reading the riot act to a drunk, who was having trouble working out exactly who had all the power in his discussion with the tall sergeant behind the desk. As he was passing, she broke off from her debate with the twelve cans of Stella and still-standing man, and called out to him.

"Inspector! Inspector!"

Judas stopped, then stepped around the drunken man and leaned up against the desk.

"How may I help, Sergeant?"

"This was delivered this morning. The envelope was clean when it was handed in – by a young chap, looked like he'd been sailing, ruddy complexion, big hair, gilet, know what I mean?"

"I do. Was there any message?"

"Yes, sir. The young man said the truce had been broken and you'd know what this meant."

Judas went cold. The drunken man had taken to staring at him and breathing on him at close range. His breath should have been given a nine-month suspended sentence on its own.

"Would you mind taking a step or ten backwards please, sir? You're interfering with police business."

The drunk shuffled to one side. He refused to go back or forwards; this was his small victory against 'the Man'. Judas found it amusing and couldn't help but give the old soak a point for lateral problem solving.

"Sorry, Sergeant, he said that the truce had been broken?"

"That's right, sir. Didn't look very happy. He said that if you wanted anymore proof then you were to listen to the river. It would tell you all you needed to know. You'll have a time of it though, sir, listening to the river that is. Those horns have been going since I came on duty at 2am this morning. It's a bit of a racket. Sounds sad, mournful. Like a funeral if you get me, sir?"

Judas took the envelope and made his way to the lift and up to the 7th floor. A police probationer, still wide-eyed and excited about everything, tried to get out of the lift with Judas and had to be gently coaxed back inside by one of the older officers. As the lift doors closed Judas heard him say something about being off limits and best avoided.

Judas found Lace ensconced in a book that was almost as big as she was called 'The Pyrates'. Clearly her last meeting with Captain Kidd had interested her to the point that she wanted to know more about him.

"Morning, Lace, do you know what's happening with the boat horns? Front desk says that they've been sounding since early this morning. Anything from the RNLI, or the Coast Guard?"

Lace closed her giant book and dropped it onto her desk. It sounded like someone slamming a door.

"We had a message from an Inspector Felix, he says that you and he are old acquaintances. He's based down at one of the 'special' departments, wanted to know if this was anything to do with the Museum."

Judas removed his Frahm City coat, hung it on a hanger then hung the hanger on the coat stand. He was still holding the envelope that Sergeant Patel had given him and noticed that the stain at the bottom corner was getting bigger. He slipped his fingernail under the flap and drew it across the top of the envelope to open it. When he turned it upside down, a small string ring, identical to the one that he was wearing slipped out and landed on the green leather blotter that covered the top of his desk. It was the same ring in size and shape; the only difference between them was that this one was soaked with blood. Judas took one look at it and shook his head. He knew what the horns signified now.

"Lace, can you find Angel Dave for me and bring him in, please?"

Lace stood up quickly, put her coat on, and began to load it with her ASP, mace and nylon cuffs.

"It's funny about the angels isn't it, sir? I've seen plenty of them moping about, but none seem to fancy flying today. It's like they're frightened to get up there."

Judas turned to the window and gazed out. Lace was right. The sky was clear; no angels were home.

"Strange," he mumbled to himself.

Judas picked up the string ring again and held it to the light. It was such a delicate little thing but when it was soaked with blood it became sinister and evil. It was clear to Judas that something terrible had happened during the night, something so foul that the River had revolted.

21

FOOLS AND ANGELS

He watched her fighting with the cord and the wind, and it made him chuckle then smile. These little creatures, so eager to fight in *HIS* name, so ready to race into conflict because they thought they must. They had a choice, if only they would use it. All of these ready-made crusades. What for? For land, for religion, for oil, for people that had no right to ask them to lay down their lives? Free will. The gift that just keeps on giving. Lucifer was feeling angry again. He'd watched the woman tie the flag to the post and revelled in the sound of the anguish of the River. There was so much pain in its waves and tides now. Instead of slate grey, it would have looked much better *blood red*.

The breeze had cracked the flag once or twice before it unfurled properly and flew straight and true. Then, there had been a dip in the wind and Lucifer sensed something. It was like a call, a summons perhaps? He saw the flag pulse and the air shimmer around it. It was some form of base magic, childlike and impotent – trivial. Regardless, his plan was taking shape once more. There would be more pain and more questions for his dear friend Judas. His will would soon be shattered, and his purpose smothered. What better way to show the universe where the true power lay? Temptation and desire would always trump belief and kindness. The soul of Judas Iscariot had become a trophy for Lucifer, and he felt as though all it needed was for the Betrayer to be nudged an inch or so more to the side and he would have it.

The woman succeeded in running the flag up the post and then clambered back inside. He toyed with the idea of ripping the flag to pieces, but he decided to let them all play a while longer. Let them enjoy their hopes and soon enough he would gift them their fears instead. She had not seen him as she worked. It was intentional and now he was alone again, watching the world below flow by. And when he looked to the skies? They were empty and barren. The winged slaves had sensed his presence and refused to take to the sky. He could feel them down below with the human ants, shuffling around with their beautiful wings clamped to their sweaty backs, afraid to use them, afraid to claim their place above *HIS* children.

"No matter!" said Lucifer, the first of the fallen, the most beautiful, the Morningstar.

The sun came out then and for a second the lament of the river was stalled. Lucifer stretched out his mighty black and silver wings, and he was magnificent to behold. Only one other could stand against him, and he was far away, fighting in another war, in another time. The field was clear, and Lucifer was going to plough it up and scorch it.

Poor little Lilith, she thought that he was her Lord and Master, that he would deliver Adam the first man to her so that she might destroy him for cheating her with love. Adam would soon meet his end, and Lilith might join him, and as for the Sin Eater, the preposterously named Huxley

Montague? Well that little bastard had been diverting the sinners away from his domain for far too long. Lucifer intended to have his soul and every single one he was carrying. The Lord of the Dark Places demanded his due, and if he had to pull this city down around them, he would do it, with a smile on his lips and his hands red to the wrists in blood and gore.

22

___

ROYAL

Huxley smelled like coconut. He'd taken a shower and used the only washing gel to hand. At first, the sweet smell had caused him to gag and pull the shower curtain back to escape the stench. Then, like sunlight crossing a field behind a cloud, the smell stopped making him feel queasy, and he started to like it – very much. He'd started to relax after his second shower and felt comfortable walking around. The man, his protector, was quiet and steady. He would talk if spoken to but could just as easily drift around, making no noise and requesting no audience. Huxley thought he was troubled and the 'sins' were quite vocal about something they called 'his burden'. Huxley decided not to pry and tried to be amenable. The flat was small but well maintained. It was spotlessly clean and it felt comfortable, if that was the right word. It felt safe, so as a result it *became comfortable.*

Robert, his host, had been a Royal Marine Commando. A select bunch it seemed. There were pictures, not many, on the wall. Robert was obviously a modest man. Most of the pictures depicted a young man, full of hope and focus. One picture showed a before and after image of his troop when it began its basic training and another on the completion of that training. Of the eighty-two that started only fifteen remained. *It must have been hard going*, thought Huxley. Someone had used a black marker to draw over the face of the men who had failed the course. There was also a steel dagger mounted on a wooden plaque. Underneath the weapon was an inscription. Huxley was about to read it aloud when Robert spoke.

"To Sergeant Robert Blackwell, on the occasion of his not being caught for crimes that he should have been punished for. May he live long and prosper, but not anywhere near me. Signed, Sergeant Waltho, 297 Troop. Per Mare Per Terra Per Scooter."

Huxley turned quickly.

"Please forgive me, I was just looking."

"There's nothing to forgive. That's me, next to the third black blob on the left, second row. Big ears and spots. The lad above me and to the right was Wally Waltho. We came from the same place and became friends. He was always getting into trouble, and I was always getting him out. My mum, dead now, God rest her soul, wasn't a fan of Wally, she thought he led me into trouble and then did a runner at the first sniff of it. She was right of course. But, I liked a fight, and I thought there was something heroic in fighting for people less able than me. We all learn don't we – eventually. Right, now that you've had a bit of a scrub, shall we eat?"

Huxley nodded and followed Robert into the kitchen. A curry had been created. It smelled amazing and he suddenly realised that he hadn't eaten for some time. Food that was. 'Sins' he was full of.

"The small bowls in front of you are chopped cucumber, coconut, sliced peppers, raisins, sultanas, and the green stuff is spinach. There is a jar of curry flakes at your elbow if you like your Indian hot, and sour cream over there in the blue bowl if you want to calm things down a bit. Naans are under the tea cloth, water in the tap, and the beer is Cobra I'm afraid. But it's wet and kills a curry in a hurry when you need it most. The food's not exactly Indian by design, it's a Royal Marine take on a classic. Dig in, I hope you like it."

Huxley looked down at the table and almost passed out. The smell and the scent of the spices and the curry sauce were incredible, and his mouth filled with saliva.

"I'm sure I will, but before we start, may I please offer my thanks to you, for letting me find refuge in your home and for treating me so well."

The other man smiled, then another expression took its place. It was a nasty, low, evil look, and as it took hold of the man, Huxley saw him reach for one of the jagged knives on the table and he began to panic.

"Oh, you think you're safe?" asked Robert.

Huxley was looking for a way out. He could not pass the man and escape through the rear door and if he turned around and ran for the front door, he would have a six-inch blade rammed between his shoulder blades. Today was yet another wretched day. Then Robert began to shake, then he started to giggle and laugh. He placed the knife down and lifted his beer bottle instead.

"The look on your face! Sorry mate, old habit, bit of gallows humour, couldn't resist it. You are as safe as houses here, and it would be a brave man, woman, or monster, that came through that door looking for you. The Black Museum and the inspector have done some good deeds hereabouts, and are owed more than one big favour. You don't need to thank me, honestly you don't, just relax, eat your curry, then we can put a Jason Bourne film on and I'll tell you which bits are real and which bits are Hollywood."

Huxley let out a huge gasp of air, then all of his muscles unclenched at once, and he appeared to slump in his chair. He'd had a rough couple of days and to be honest, some gallows humour was what he needed right now.

"I thought Jason Bourne was a Marine, the American kind?" he said.

Billy choked on his Cobra and was about to put the world to rights when he noticed that his guest was smiling now.

"Not bad, Mr. Montague, not bad at all. Now, first things first, the American Marines are not really commandos, so we don't speak about them in the same way. Secondly..."

The conversation lasted longer than the meal. Huxley was perspiring now, and he could have sworn that his sweat smelled of Korma, or was it Madras? While he was working out which one it was the table was miraculously cleared and wiped down. He wanted to volunteer to do the dishes or contribute in some way but everything was done so quickly and so smartly that he dared not intrude. Robert offered Huxley another beer, and then sat down in what he called the 'Chair of Power', or the only single chair in the house. He reached for a remote control and surfed through a couple of content platforms. On one there was a jewel heist in a casino that had been overrun by zombies, another had a full listing of Merchant Ivory pictures, lots of corsets and swooning under a raunchy Mediterranean sun, and finally, the Holy Grail, a selection of super spy films featuring actors that were too young to get a role in Star Wars, or too old or the wrong nationality to be the next James Bond. They settled for the spy.

Huxley started to doze. His head began to bob, and he

knew that he had asked to be excused at least three times so far but the ex-Marine would not hear of it. Huxley really wanted to sleep but he also wanted to hear more about his host. It was only when the second movie in the franchise started that he did. The Royal Marine's story was sad, as he had expected it to be. Something inside told him that this resourceful man, would not, should not be living alone, unless he had chosen to be. As Huxley had surmised, correctly, there was something huge and devastating in this man's past.

"I was in Bosnia from the beginning. A lot of it was before the balloon went up, doing a lot of talking to the special forces there, slipping across the border every now and again, making sure weapons got to the right people, and making sure the weapons with the defects got to the wrong people. Lots of *living in country* as the press and the weekend warriors like to call it, and then there was the sneaky-beaky stuff that I don't talk about. I was away for a long time you see, and when I did get back, I was twitchy, and that made the wife uncomfortable, and my little girl Sara, well she was scared of me. The look in her eyes destroyed me. There were times when I wished that she wasn't mine. Sounds crazy doesn't it? I loved her so much that I wanted her to be happy, and if that meant that she was someone else's? I'd have swapped that for the fear in her eyes every time."

Robert took a swig from his bottle. He was not drunk. He should have been, but he wasn't, regardless of his mental state. He was still primed, and he still looked very capable indeed.

"Can I ask what happened?" Huxley asked.

"Why not," said Robert.

"Well. What happened to your wife and the girl. Sorry, your daughter, Sara."

"It's okay, I don't feel uncomfortable talking about them anymore. In fact, the more I do the closer they feel. They were killed by a Bosnian Witch. We'd flattened this old church, it looked like a ruin and the top brass were convinced that it was being used by the enemy as a staging point, so they levelled it from the air and then we went in to sweep up any ordnance that was left behind. It turns out that the building was in use, just not by the enemy. A coven met there regularly. The locals we spoke to said that it was a dark place and should not be trifled with. But we did, and afterwards, well, men started going missing. We found bits of them here and there, but it was clear that we'd been marked for death by someone who knew the country a lot better than we did. We were all evacuated and sent home for some much-needed rest and recuperation. Only problem was, whatever was wiping us out, followed us back home."

Huxley reached down for his bottle of beer, and after scrabbling around a bit, he found it just to one side of the sofa. He also found that it was warm and he thought about pretending that it was spent, but his host's eyes were upon him, and they were clear and alert. Huxley downed the warm lager and volunteered to liberate another pair from the fridge. When he returned from the kitchen, Robert flicked the caps from both new bottles with an annoying ease. Huxley sat back down and started to drink the ice-cold lager. Robert did the same and when he had downed half of it, he placed his bottle back down on the side table next to his 'seat of power'.

"This witch found us. How she did is a mystery, but there she was, bold as brass, standing on my doorstep and telling me that my days were numbered because of what I had done. I tried to take her down, but she had the strength of ten men and I got knocked about. She said, just before she knocked one of my teeth out that she would not kill me in front of my wife. Then she just vanished.

"A week or two later she reappeared and gave me a note with the address of an old derelict car wash on it. Whilst I was reading it she blew some orange powder into my eyes and any chance of escaping her was gone. She'd cast a spell on me you see. She could now see through my eyes and once I'd read the note I was compelled to turn up and take my medicine. The place had been shut for quite a while, local businesses had been lining up to steal it from the council, but there were no takers, it was a dead end, from a business point of view. When I got there she told me that the old building I'd blown up was also home of the ancient order of the White Witches of the Bosnian Order. We'd killed twenty-eight of her sisters and I was number 28 on her list. A life for a life. Simple.

"The witch said something in ancient Bosnian, if there is such a thing, and I marched over to this wall. I was helpless, couldn't refuse her anything, then she tells me that she is going to bring the wall down on me and I would die the same way as her sisters. Crushed by falling rubble was her sentence for me. Just before she pulled the bricks down she showed me a picture of my girls, both dead, lying in bed with strange stones resting on their eyelids. They were dead the moment I set off for the car wash."

Huxley shifted in his chair. He was anxious and felt awkward in front of Robert. He was used to taking on the sins of others, but they were normally already dead or dying. The man continued.

"So there I am, preparing to be flattened, howling at the moon and crying my eyes out when the inspector appears. The witch turns on him and starts to fling her spells about but the inspector just takes it all, and then this angel swoops in and together they put a stop to her capers, and save my life in the process. He questions the witch and they come to some sort of agreement.

"After that they took her to some special holding place and she was able to travel back to Bosnia by touching some magical object. I owed the inspector my life and at first he wasn't interested but I have some skills that he said could come in useful, and the rest is ancient history."

Huxley listened to the tale in silence, pretty much, and at the end of it he had made a decision to help this man.

"Robert. You have your special skills, as do I. But I have been thinking, there is a lot of sadness in your life, and you carry the weight of it around with you. What if I told you that I had the power to take those bad memories from you, that I could give you peace and help you forget the dark horrors that plague you?"

Robert finished his beer and placed the can on the sideboard.

"Hypnotism? I've tried that my friend, no joy I'm afraid."

"Oh, this is much more involved than mere hypnotism. All you need do is allow me to say a few words over you and the bad thoughts, let's call them that for now, react to my voice and decide to leave you, the host, and come to me instead. I absorb them, they can do no harm to me, and then, at a particular place, I release them, and they are transformed."

Robert sat forward; he was interested.

"Transformed into what?"

"Well, they are cleansed, and then they may go on their way."

"Go where?"

"Heaven, of course."

Robert stood up and paced around the room. Huxley

thought that he may have overstepped the mark and had upset the man. But he was wrong. Robert turned around to face him and there was a big, broad smile on his face.

"When do we start?"

"We can do it now if you like. Just lay down on the carpet on your back and close your eyes, Robert."

Robert did as he was told and Huxley knelt down by his side, and held one hand over Robert's chest. When Huxley began to chant, the lights in the flat performed a theatrical pulse, and the microwave oven started to chirp.

"Don't worry about that, Huxley, it'll go off in a second."

Huxley continued chanting. It was a language that Robert had never heard before and try as he might, he could not work out what part of the world it had originated from. A few minutes passed and nothing had happened, but Huxley continued. His voice was steady and flat. Then Robert noticed a small dark shape forming just beneath Huxley's hand. It grew in size until it resembled a black cricket ball. Huxley then moved his hand from above the dark shape to beneath it, then he curled his fingers around it so that it shrank and fitted into the palm of his hand. Then he casually lifted his hand to his mouth and ate the dark shape. Robert was taken aback at just how nonchalantly he'd performed the act. But it was not over yet. Huxley signalled for Robert to lay back and to close his eyes once more.

The next shape to appear was not so dense – it was, however, very angry, and it buzzed like a giant bluebottle. Huxley had to work a little harder to wrangle this one, but he managed it fairly quickly and consumed it. Four more times Huxley called the sins out. They obeyed him as he said they would and when at last Huxley stopped chanting,

Robert felt something that he had not felt in over twenty years – peace.

Robert thanked Huxley. He was a new man. He felt completely different; he'd never experienced something like that before; all these things he said and more. Huxley was exhausted but also polite, so he tried to keep his eyes open and listen to his host, but the effort of performing the ceremony had wiped him out and he fell asleep. Robert did not want to move him and retrieved a blanket and a pillow from his guest's room and covered him up. Then Robert, feeling slightly light in the head, took himself off to bed to dream about winning the lottery, or flying, or anything but the horrors he had witnessed. They were gone forever, never to be dreamed of again. He was fast asleep when the door was expertly forced from outside. Normally, he would have heard the footsteps on the tiled pavement outside the flat and woken up. Not this time.

Lilith crept inside the flat. The door had proved easy to open and now here she was, standing in the middle of a room in the dead of night. The creature that would finally lead her to Adam, the First Man, was in one of the bedrooms and he would talk to her, or die. The first room she entered was empty. There were clothes hanging in the wardrobe, shoes on the floor, and toiletries in a small blue wash bag. The bed was not made though; there were no sheets or pillows, which she found odd. The second room proved to be the right one. A man was sleeping under a fluffy white duvet. She crossed the room without making a sound, but the man twitched in his sleep. She reached out to grab the corner of the duvet but suddenly there was movement, fast, disciplined movement. Her hand was grabbed and twisted, and it was all she could do to stop herself from being thrown to the floor.

The fight ebbed and flowed. Lilith was not of this earth, and she had a power that made her strong and fast. In the darkness she had mistaken this man for the Sin Eater. He was powerful and well-trained; it was going to be a shame to have to kill him. Her opponent moved well and had already landed a few heavy punches on her, but he was just a man, so she waited for him to lunge at her, then casually snapped his neck. He was dead before he hit the floor. Lilith found the light switch on the wall and pressed it. The room was a mess. What furniture the man had was upended and the bed was almost stuck to the ceiling. He lay at her feet, broken and bent out of shape. Lilith stepped over him and left the bedroom to start searching the rest of the apartment.

Huxley had seen the tall woman enter the room. He had wanted to cry out to Robert that there was an intruder, but his words had deserted him. He heard the fight, and knew that he could not offer anything in the way of support to his new friend, and so he ran. He eased through the open door and sprinted for the Tube station across the road. He used his bank card to operate the barriers, ran down the stairs, and barged his way onto the platform. A train was just about to depart, and he launched himself through the open doors just as they were closing. The train called at four more stations before Huxley realised that he had no shoes on his feet. The sins inside him were being very quiet. Maybe they could sense his shame, because, however you skinned this particular cat, he had run away and left Robert to die.

23

THE BLOODY VENUE

A large black raven swooped down out of the sky and liberated a chip slathered in tomato sauce from a surprised tourist, who shrieked far too loudly for Cat Tabby to take her seriously. Her travelling companions whipped out bulky cameras from backpacks and slim phones from pockets so quickly to record the hilarity that Cat Tabby was taken aback. There were lots of sightseers and tourists bustling around the Tower of London today, so much so that Dick Whittington had to shoulder an older lady out of his way in order to get to the vacant bench she had been heading for. Once there, he had spread his long legs and put both arms out and across the top of the bench, signalling to all and sundry that he did not want company. That was where he and Cat Tabby sat now, waiting for the Mundane Folk to clear off so that they could talk to a ghost about a fight.

Soon, the crowds began to thin, and the bins began to strain under the weight of discarded sandwich packets and well-thumbed tour guides. Dick stood up to stretch his legs; the left one was always susceptible to pins and needles and he hobbled the first few paces until his circulation got back to work. Cat Tabby teased him about it often, but he was too excited about the meeting he had arranged to bandy words with his human partner. A Beefeater saw Dick moving out of the corner of his eye and moved to inform him that he needed to get his skates on because the Tower of London was expecting some special guests this afternoon and unfortunately the general public were not invited to attend.

The Beefeaters, or to give them their proper name, the Yeoman Warders of Her Majesty's Royal Palace and Fortress the Tower of London, and Members of the Sovereign's Bodyguard of the Yeoman Guard, were buzzing around, shooing the stragglers through the gate. A Royal Navy ship had moored nearby, and as custom demanded, the captain of the vessel must honour the tower with 'the dues', those dues being a small wooden barrel of rum. Most of the ship's crew were still onboard but the captain and a few chosen men and women had drawn lucky straws and were expected shortly.

"Sir, might I ask you to leave now, the Tower of London is closing for the night. The quickest way out, and the least arduous, is the other gate. Less of a squeeze and entry to the Tube station is closer."

Dick performed the smallest of bows and then smiled at the Beefeater.

"It's so good to see the old ways being kept alive, my good Yeoman. The King must receive what is owed, it is only right and proper to honour him so. We shall be away now, thank you."

The Beefeater smiled in return and waved the tall man away. It was only when he was standing to attention with the other members of the guards that he remembered what the man had said, and it confused him.

He said 'we', but there was only one man there?

Cat Tabby had trotted after his friend and then, when they were absolutely sure that they were not being followed or could be seen from any of the windows above them, they stepped through one of the stone walls and disappeared completely.

The secret chamber they had retired to was snug. It hadn't been used in a while and there was a thin silver film of dust over the chairs and the table. Dick took his lighter from his pocket and kissed the wick of the candle with its flame, and then pulled one of the chairs out, cleaned the surface of it with a handkerchief, then sat down and closed his eyes. Cat Tabby explored the room, sniffing for secrets.

"Why couldn't we have just come here straightaway, Cat?"

"Because, dear Dick, the magic only works when the Mundane Folk are far away. It wouldn't do for one of them to stray this way; beyond the other door are places that no human should tread."

Cat Tabby motioned towards a large wooden door with grey iron hinges on the far side of the room with a paw.

"I walked those corridors many years ago, my friend, and they are no place for any but the Under Folk."

"And when can we expect our friend to appear?" Dick asked.

"He will make his entrance soon enough. Remember Dick, he's not all that fond of me, or you come to that, but this is by far the best place to hold the fight. It will pull in a fortune, and we must use the promise of the gold to win him over."

There was no answer from Dick this time and Cat Tabby padded across the floor so he could see his friend better. Dick's eyes were closed, and the sound of his snuffling started to intensify. Cat Tabby leaped up onto the table, settled down in front of the candle and watched the flames flicker, dreaming of luxury and wealth.

The candle had burned down by a quarter when the sound of keys in the door woke Cat Tabby. Dick was not far behind. The large door with grey hinges opened and a cold draught slipped in to say hello. Dick pushed his chair back and Cat Tabby edged closer to his friend. A deep voice sounded from the darkness beyond the open door and then a tall form stepped into the light.

"Well met, Sir Richard, and a warm welcome to the Tower of London to you, Cat Tabby. I am here as requested, but I do not have as much time as I would like. The Navy has arrived and tradition dictates that I, Captain Blood, attend the revelries, such as they are. So. What is that you want and how may I help?"

Dick offered the captain a chair, and Cat Tabby moved across the table to sit next to Dick. The captain sat down and moved his sword and scabbard to one side then placed one large, gloved hand onto the table, but kept the other on the pommel of his murderous-looking blade. This action was not for dramatic effect. Blood was an old soldier and an adventurer. He was also a bit of an anarchist and best avoided on a battlefield.

"An acquaintance of ours, and I believe of yours, Captain, has just had word that a mortal enemy of his has returned to this fine old city's dirty and bloody streets, and requires satisfaction, with the tip of a spear or repeated blows to the head with a stone club. We, that is Dick and myself, have persuaded this other party to let us arrange the meeting of the two foes. It only seems right that a clash of Titans should be seen, and enjoyed – and paid for. And, more importantly, for the victor to stand tall and lay to rest any old rumours that may have circulated since their last meeting. We have been talking to most, if not all, of the major players in the Underworld, and they all want to be a part of this event. The attendance will be huge and the betting – well you know how our lot like to wager – will pull in a pretty penny, and we would like to share that with you, Captain."

Captain Blood looked into the flickering flame of the candle and his fingers started to make small circles in the dust. They didn't have long to wait for the first of his many questions.

"What percentage of the gate receipts can I expect?"

Cat Tabby and Dick Whittington started low, just as the captain had started high, and met somewhere just shy of a quarter of the gate.

"How many are we to expect? How will they arrive? Who will handle the drinking and the gaming on site? Will there be an undercard? Who will police the crowd? Where will the gold be collected and stored? When and where will the final pay-out be?" asked the captain.

He was nothing if not thorough and Cat Tabby was kept on his toes. Before the candle finally sputtered its last the captain stood and then reached out across the table. Dick Whittington shook his hand and then the captain turned around and opened the door. He stepped into the dark space beyond but did not disappear entirely; he had one last question it seemed.

"And what of the Black Museum, Cat Tabby? I presume that he does not know of this ... *event?*"

Cat Tabby arched his back and stretched; his small claws scratched the wood of the tabletop.

"I won't lie to you, Captain. He doesn't but if he does suddenly get to know, then whoever it was that told him will lose their lips. Besides, why would anyone miss the chance to make a fortune? We're talking the King of all fortunes here, bigger than the Crown Jewels, many times over."

The captain did not turn around and his words came over his shoulder.

"Remember, Cat Tabby and you, who was once the Mayor. Only I have the keys to the Tower, and all those wretched souls that wander the ramparts and the battlements are my soldiers, and they will do as I command. You will not escape this place if you speak or act deceitfully. I make no threats, but it would be wise to heed my words lest something terrible befall you."

The captain did not wait for an answer or any assurances, he did not need to. The door closed behind him, and the draught left by his side. Cat Tabby looked at his friend.

"We've got the bloody venue!"

"The venue is going to get bloody, more like," said Dick.

It was pitch black inside the walls of the Tower and even the ravens had decided on an early night. The odd couple made their way to the special exit by the river, staying well under cover and hugging the shadows as they went. As he padded along, Cat Tabby was thinking about the captain's question regarding Judas. Something drastic may have to happen to the Master of the Black Museum and his colleagues if they became involved. Everything would start to get tricky then, so what they needed was a diversion.

A man watched them walk away from his hiding place in the shadows. He'd heard every word they'd said to the captain and every word they'd said to each other so far, and he knew exactly who needed to hear it.

24

NOT SO CUNNING

Angel Dave was sitting next to an old-fashioned chimney stack on the roof of a building in Mornington Crescent, North London. Across the road from his perch was the old Black Cat cigarette factory. Now that inhaling nicotine and other assorted chemicals had gone out of fashion, the Art Deco block was home to a number of advertising agencies, PR hubs and Pharma specialists. Angel Dave knew this because he had a friend who worked in the post room of the building; he also knew that one of the dirty, almost derelict houses across the road had a basement, and in that basement was the person he had been sent to find.

Charles Murrell, also known as the Cunning Man, was wanted for questioning by the Black Museum in connection with the murder of the Gilded Goat. The Goat had been an Under Folk face. He was a real goat, but he was able to walk on two legs, and spent most of his ill-gotten gains on suits by Ozwald Boateng and Paul Smith, and artisanal cologne and horn cream. He had been convinced that there was someone, somewhere, with the magical skill to turn him into a human being. Unfortunately for the Gilded Goat, the one he'd been told possessed such a skill was Charles Murrell. He'd played on the goat's naivety and desperation and convinced him to part with a large sum of money that wasn't his, as payment for the spell that would make the goat's dreams a reality. Whoever had caught up with the Gilded Goat – it might have been the gang whose gold he had stolen, or the Cunning Man's bodyguard, an eastern European Golem with hands made of stone and a conscience as cold as a brick – whoever it was, they'd been brutal with the Gilded Goat, and the sight of his poor, dead, mutilated body had turned the strongest of stomachs.

Mornington Crescent, a neighbour to cosmopolitan Camden Town and industrial Euston, had deep roots. There was lots of magic here. The canals at Camden Lock had transported a lot more than coal up and down the country. The narrow boats transported all of the members of the Under Folk that preferred to keep their business secret, and Camden Town was its hub. There were still way-stations, coaching houses and taverns for travellers hidden in plain sight here. Look down a side alley at sunset and you might see a door with a sign above that read 'The Silver Horn'. You might have lived in the area for all of your natural, and never seen it before. Blink twice and it would be gone. Or pitch out of a pub at closing time and stick your hand in the air for a Black Cab. You might see a carriage drawn by white horses instead. The many sides of the waking world were visible in Camden Town, if you knew where to look.

Angel Dave did not need to guess why the Cunning Man had chosen to hide here. It made perfect sense. So, he made a mental note of the number on the door of the house he had been staking out then leaped into the air. He had a report to make.

25

THE THIEF TAKER GIVES

Anthony St. Ledger Jnr scratched at the left-hand side of his neck. The white collars he preferred to wear were high and he would not attach one to his shirt if it were not starched to within an inch of its life. He'd been wearing the same one for three days now and it had begun to chafe. He hated the thought that someone would see him with a grimy collar, but needs must. The Thief Taker watched the mighty Met from across the road. He was always in awe of it. The sheer size and reach of the 'Force' scared him and thrilled him in equal measure. He waited until a group of the *mundane* walked up to the main door and joined them.

St. Ledger wanted to raise both hands above his head, close his eyes, and bathe in the rays and the warmth of the righteous, but he was a law keeper from another age, and the way he plied his craft would never have been accepted here. He waited for the bulk of the party he had followed into the Yard to be processed before slipping past them, then with a sleight of hand he had been taught by a

Newgate pickpocket once upon a time, he fished a warrant card out of a constable's pocket and made his way to the lift.

When it arrived the lift was empty, and St. Ledger smiled – so far so good. He stepped inside and stood with his back to the metal wall of the box. It felt flimsy and it bowed as he rested his shoulders against it. Anthony looked down at his feet, wondering whether or not he would make it to the Black Museum at all. The doors started to close and were nearly shut when a hand thrust itself between them and they were forced to retreat. Three young policeman and a policewoman stepped in. It was clear to the Thief Taker that they knew each other well, and one of them tried to continue a conversation that had started outside, but lifts are conversation killers, and no one wanted to keep it going so when they reached the 7th floor, they did it in silence.

When he moved to exit the lift one of the officers placed a friendly arm on his shoulder.

"That's the 7th floor, sir. Management and Ops are 8 and 11."

St. Ledger turned to the young man and smiled.

"This is me, thank you."

As the lift door closed, and the surprised faces of the young police officers were wiped from his vision, he suddenly realised that he was interesting again. The last time that had happened had been hundreds of years ago, and it put a small but welcome spring in his step as he walked down the corridor with the awful neon lighting that led to the office of his friend, Judas Iscariot. The Master of the Black Museum.

He knocked on the door even though it was already open. It was polite if nothing else.

"Anthony St. Ledger Jnr, son of the more famous and

slightly less dashing Thief Taker of old London Town. May I enter?"

"Yes you may, you ragged old peacock. Come in and have a coffee, you look like you need one," said Judas.

St. Ledger Jnr performed an elegant bow and stepped inside. He was wearing a cloak and he removed it with a theatrical swoosh that would have had a Spanish Bullfighter applauding, and casually cast it over a waiting hook on the coat stand.

"If that old cloak puts as much as a smear on my new coat you will be paying the washer-women to clean it for me." Judas was not in a good mood, but it was clear he was happy to see a friend and an ally.

"That old rag? Dark blue, is that still a thing?"

"If you could only afford that coat, Thief Taker..."

"You have me there, Master of the Black Museum. I have news for you. We can talk the Frahm Winter collection at another time, perhaps?"

Judas boiled the kettle once, poured the scorching liquid into the Thief Taker's mug, emptied it, then boiled the kettle again. He hated a warm cup of anything, and would never offer one if it were not molten. When he was satisfied with the colour of the brew and the temperature of the china, he handed it over.

"Thank you, Inspector," said St. Ledger.

"You are very welcome, how long has it been?"

"The last time we worked together was on that Spring Heeled Jack case. Most of my cases have been interesting but that one, it was crazy."

Judas gestured towards his desk and took a seat behind it. The Thief Taker followed and sat opposite.

"There is something you need to know. It's a rather large something in fact concerning a giant, and another giant."

Judas sipped from his mug and felt a heavy weight on his shoulders. The Archangel Michael, Heaven's hardman, bodyguard and destroyer of all of God's enemies, had rested one of his great mitts on him once, and it had felt similar. He was about to hear something that would not make his life any easier. He knew the tone, and he knew the words that followed would not make him smile. He drank from his mug more deeply, not caring whether his lips were scorched by the molten mocha, and raised his eyebrows.

"I have been employed by one Gogmagog, head man of the Guildhall Under and all-round bad guy, to follow Cat Tabby and Dick Whittington. Before you ask, it's because another giant that goes by the name of Corineus has been sighted in London and Gogmagog wants him dead."

Judas spluttered and some of the nectar recently extracted from his expensive, hand-rolled coffee beans made a mess of his expensive, hand-made shirt.

"Corineus and Gogmagog! I thought Corineus was dead long ago, and the other was busy strangling cows for fun."

"I wish it were so, but Cat Tabby has found the giant Corineus and has decided to make a few quid out of it by setting up a fight between these two old rivals – to the death. Gogmagog knows there are still folk that whisper behind his back that he is not truly the king of the giants, and he will do anything to set that matter straight. Cat Tabby has been playing him like a kipper and Gogmagog knows this, so he hired me to keep an eye on him. I know where Corineus is, and I know where the fight is going to happen!"

Judas peered down at the small brown stain on his shirt. It had started to spread right before his very eyes and normally this would have sent him searching for a damp cloth or a tissue, but right now he couldn't be bothered. The crime committed amongst the Under Folk was endless. He could see how that might please the Almighty, it might even cause *HIM* to smile, but Judas was still serving his jail sentence and there was no sign of a pardon. Only Lucifer the Morningstar had offered him a way out. Maybe he should shake the tree and see what falls out?

"Inspector?" said St. Ledger.

Judas refocused and returned his mug to the table.

"Where and when?"

"The 'where' is the Tower of London. The 'when' is soon, I'm afraid."

"Is that turncoat Captain Blood involved in any of this?" Judas already knew the answer but asked the question anyway.

"Nothing moves in that place without the good captain knowing about it or allowing it to happen. Cat Tabby and his friend were there only yesterday."

"And where is Corineus hiding?"

"He's on a ship called the Zennor down in the harbour at Canary Wharf. I say on the ship, but I mean inside it. I think that the sudden and unexplained sinking of another large boat was Cat Tabby's handiwork too. The Zennor has been miraculously stopped from setting sail."

"Or escaping," said Judas.

"Precisely, Inspector. Our furry friend has big plans for this fight. You could fit half of the Underworld inside the venue, and it's right on the river so it's easily accessible to one and all."

Judas stood up and St. Ledger rose with him.

"This is just what I don't need. I've got two murders to solve, the Mudlarks have declared war on the rest of the River Gangs, and I have a Sin Eater called Huxley Montague in a safe house because his life has been threatened." Judas wandered over to the big map on the wall. St. Ledger stood next to him.

"A lot of pins there, Inspector. I don't suppose they signify tourist spots?"

"Unfortunately not, Anthony. There has been a rise in incidents down on the Embankment of late. Something's rattled the natives."

"I was going to call on you a while back, Inspector. Do you know anything about a company called First Garden Creations? It seems that everywhere you turn, someone or something is talking about it. Lots of strange things happening – magic folk disappearing, and covens and burrows being emptied. Just wondered if you had heard anything?"

Judas picked up a red pin from the box underneath the map, then carefully pushed it into the map.

"Constance Amelie Cockle was murdered by person, or persons unknown and her poor little body washed up just here. Her corpse was found by one of her kin, then the King of the Mudlarks sent me a blood-stained ring and a note telling me that war is coming."

St. Ledger nodded his head.

"Anthony, would you be able to help me with something? I know that you've already done more than you should have, and to ask a favour would seem impolite right now. Would you do a bit of digging and find out what you can about this First Garden Creations for me?"

"You helped me once upon a time, Inspector, when you needn't have, so I'm all yours. I have a question though; hope you don't mind me asking?"

Judas turned to St. Ledger; he had an inkling of what was coming.

"Ask away."

"Well, Inspector. Gogmagog has offered me a pretty payment to find this Corineus, and to be honest, I could do with the gold. Is there any way that we can work this so that I can get what's promised without being pulped by the giant in the process?"

"Leave that with me, Anthony; whatever happens you will get paid. I have some operational funds that I haven't used and there's always the Black Museum. The inmates know where the bodies are buried and where the gold is hidden so we'll sort that afterwards."

"Thank you, Inspector, much appreciated. I'll make some enquiries then drop back here when I can. A pleasant evening to you, Inspector."

Judas watched the Thief Taker Jnr wander out of the office, then turned back to the map and the newly pinned pins. It was while he was trying to work out exactly where Constance had been killed that he realised St. Ledger had just strolled into the Black Museum without anyone knowing about it.

"Security will have to be stepped up!" he said to what he thought was an empty room.

"Beg your pardon, sir?" said Lace.

Judas turned away from the map to greet Lace. He was glad to see her. Ever since losing Sergeant Williams at the battle of Clapham Common the Black Museum had been different in so many ways.

"I was just musing on the fact that one of the Under Folk, one of the good ones, has just waltzed straight into the Yard, marched past the front desk without so much as a glance, then popped up here for a chat. Good work on his part, sloppy on ours. I'm going to have a word with Sergeant Henshaw about it, he normally has a good idea or two. But that's for another day. How did you get on with the flag?"

Lace reappeared from the dingy kitchenette with a mug of something khaki in colour. As she walked, little slops of tea escaped over the rim of the mug, staining the string and tab of the teabag.

"I've got some new coffee in there with a grinder and all the other paraphernalia, why not give it a go?" Judas suggested.

Lace plonked her mug down, removed her jacket and hung it over the back of her chair. Then she took a rather loud slurp of tea.

"Coffee, sir? Tea is the choice of the champion! Besides, I'm a heathen."

She took another noisy slurp, and let out a contented sigh.

"Ahhhhh, nothing better on a rainy Thursday than a hot brew. If you're nice, I can bring in a box of Tetley Tea, the gold standard of bags."

"Clearly, it would be wasted on me, Lace. Now, on to more important things. Did you get the flag and were you able to hang it from the bridge?"

"I did and I was, sir. When the flag reached the top of the flagpole I heard a sort of a humming sound. It didn't last long, but it was definitely something to do with it. And when I got back down to ground level a note was waiting for me. Here it is, sir."

Lace removed the note from her pocket and handed it over to Judas. The paper was thick and ragged at the edges. There were no holes in the side to suggest that it had come from a notebook. No, this was watercolour paper, made in single sheets. Judas lifted it up to the light and there, in the bottom right-hand corner was a watermark. It consisted of two capital letters and a rather crude skull and crossbones.

"The letter C and the letter K. Your new karaoke partner works fast it seems, Lace."

He read the note out loud.

"*All guilds, gangs and watermen of the great river have been summoned to the Tower Under Water at the turn of the 3rd tide. The hempen halter and a dance with Jack Ketch awaits those who decline.*"

Judas smiled and reread the note to himself. Then he checked his watch and decided that the Underworld could look after itself for the next few hours because he was tired and needed to sleep.

"Well done, Sergeant, well done indeed. We have a bit of a gathering tomorrow at the Tower Under Water. I haven't been there for years and if I was being really professional I would go and take a look to see if anything has changed. But I'm pretty confident that we two can handle a hundred or so bad-tempered water folk in a tight space. Aren't you?"

Lace smiled.

"What could go wrong?"

Judas put on his coat, and flicked a small piece of lint from his sleeve.

"It's going to be a long day tomorrow, Lace. If things go the way I hope then you may have to take a trip downriver. It will be dangerous, and you'll have to be on your toes. Take this now, and keep it safe. It will open a few doors for you, and keep you alive if things go wrong."

Judas removed the string ring from his finger and handed it to Lace. She slipped it on. It was very loose, so she used her teeth to pull on the knot and tighten it.

"That won't be slipping off any time soon."

"Goodnight, Lace."

"Goodnight, sir."

UNDER THE DARK WATER

In the corner of his room, a sunrise was in progress. Judas had been swayed by some advertising that he had seen on the bus and purchased a lamp that grew brighter gradually, supposedly mimicking the rise of the real sun outside. It was said to improve the quality of one's sleep and help you to seize the day, leaving you energised and ready for anything. Judas got out of bed feeling exactly the same as he had done for the last thousand years. Regardless, he showered, shaved, checked for grey hairs, of which there were none, got dressed and tried to make a smoothie out of what remained of the bags of frozen, pre-chopped fruit in the freezer.

It was half successful really; the smoothie needed some yoghurt or fruit juice, of which he had neither, so he used milk instead. It wasn't bad but it wasn't great, and he poured the half that remained in his glass down the toilet. He made coffee, put it into one of his 'cups-for-life' then left the flat. He'd been dreaming of the witch again and really wanted to see her. Finding the time was the difficult bit, and he was aware that if he left it any longer, she would find someone else. These thoughts occupied him for his journey to the Yard. His coffee was cold and untouched when he reached it.

Sergeant Lace was already in residence when he got to the office. She looked well slept too.

"Morning, sir."

"Morning, Lace. We'll be heading off shortly, shall we have a – what do you call it – a 'brew' before we go?"

Lace jumped up and went in search of her teabags and two clean mugs. Judas took a seat by the window that he'd had engineered so that angels could enter the office without causing a disturbance in the lifts. The sky was busy again, and as he watched the angels crisscrossing the sky he suddenly thought of Angel Dave.

"Lace? Have you seen or heard from Angel Dave over the past two days?"

Lace placed a mug of tea in front of him and sat down in the chair opposite.

"Can't say I have, sir. I know he was on a watching brief for Charles Murrell. But he hasn't been back to the Museum, not as far as I know."

"Okay, thanks. When I get back, I'll try and find out what he's up to."

They sat in silence and drank their tea. When Judas finished his, he looked up to see Lace was staring at him.

"It was far better than I expected, Lace, a very enjoyable *brew*. Thank you, I shall never speak ill of tea again."

"Have you ever tried fruit tea, sir?"

Judas stood up quickly and made his way over to his desk. He picked up his warrant card and donned his coat.

"Shall we go?" he said.

"That's a 'no' then, sir?"

"It is, unfortunately."

Judas walked along the Embankment towards the City, accompanied by Sergeant Lace. They dodged the tourists, weaving in and out of the crowds; there was no such thing as walking in a straight line in London. At Blackfriars Pier, Judas stood on the floating pontoon for a ferry. Lace watched three river taxis fill up with people then pull away; all the while Judas looked in the other direction. When another river taxi pulled up, Lace coughed politely. Judas turned around and smiled at her.

"Our ride approaches, Sergeant Lace."

Lace turned back to the water and saw an old man leaning on his oars below them. His boat was unusual. At first glance it looked like an oversized coracle that had been balanced on top of a broad-beamed canoe.

"Well I never, if it isn't the Master of the Museum himself! Old scar neck, the noose dodger!" said the boatman in his raspy, croaky voice.

"Well met, old Winkle! It's a pleasure to see you still alive. What's it been, 500 years?"

"Closer to 700 I think, sir."

"That long? Well, it's good to see you, may we come aboard? This is my new sergeant. Old Winkle, meet Sergeant Lace. Sergeant Lace, this is my boatman of choice, Old Winkle. He knows everything that goes on down here on the water. If you are in need of information, this man is the first port of call – pardon the pun."

"Pleased to meet you, Sergeant, come aboard."

Judas stepped onto the boat, followed closely by Lace. They sat behind the ferryman, looking forwards instead of backwards. Winkle stood to row like the fishermen in the Mediterranean and although he was short and wiry, one look at his rounded shoulders told you that this man could pull a shire horse through a hoop. The odd little boat defying all expectations surged through the water, even against the tide.

"I hear that there's a gathering of the River Gangs at the Tower Under this morning, Inspector," said Winkle. "Is that where you are heading?"

"Just as I said, Lace, he knows everything that happens above or below the waterline. Yes we are, my good Winkle, so get a move on. You might well be getting old. The question is, are you getting slow as well?"

Lace felt the boat lean forward and soon white water was coursing down its sides. They reached Tower Bridge in no time and Lace was surprised to see that the old man was not even breathing heavily.

"Here we are, sir, Tower Bridge Quay. Now I'm sure you remember the way, just don't forget to pay!"

Judas reached inside the outer pocket of his Frahm City coat and produced a gold coin. It was slightly smaller than a 10p and from where Lace was sitting, it had been in use far longer than it should have. There were nicks around the edge and the details on both sides were just smudges now. The ferryman was shocked and surprised when Judas pressed it into his hand.

"That journey is never worth one of these, sir. It was no more than the flexing of the oars. If you haven't anything smaller, you can owe me, just like in the old times," said Winkle, holding both palms outwards, reluctant to accept the payment.

"Take it, or I'll take it back, you old fox. Think of it as payment for all of the times that I put you in harm's way and you didn't grumble."

The old man dropped his hands and then reached out to take the coin. It was very bright against the dark of his lined palms.

"Thank you, sir."

"No, thank you, Old Winkle. Now listen to me, and listen carefully. There is going to be a big event happening near here. Take my advice and don't attend. If you do, which I think you will no matter what I say, keep the boat near."

Old Winkle put the gold coin away inside the pocket of the leather jerkin he wore.

"I will, sir. And if you need any help with anything, don't leave it another 700 years."

Judas stepped out of the coracle and onto the quayside. Lace jumped out after him. Before they left, Judas turned back to the boat.

"And another thing, if I catch you referring to me as old scar neck again, I'll give you a guided tour of the Black Museum and leave you there for a bit."

Old Winkle pulled on his oars and the boat found the channel quickly and began to slip away. The old man shouted something but the sound of a large ship's horn blowing from nearby obscured it. Judas shook his head, smiled, then turned away from the water. They'd be getting much closer to it very shortly and hopefully they'd be able to walk away just as easily. The gate that led to the passage that would eventually take you down to the Tower Under was firmly locked and looked as though it hadn't been used in a long time. Paper cups and flyers for club nights had been blown up against it and there was the unwelcome but not unexpected smell of the outdoor urinal. Judas reached inside his pocket once more and produced a black key. It looked as though it should be accompanied by a steel ring and some friends.

"Here we go then, Lace. Keep an eye on the gangs and watch my back, will you? It won't be the first time that someone has buried a boat hook in it."

Judas inserted the key into the lock and the door swung inwards with a groan. They stepped inside and Judas made sure to lock it behind them. The passageway that led away from the gate was straight and true and steep. Lanterns had been hung on the walls at regular intervals; it was well kept, the stairs had been brushed, and no cobwebs hung from any rafter. Judas noticed Lace taking it all in.

"The funny thing about sailors is that they hate mess and being untidy. The Devil makes work for idle hands, sort of thing."

They walked on and shortly Lace started to pick up the sounds of life up ahead. Then, after not more than a hundred metres they turned a corner and stepped into hall of the Tower Under.

There were lots of people milling around. There were also lots of the Fae here too: fairies, gnomes, creatures that went on all fours and all eights, centaurs, angels here and there, and many more. Lace had never seen so many different creatures all in one place. The hall was well lit, and it was very warm compared to the passageway that they had just come down. The ceiling was high and painted on it were all the waterways hereabouts; smoke from the pipes of the sailors had stained it light brown but nonetheless it was impressive. Along the walls of the hall were small tents. Each one was different and so was the nature of the business that went on inside.

Judas whispered to Lace.

"Watch this."

Lace scanned the hall and sure enough the crowds began to thin and some of the tents closed early. A rather putrid old orange landed at their feet with a splat. Someone had thrown it from the back. Judas stepped over it. Then the whispers started.

"The Black Museum is here."

"Quick, hide the spices!"

"They've ruined my sales for the day."

And there were some whispers that went much further than that.

Judas just smiled and made his way towards the back of the hall. When they reached it they found the Captains of the River Gangs sitting around one large wooden table under a brightly painted awning. They were all drinking, as usual, but their mood was subdued. They were trying to appear calm and collected, and failing. The tavern keeper appeared. She was a round lady, hard looking. Tattoos wound their way up and down her arms and she was also wearing ink around her neck. Her hair was jet-black and when she turned her eyes on them, Lace realised that they were the eyes of a cat. She was wearing an apron – *that moved.*

"What can I get the Master of the Museum?" she asked.

"We'll have whatever they're having if you please, my lady."

The tavern keeper performed a small and rather dainty curtsey. Then she hissed twice and the heads of two cats appeared at the top of her apron. They looked at their mistress but didn't move any further, and when she realised that they were pushing their luck – again – she roared at them, and they moved very swiftly.

"Get these two fine folks their beer right now, you saucy pair!"

The cats disappeared inside the tavern and two young ladies returned almost immediately carrying a wooden jug and two tankards. These they placed on the table opposite the captains. When all was well, they turned back to their mistress with heads bowed.

"All right then, in you come," she said.

The two young ladies fell forwards, turning from girls into cats, then they jumped up and disappeared inside the apron once again.

"Apologies, sir, they do get a bit cheeky when royalty comes to call. If you need anything else I'll be right here."

"Thank you, my lady, we will settle up when we leave." Judas pulled out a stool and sat down.

"Light Horsemen, Lumpers, Heavy Horse, Night Plunderers and Game Lightermen. Welcome, and thank you for heeding the call of the flag. It is much appreciated. Most of you know my sergeant, and by now you must all know why I have asked you here today. The Mudlarks are in mourning; two of their children have been murdered in a most horrific way. A note was pinned to both bodies announcing that the killing was ordered by you. I find it hard to believe that any here would commit such a crime but as yet I have been unable to discover any other leads. And I tell you this now, in all honesty and to be clear and just, I have received a token from the King of the Mudlarks, a bloody token that means only one thing – war is coming."

The captains shifted on their stools. A couple took a long pull from their pots. One tried to hold a flame to his dead clay pipe and Judas could see that his hand shook. The captain of the Heavy Horse was the first to speak. He was a broad shouldered individual with incredibly hairy forearms. His head was clearly human, but from his elbows down he could have been a bear.

"The Heavy Horse have nothing whatsoever to do with this heinous and unholy crime."

There were murmurs from the others; each one denied in their own way to having anything to do with the deaths of the Mudlarks.

"So, what is to be done then?" Judas took a moment to take a drink and let the suspects sweat a bit.

He looked across the table at them, scanning each face for a sign or a twitch that told him lies were being served up alongside the beer. Each one held his gaze though, and stared back at him defiantly. Judas tried again.

"So, you, the River Gangs, have seen nothing, you've heard nothing, and not one of you, unless I'm mistaken, has sent any note of condolence to the Mudlarks?"

The Captain of the Light Horsemen muttered something to the others, and they nodded or tapped the bowls of their clay pipes on the surface of the table.

"I haven't had cause to arrest anyone of late and I might be a bit rusty, but my sergeant here, well, she carries a cannister of chemical eye bath that will blind you, and a magic metal pole that extends at a rapid rate. Back at the station they like to call it the muscle breaker. Now, unless one of you, or all of you start talking I will turn a blind eye and allow her to take one or two of you into custody. Then, when we get you back to the Black Museum I will person-ally take you to meet a couple of the inmates and let them show you around, for a decade or two."

Lace stood up quickly. The ASP she always carried about her person was already in hand and she quickly flicked it out so it was fully extended, with a very impressive sweep of her arm. The sound it made added to the theatre. Judas presumed she was going to stop there but Lace had other ideas and she swung it down on the table and shattered two of the clay pots that the captains had been drinking from. There was a lot of action then. People were falling off stools, other patrons were making a break for it, thinking that a fight was about to happen. Cats started appearing from nowhere, turning into young girls right in front of their eyes and then back again, voices were raised, curses and threats started to colour the air, and then, the pièce de résistance. Lace took two quick steps to the left then gave the captains of the Lumpers and the Game Lightermen a face full of MACE.

Judas was impressed; it was overkill, but it was good overkill. The Captain of the Heavy Horse held out one hand, palm upwards. His long knife was in the other but from where Judas was sitting this was just for show.

"Hold hard there! There's no call for violence at this table! None here are guilty of the murders, we work the same river. There are too many eyes and ears on it for one of us to have any secrets from the other, and on no account would any here throw their lot in with another gang. There are rules that we live by, believe it or not. More importantly, Inspector, the Mudlarks are the intelligence on the Thames. We buy all of our secrets from them and learn what trade is coming up or down, for a fee of course. Why would any of us queer that pitch? They make us rich, after all."

All around them, normality was starting to assert itself again. Cats were jumping into aprons and stools were being righted. Shocked and stunned patrons drifted back, sensing a cessation in conflict.

"Lace, would you ask the lady of the house to tend to the captains please? Tell her that good clean water followed by some grog should do the trick."

"Yes, sir. If it's okay with you I'm going to take a *few statements* as well."

"Fine by me, Sergeant. If they decline to answer your questions feel free to persuade them."

Lace smiled and gave her ASP a couple of swooshes through the air. Judas turned his attention back to the remaining captains, the ones that could still see where they were going.

"A few nights from now there will be a great gathering, and the main event of said gathering will be a fight to the death. There will be many of the Under Folk there, in fact I'd go so far as to say that the taverns and the streets of the Underworld will be empty. There will be a lot of gold flying around, old scores will be settled and deals will be done, for one perceived slight or another. I'm telling you this because I don't want you to attend. I can't order you not to but I'd take it kindly if you were to remain absent."

The captains looked at each other then back at Judas. Suspicion was writ large on their faces. And the very idea that the Black Museum would dare to order *them* to do anything? Well that was never going to happen, none of them would last long as a captain if it was known that they could be pushed around. Judas saw all of this in the blink of an eye and decided to ram his point home.

"If you attend this fight you will almost certainly come face to face with the Mudlarks, every single one of them, and if I cannot tell the King where he can find the murderer of his children, then all of you – and many of the Mudlarks – will be feeding the ravens come sunup. It's inevitable."

"If we don't attend, Inspector, the Mudlarks will think us guilty and turn on us anyway," said the captain of the Heavy Horse, astutely.

Judas shrugged his shoulders in resignation. He had to concede the point. Not being there showed weakness, everything was tilting the wrong way – again.

"It's over to you then. If you get off your backsides and get your people out onto the river and help me find the killers, this could all end well. If not, it's war, and the clever money would be on the Mudlarks seeing this one out, because as you said, they have all the intelligence and if they don't wipe you out by force they'll certainly strangle every gold piece from your coffers by drying up your trade routes. Think about it. I know the Mudlarks are."

On their way back up to the surface both Judas and Lace were silent. The enormity of the situation had hit home after their conversation with the River Gangs. They had hours, not days, to find the killers.

27

SECONDS OUT

The screen on the wall could have served as a dining table. It was state of the art, of course, and had been fitted by a technician with a remote control that had a Dunce mode installed, so that a Luddite like Adam could use it. The screen was full of mini screens. One was telling him how hot Barbados was at this time of the year, another educated him as to how is bonds and gilts were doing. There was a black and white film playing top left and some porn, good quality stuff with a storyline, occupying the bottom right. Adam saw all of this at once, taking it in like background music, but his attention was on the main screen and what was being shown made him smile like the hyena he was.

He had divided London's waterfront into colour-coded sectors. Most of them were red, indicating that they were in enemy hands. A small number were green – these he already had control of because they were not owned by the River Gangs. Cold, hard cash had secured them, and he had imagined that more of the same would have allowed him to take the River Gangs' properties. He had learned the hard way that they would never relinquish their lands. That was why the Sons of Colquhoun were so useful to him, and in the end they would go the same way as the rest of the Under Folk – into oblivion.

Adam took a circuit around the boardroom table, stopping only to call down to reception for some refreshments. As he waited for them to arrive, Adam took a quick look out of the window and over the city. Opportunity was everywhere, and he felt like a conqueror viewing strange lands for the first time; there was no one to stop him. One of the reception team buzzed the intercom and he let her in. She was carrying a silver tray with the fruit of the day, assorted mineral waters and sandwiches, enough to choke a donkey. When the door closed, Adam helped himself to a tuna and mayonnaise sandwich and sipped on a bottle of something that tasted vaguely of strawberry.

The phone rang; it was the internal line, not his mobile. He pressed the blue button on the strange octopus-shaped thing on the table that he used for conference calls.

"Yes?" he asked.

A familiar voice filled the room.

"Everything is going according to plan. The River Gangs are at each other's throats, all business on the river itself has shut down, but that's just the semi-good news. The real good news is that there is going to be a fight between giants in a few days, and the word on the cobblestones is that the Underworld below the Underground is going to be empty because they're all going to watch it."

"Are they really?" said Adam.

"They are indeed," said the voice.

"And the River Gangs? Will they be attending?"

"They have to."

"Tell me why?" Adam asked.

"It's a saving face thing. They have to go to show they aren't afraid, and they can't not go because it would look weak. It's an added bonus really."

"How so?" Adam knew the answer, but he just wanted to hear the voice on the other end of the line confirm it.

"What if something big happened at the fight? What if there was a fire and all the gates were locked? What if there was an explosion, faulty wiring – that sort of thing."

Adam drank what remained of his water.

"Could it be done?"

"If you pay me in advance, it will be done."

Adam thumped the table.

"Well, make it happen and you can name your price."

There was a chuckle from the other end.

"And will you be needing a front row seat to see the fight? They're going fast."

"Of course I will, and a quick way out," said Adam.

"Consider it done, I'll send you the ticket along with my price."

Then the line went dead. Adam helped himself to another sandwich then took the idiot-proof remote control from the table and started to change the colours of the waterfront properties from red to green. Cat Tabby had done well so far.

28

THE TURNING TIDE

Sergeant Lace kept checking to see that the string ring the inspector had tied around her finger was still there. She'd only done it about twenty-five times so far. She was in a tunnel under the Embankment somewhere; the guide in front had turned left and then right so many times she had given up trying to count them. If she got lost down here there would be no way out. Hence, the repeated checking of the ring. It guaranteed her passage to the King of the Mudlarks but that was it; after that she was on her own. Lace tripped but did not fall and when she looked down at the floor was surprised to see there were neat, well-scrubbed flagstones underfoot. She walked on and soon she saw the flicker of candlelight ahead.

If the Tower Under the Water had been an eye opener, the Hall of the Mudlarks knocked that into a cocked hat. The first thing she thought was that it looked brown – lots of brown panels and shapes – but when her eyes had adjusted properly she saw that the whole hall was made up of highly polished bits of dead ships and boats. Here and there were keels, anchors, decks. Windows were circular and small; ropes crisscrossed the air above her; masts pointed in all directions – some were so big they had become walkways; others had been transformed into rows of seating. It was incredible to behold and Lace, forgetting for a second that she was putting her head into the mouth of a very hungry and angry lion, marvelled at it.

"DIY SOS eat your heart out!" she exclaimed.

There were hundreds of people milling about; men, women and a lot of children. The mood was sombre. No one was smiling, and Lace knew why. The guards at the entrance to the hall were talking in hushed tones with the messenger. He was frantically pointing to his own finger and then back at Lace. She reached inside her jacket and checked to make sure her ASP was still there. Her movement caught the attention of the guard and then all hell broke loose. Suddenly, Lace heard movement behind her, and she responded accordingly. The passageway that led up to the door to the hall had been fashioned in such a way that you could walk up to the gate easily, but walking away was another story. In hidden gaps in the walls of the passage Lace counted at least four more guards. They came forward slowly; huge, jagged cutlasses in one hand and daggers that looked like they could skin a wrecking ball in the other. Lace flicked out her baton but never got to use it because her arms were pinned, and a bag was pulled over her head. Then she was hit hard and blacked out.

When she woke up she was tied to a chair. She must have been out for a while because her wrists and ankles hurt from the tightness of the rope used to subdue her. Her mouth was dry, and she had body ache to go with her headache. The room was circular, wooden walls of course, and at one end was a noose attached with the whitest rope she had ever seen, hanging from a yard arm. Lace moved her head from side to side in order to loosen her shoulders. The guard behind her, who had been so silent she didn't know he was there took two steps forward and laid the flat of his cutlass on her shoulder.

"Steady there," he said.

'Any chance of a cup of water?" she asked.

"Not much," the guard replied.

"Any chance you could take a look at my finger then?"

"And why would I be looking at your finger?" said the guard. His voice had softened slightly.

"Because I'm wearing a ring that your King gave to my boss. It's supposed to give me safe passage through your lands," she said.

The guard shuffled backwards and Lace heard him sheathing his sword. Then he appeared to her right and without taking his eyes off hers, he reached for her wrist. His hands felt warm as Lace stared into his eyes. He had pupils the colour of mint. Very green and pure. She watched as they looked down at her fingers and then smiled as they widened.

"Why didn't you show this to the guards at the gate?" he asked.

"Didn't get a chance. Reached inside my jacket and the next thing I know I'm here holding hands with you." Lace grinned as the young man released her wrist.

"I meant no disrespect and I am certainly n-n-not the type of Mudlark to take advantage of a lady," he stammered.

"A lady? Me? Only on Fridays. Now, can you loosen these bonds? I have to speak with your King."

The young guard took a small clasp knife from his

pocket and sliced at the rope. Then he helped her to her feet and waited as she rubbed her wrists and ankles. When she felt she could walk without tumbling over every couple of steps, Lace allowed the guard to help her down another passage and back into the main hall.

"Where now?" she asked.

"We must go to see the Bosun. He's the Lord when the King is not here, he'll know what to do."

They leaned on each other as they walked and the guard looked up to get his bearings, then pointed forwards. Lace looked up and saw that they were nearing the side of a ship. Not just a ship, this was one of those triple-decked affairs that Errol Flynn cavorted over in the old movies. Hundreds of cannons had their noses out, looking for the enemy, she presumed. As they got closer, Lace could see that an opening had been cleverly cut into the ship's side. There were more guards everywhere. One of them saw them approach.

"Where are you heading, young master Hornpipe, and who might this be?"

"She was stopped at the main gate and bundled off to the bilboes," he said.

Lace chipped in.

"Wrongly bundled off!"

"Is that so?" asked the other guard.

Hornpipe motioned towards her hand.

"She wears the King's ring, see there."

Hornpipe was trying to instil a bit of urgency, hoping to avoid any blame for the confusion.

The other guard looked down. At first the look on his face was of resignation. This must be another one of those poorly timed jokes ... then it changed to wonder and alarm.

"I need to get her in front of the Bosun, right now!" said Hornpipe.

"Her? My name is Sergeant Lace of the Black Museum."

The colour drained out of the other guard's face, who turned on his heels and started barking orders at anyone standing nearby.

"Make a lane there! Make a lane! Send word to the Bosun! On your toes now!"

Lace tried standing on her own two feet again and found that she could.

"Thanks for the help, Master Hornpipe, I can take it from here."

The young guard with the emerald eyes tugged at an imaginary forelock and smiled a little, crooked smile.

"I think it best that I come with you, just in case you stumble or need my help."

"How very gallant of you," said Lace.

The Bosun was a woman. She was younger that Lace had imagined. In her mind the Bosun was always a terrifying ogre of a man. She was standing at a table surrounded by people. There was a lot of jockeying for position and overlapping conversation; the mood in the room was tense. As they drew near, Lace could see the guard speaking into the Bosun's ear, and pointing at his finger to reinforce the content of his story. The Bosun's head snapped backwards as if she had been slapped, then she pointed to her ear and the guard repeated his story. Or at least that is what it looked like from where they were standing.

The Bosun stood up quickly then Lace heard a high-pitched whistle. It was shrill and piercing, and within seconds the room was empty save for Lace, Hornpipe and the Bosun.

"Pray, take a seat. I'm told that you have been waylaid and assaulted while about the King's business. Is this true?"

Lace sat down and rubbed at her wrists.

"It was a mistake I think ... feelings are running high, and I did come unannounced," said Lace.

The Bosun looked over her shoulder at Hornpipe, but he remained silent.

"That is a brave and honourable thing to say. What do you call yourself?"

"I am Sergeant Lace of the Black Museum at Scotland Yard," said Lace.

"The Master of the Black Museum's newest recruit? It's a pleasure. I am the Bosun, simple as that. I wish I could have kept my old name but when you call the tune, you lose your name. Them's the rules, unfortunately. I can see that you wear the ring so we will dispense with any further questioning on that score. The King is in mourning and is indisposed for now, but he will be able to talk with you shortly. Now, apologies for your treatment, Sergeant Lace of the Black Museum. How might we make amends?"

Lace stood and wobbled a bit. Hornpipe reacted quickly and placed a reassuring arm around her shoulders.

"I'll think of something," said Lace.

The Bosun caught her eye, looked at Hornpipe, then back at Lace. She smiled.

"I'm sure you will," said the Bosun. Then she returned the whistle to her mouth and blew on it. Lace and Hornpipe were nearly trampled in the stampede.

LACE WAS HAVING her second sleep when she heard the whistle again. Hornpipe stiffened next to her. They had become 'close friends' quite quickly after he had tended to her wounds. What followed had been unexpected – but reciprocal. They tumbled out of his bed and scrambled across the floor, finding each other's clothes before their own, which was a strange magic in itself. Lace had only just donned her leather bomber jacket when there was a banging at the door. The King was in council, and they had been summoned.

The Council room was big and dark. In the middle of the floor stood a great ship's wheel. The King of the Mudlarks sat next to it on his throne. He looked tired and there were dark circles under each eye. In better times he would have looked as though he had been burning the candle at three ends. Lace was ushered forward, and when the King saw her he stood.

"You have been harmed, Sergeant Lace? I offer you my apologies, some of my people have grown angry and resentful. Is there anything I can do to make amends?"

"Absolutely not, Your Highness. I have been looked after well after the initial confusion."

The Bosun was sitting nearby and stifled a laugh with a cough. Lace coloured but continued all the same.

"My master has sent me to you with some news. Not the news you yearn for, but important news all the same. May I share it with you?"

The King reached across the great wheel and pulled down on one of the spokes. Lace heard levers creaking and ropes pulling through tackles somewhere and the floor she was standing on began to move. Screens dropped from the rafters and soon, only the King, the wheel and Lace remained. The King stepped down from his dais and walked past Lace to a door on the other side of the room. He produced a key the size of a toasting fork from the folds of his gown and inserted it into a keyhole that Lace could not see. There was a click and the door shuddered and opened. Inside the room, hundreds of black candles had been lit and stood on any surface that could take them. Already, grey wax formed small hills at the base of each one. And in the room, on planks of wood resting upon wooden barrels were the bodies of the murdered Mudlarks.

The King crossed the room and sat down on the only chair. He turned to Lace and gestured towards the children.

"I have sat here in this chair for what feels like days. In my mind I perform scenes from a play. In one, I am able to bring them both back by giving up my eyes or my heart. In another I arrive just in time to stay the killers' blades and butcher them instead. Recently, I have seen myself on stage, dying of a broken heart. Take a look, Sergeant Lace. See what we are fighting against."

Lace knew she had to. Not to look would have caused the King more pain, and she didn't want that. He'd suffered enough already. So, she crossed the room and lifted the first shroud. It was the boy. Whoever performed burial duties amongst the Mudlarks had done a good job but here and there the tips of a scar, or the knot of a thread used to sew body parts together could be seen, and Lace gasped. Then she lifted the shroud that covered the girl, and the King sobbed.

"Beautiful Constance! Shattered and destroyed! Who could have done this? Why would they have done this?"

The King stood and kicked his chair away. It shattered against the wall.

"We found her face down in the mud not far from here. The water had turned her over and we may never have found her if the birds had not called out to us."

"I know this is terrible, my Lord. There was another note?" she asked.

The King removed the note. Again, it was written on a piece of oiled sailcloth in black ink, then sealed with hot wax. It was the same message as before and signed by the rest of the River Gangs. As she read it she noticed the King's hand shook.

"My Lord, the Master of the Black Museum sends his condolences, and he wants me to tell you that he will stop at nothing to find whoever was responsible for this hateful crime. He says that the pieces of the puzzle are starting to fall into place and requests that you hold back your forces. He needs another forty-eight hours."

The King looked down at her. He was a very tall man, and she saw his face turn from a grieving father to an avenging warrior in a heartbeat and it caused her to step back.

"I have the utmost respect for the Black Museum and its Master but time and tide are against you now. I can only give you twenty-four hours and then we go to war."

Lace had the good sense not to argue with him, but she pressed on hoping that the next piece of information might sway him.

"My Lord, an event has been planned for two nights from now. It will take the form of a fight between giants and huge crowds are expected. DCI Iscariot believes the killers will be there. In fact, he's certain we will be able to flush them out of hiding. But it will take forty-eight hours."

The King handed Lace the note who rolled it up and put it inside her jacket pocket. He saw the string ring on her finger and pointed at it.

"You're brave, Sergeant Lace, and I will give the Black

Museum forty-eight hours, but no more. Answer me this before you go. Will the other River Gangs be there?"

"My master said you'd ask this. We visited them a short while ago and made it clear to them that we didn't want them to attend. As expected, they took the bait and will be there. And if the killers are from within their ranks, the Black Museum will stand aside."

"He's a clever man your master, and a devious one. We will come to this fight and we will have our revenge, one way or another."

Lace nodded in agreement; there was little else she could do. The King walked from the room, followed by Lace, and seconds later they were back in the Council room of the Mudlarks. Only the Bosun and Hornpipe were still in attendance. The King sat back down on his throne, tipped his head back and closed his eyes for a second. When he reopened them the stern look of an embattled leader had returned.

"The Bosun will show you the quickest way out. Good luck, Sergeant Lace, I hope to see you again, in better times. Give your master my thanks. Remember, Lace, forty-eight hours and then we begin, culprits or no!"

Lace turned away from the small throne beside the great wall and she was almost at the door when the King spoke again.

"Oh, and Sergeant Lace. I hope your intentions are honourable with regard to young Hornpipe here, we Mudlarks take certain things very seriously indeed."

Lace tripped and almost fell. Luckily the Bosun was near and caught her. She whispered in Lace's ear.

"It is but a joke, Sergeant, a bit of levity, something to smile about when the sea is against you."

Lace turned to face the King. There was the faintest

smile on his face, but it was still a smile, and it gave Lace hope that they could solve this case in time. The Bosun did not lead Lace all the way to the surface; Hornpipe volunteered to take her the rest of the way. The five-minute trip to the surface gates took rather longer but Lace did not complain. Neither did Hornpipe.

29

THE PINK LION

He could just make it out through the foliage. A creature of some sort; not one that he had encountered before. It had unusual colouring and a round body with lots of bright yellow hair. It had not moved for at least an hour. It was obviously an apex predator because it stood so still, and its eyes never wavered. Angel Dave was going to be devoured, and there was nothing he could do about it. He closed his eyes and waited for death. When he reopened them it was gone; maybe it had sniffed at him and decided there were better tasting creatures nearby? Angel Dave started to talk to himself.

I can't feel my legs, have they been eaten? No, I can feel something now, at the small of my back, a tingling. I'm not dead, not yet anyway, but I am in a cage. It's all around me, a mesh of some sort. If I was able to flex my wings I could test its strength. The feeling in my arms is coming back to me and I can move my neck.

Angel Dave pushed himself up using his arms and tried to lift his wings. The one on the right obeyed him, the other was still out on strike and had decided not to go back to work just yet. Using his good wing, he levered himself into a sitting position and after he had caught his breath, he vomited all over his legs. He had the mother and father of all headaches, his eyes watered and each time he moved his head he felt waves of nausea crashing down on him like breakers on a beach. Angel Dave lifted a hand and pressed it gingerly to the side of his face. It was swollen but no bones had been broken.

His lazy wing started to respond after an hour and the headaches subsided, so his mind was able to start piecing together the events that had led him to this point. He remembered the Golem's face now and the strength of its ferocious hammer blow, and then he recalled falling. The stench from his own vomit was starting to get fruity now and Angel Dave decided to attempt an escape. He used a wing tip to prod at the mesh of his cage and was surprised when the mesh ripped easily. He stood and the ground beneath him started to flex. Angel Dave reached out to grasp one of the cage's bars to stop himself from tumbling over, but missed and instead of hitting his head on steel, he fell through the mesh and landed on grass.

Angel Dave stood up quickly and vomited once again, this time managing to avoid his clothes. Instead, his projectile belly contents coated an orange creature with two small horns that had crept up on him. But the creature did not move; it rolled back on itself and then rolled forwards again to resume its original position. Angel Dave suddenly realised where he was. This was no prison cell! He had not been captured; he had fallen into a garden full of children's toys, and he had made an unholy mess of the trampoline. The Pink Lion was nearby. It wasn't at all ferocious, it was barely more than nine inches tall. He had been delirious and imagined the whole thing; the poor Space Hopper was coated in bile and there was no reason on earth that it should still be smiling but it was – bless its boots.

Angel Dave removed his trousers. He could not bear the stench any longer. He was wearing long black shorts underneath, so he was not going to offend anyone. He rolled the trousers up and stuffed them inside a composter behind the wrecked trampoline. Then he saw the paddling pool. It was half full of rainwater, but he drank it like it had just been bottled in the shadow of a French volcano. The water worked its wonders, and he felt a bit better, which was more than enough to leap into the sky and get back to the Black Museum. He had no idea how long he had been out cold; the Cunning Man could have escaped! Angel Dave felt awful, but he would feel a whole lot worse if he had let the inspector down.

Judas was sitting on the floor at the rear of the office, back against the wall. His eyes were closed, and his fingers stroked the smooth face of his silver coin. He was deep in thought, oblivious to the world around him, and trying to stitch all of the events of the past week together when something hit the window above with such force that the glass shattered. The shards had not even hit the floor before Judas was up, silver coin away and hands raised ready to fight whatever had just breached the Black Museum's defences. When he saw who had just flown through the window he relaxed somewhat, but that fury was replaced immediately with concern.

Angel Dave was cut pretty badly. A few of his feathers, most over a foot long, spiralled through the air. One hit a computer monitor and knocked it from the desk it was minding its business on. Smears of blood on the linoleum led like little red roads to Angel Dave's body. Judas marched across the glass, and he heard a snap as one of the larger pieces finally gave in and shattered. He took Angel Dave by the shoulder and gently rolled him over. The angel had come straight through the window, hit the floor and then bounced so he had come to rest on the other side of the room that was luckily devoid of glass. There was an enormous bruise on one side of his face, and as Judas had expected, that silly grin the angel wore when he was hurt or scared.

Judas retrieved the first aid kit from the kitchenette and a bowl of hot water. He sponged the angel's wounds and carefully picked out any shards of glass that had decided to stay along for the ride. When Judas ripped open the sterile dressings to dress the wounds he discovered they were pitifully small and would not be of any use whatsoever. He raced over to his locker and removed his two back-up shirts – white, double-cuffed Gieves and Hawkes – ripped the cellophane covering off and started to tear them into strips. Then he poured the liquid disinfectant from the First Aid kit into the hot water, and soaked the strips of his dead shirts in the bowl. He wrung one out and started binding Angel Dave's wounds. They say that use makes master and Judas smiled at that thought. He'd been beaten to a pulp so many times that he'd become a bit of an expert on staunching blood flow and setting bones.

He propped Angel Dave up against one of the filing cabinets and went in search of a broom and a dustpan to clean the glass up. He'd just finished setting the room to rights when Angel Dave regained consciousness.

"Inspector!" His voice was deep and he slurred his words.

"Take it easy, my friend. Rest, do you need any water?"

The angel nodded and Judas fetched him a two-litre

bottle from the fridge. He had to refill it four times before the angel was sated.

"Inspector, sorry about the window."

"Don't worry about that, the Archangel Michael breaks it every time he pays me a call. I think he does it on purpose now, just to wind me up! What's happened, who did this to you?"

"I found the Cunning Man. Just wanted to be 100% sure that he was there and decided to take a closer look."

"And the Golem did what he's paid to do?" asked Judas.

"It moves so fast for such a big thing. It caught me by the wing then gave me a clout. I got free and tried to fly away but after a few seconds I fell out of the sky, bounced off a garden shed and ended up on a trampoline. It saved my life."

"Well, I'm glad it did. Not so happy you ignored my orders though. Next time I tell you to watch, just watch, okay?"

Angel Dave looked up at Judas.

"There's going to be a next time?" he asked.

Judas fetched him another bottle of water and said, "Maybe, after you get better."

Angel Dave drained the bottle and stood up. He was dizzy and he looked a bit like a Morris Dancer with the long white bandages hanging from his arms and legs. Angels heal fast and Judas was glad to see his smile return.

"Now, tell me what happened," said Judas.

Angel Dave finished his report and when Judas looked into his face it was whiter than usual, and Judas could tell that he needed to rest.

"I want you to stay here. Do not move. That's an order. I need to step out for a second and will be back shortly – okay?"

Angel Dave nodded. He walked across the office, gingerly, chose the large sofa in the corner and fell onto it. He flexed his wings to make himself comfortable, placed his fingertips on his temples and closed his eyes. Judas watched him for a second to make sure that he was not going to pass out again and then slipped out of the office and into the Black Museum. The outer door opened with a hush, and he stepped inside. The inmates were mumbling as usual. Their voices sounded like angry bluebottles stuck behind a radiator, but he paid no attention and made his way to the Key Room as quickly as he could. Time was of the essence, and he needed to find a small rectangular tin that once belonged to a Polish serial killer.

As Judas entered he saw a flash of movement out of the corner of his eye, and when he turned to investigate he saw Simon the Zealot step away from the table rather smartly. Judas thought he saw Simon move his hand away from his pocket. The look on his face told Judas that he was up to no good and Judas would have liked nothing more at that moment than to hang Simon by his feet from the broken window in his office, and frighten him into talking.

"Judas! How opportune, I was just about to call on you. The table has a crack running through it. I was just investigating; I'd hate for it to fall apart."

Judas just shook his head and started scanning the tabletop for the object he was looking for. Simon noticed and volunteered to help.

"I have been making an inventory, Judas. If you need to know where something specific is, you have only to ask."

"I think I'm going to be okay on this one, but thank you, Simon."

Judas found what he was looking for about a hundred yards down the table. A small, grey metal tin with an image of a moustache crudely etched into the lid. He picked it up and stepped into Victorian London. Across the road was a tavern. Outside the drinking house stood four women who held each other's hands, forming a small ring. He crossed the road and as he drew nearer, the women started to hiss at him. There was nothing that Judas could do to help them. They had died a long time ago, poisoned by the man inside.

Judas entered. There was a fire in the hearth but no warmth to go with it. The bar was empty; the efforts of the women outside were obviously paying off. Behind the bar stood a man. He was of average height and build, wore a white apron around his waist and sported a moustache which had been oiled and styled so that it turned up at the ends. Judas approached the bar and Seweryn Klosowski, whose mind was elsewhere, jumped when Judas rapped his knuckles on it.

"How goes the endless torture and torment?" asked Judas.

The man behind the bar took a step backwards, as if he had been slapped around the face. He recovered quickly though and straightened his moustache by twirling the ends.

"Inspector Judas Iscariot, my jailer, and tormentor! Have a drink?"

"I wouldn't drink anything that you had poured, it would be one part alcohol and three parts poison wouldn't it, Seweryn? Business looks slow, I suppose it could have something to do with all your ex-wives outside, drumming up trade for you. Nice of them, considering."

"Inspector! Me? Poison you? I would do it you know, the first chance I had but you're immortal and there isn't a poison strong enough to kill you, more's the pity. What do you want?"

Judas pointed at the fire. There were two chairs, one on each side of it.

"Sit. I have a job for you. Do it and I'll think about having the good ladies take a break once in a while. You might get some trade, and someone other than your reflection to talk to for five minutes. Interested? Course you are, now sit down and listen."

Seweryn Klosowski was known as the Borough Poisoner – a nasty, vicious man, who in his youth had been apprenticed to a master surgeon in his homeland of Poland. No one knows exactly when he turned from healer to killer, but he left the East and travelled to Britain before anyone found out. His dashing looks and his manicured moustache dazzled many a fair lady and he must have realised, then, amongst the swooning and the coy looks he received from the local women that he had a power over them, and he used it. Wife became widow, three times over, and then the fourth, who saw her Polish prince for what he really was, sounded the alarm, and his crimes were discovered. Death was too good for the Borough Poisoner. That was why he was here in the Black Museum, watching a world go by that he could not join. His only company: the women he had wronged.

Judas sat down and watched the Pole fold his glass cleaning cloth into a neat, perfect square that he then placed carefully upon the bar. He was eating up the seconds of contact with Judas greedily. Hundreds of years must have passed since he had spoken to anyone, and Judas started to get angry.

"If you don't sit down before I count to one, I'm leaving, and any chance of anything less than terrible happening to you will be leaving with me!"

The Pole shuffled out from behind his counter and

pulled up a chair as quickly as he could. He tried to adjust his moustache, but Judas saw this coming, reached over, grabbed the end of it and yanked it as hard as he could. There was a ripping sound, like an old cotton tea-towel being pulled apart, and when Judas pulled his hand away half of the Borough Poisoner's moustache was in it. The poisoner looked stunned. His eyes widened and his mouth opened. At first, Judas thought that he'd forgotten what to say when he was in pain, because no sound came from that orifice. Then the floodgates opened and Klosowski howled so loudly that it drowned out the hissing of his dead wives outside. When he stopped sobbing and touching the bare skin where his facial hair had lived, he trembled and rocked. Judas watched him, feeling no pity whatsoever. He really wanted to grasp the other side of the moustache and pull it off. His interrogation would have gone oh so smoothly if he had, but he heard something then that stayed his hand. He tilted his head and heard laughing from outside the tavern. The hissing had been replaced by merriment, and who was he to deny the dead wives a moment of happiness?

The Borough Poisoner looked up at Judas. He did not need to say a word to his jailer to tell him what he was thinking; his eyes had already written pages.

"What do you want from me?" he said.

"Once upon a time you were a member of the Polish underworld. You were admitted into the dark circle after making the usual sacrifices, and then they let you pass through and into their *Dark Realm*. I have walked those pathways and seen what happens there, and I know that certain accommodations are made there with the Golems. Cretins like you swap years of your life for their protection; a stupid bargain made by ignorant people because the Golems take a lot more than that, don't they Klosowski? You swapped the remaining years of your life to escape from the noose, and your Golem didn't come and save you, did he? They might appear to be slow but they're not, are they? But – and here's the unusual and tricky bit – once a connection is made between a Golem and another, the link is always there; unbreakable and everlasting."

Klosowski licked at his top lip; it was raw and pink and there were tiny red dots appearing as the blood started to venture forth.

"That is correct," said Klosowski.

"Good. I want you to pass on a message for me, but not *from* me, you understand? Carry a message to your old friends and let it be known that vast sums of gold will be changing hands at the great fight between the giants. The fight will be happening very soon, and they should make sure that their partners and employers are there. If the message is passed on, and the person I'm looking for attends the event, I will make good on my offer."

"The Golems? Very tricky indeed, hard to understand their magic and their ways if you do not speak the language and understand the forms. It's good that you came to see me, Inspector. Lucky, if I may say so. Anyway, the Golems are, how you say, tough to negotiate with. I'll need a few assurances and some money."

Judas raised a hand in the direction of the Pole's remaining facial hair and the poisoner stopped talking.

"Stop right there! The majority of Polish magical muscle has been pimped out to all manner of filth and charlatan this past century, so don't start giving me all that twaddle about the purity of Polish magic and the indomitable spirit of the Golem protectors. I'll say it one more time. I want you to pass a message on to all of the Golems working for anyone in the Under Folk in London. I don't mind who you pass it to, just make sure you whisper my message into as many of their big stone ears as you can."

Klosowski kept one hand over what remained of his moustache and smoothed his dark wavy hair back with the other. Judas could see and hear the cogs of deceit whirring inside the man's head, but he was fairly sure, no, make that entirely sure that whatever the Polish poisoner was concocting inside his lop-sided head, he could counter it when the time came. For now, he just needed some words to travel fast and travel widely. Judas leaned forward and whispered into Klosowski's ear. Then he repeated it once more for luck, stood up and walked to the door. Outside, the world carried on. In hues of gold and grey, people walked past but only as shadows, horses pulled carriages and carts with nothing on them and no one inside. Life could be seen but it could not be lived. Judas turned to the women that Klosowski had murdered in the real world, who smiled at him instead of hissing, and he felt good for a second. He gripped the metal tin in his hand and the Black Museum pulled him back. He replaced the tin on the table in the Key Room and looked around for Simon, but of course the slippery snake had disappeared.

Judas tapped his index finger against his forehead until it made a knocking sound and he pondered.

Why did I think that Simon the Zealot would make a good custodian of the museum? What was I thinking? Judas old boy, you're looking for redemption so hard, and you want it so badly that you're projecting it onto others. You think that if you save a few, things will go easier. You're an idiot. Now get back to work.

Judas returned to his office to find Angel Dave chewing the fat with Sergeant Lace. The angel looked much better, and had removed some of his bandages. The wounds he had suffered had practically disappeared already, which was a good thing, and there was something different about Lace too, but he couldn't put his finger on it. Whatever it was would have to wait.

"Sergeant Lace, you okay?"

"Yes, sir, *very okay*."

Judas looked at her. She was smiling. She often did, but he thought her reply was a little odd. It was probably nothing, so he let it go.

"Angel Dave, you feeling better?"

"Almost 100%, Inspector, give or take 100%."

Judas smiled at them both. They looked worn out and battle scarred. He wondered exactly what he had done to deserve their loyalty. He was the original sinner, wasn't he? The big bad wolf, the man who tried to destroy Christianity. Judas scratched his head; he was perplexed but very grateful. As he flicked through his police issue notebook, he read some of the earlier entries. Sergeant Williams' name was sprinkled everywhere. He closed it and tapped it on the desk and with each tap he remembered the partners he'd had and the friends that he'd made. All of them had passed away into the folds of time, leaving him on the battlefront and alone. He grieved them all – every single one of them – but this wasn't the time or place to sit back and relive old times, there was plenty he could do to make the present a better place, starting with Corineus.

"Lace, I want you to hold the fort for me. I'll let the front desk know that your orders are my orders, and they are to jump if you tell them to. Secondly, I want you to contact Wulfric, the Warden of the Church Roads. Tell him to expect my call and that I will need him to help me take a package from East London to a certain train station. He'll know which one; if he's suffered a bout of short-term memory loss, just say it's where *she* is. That will jog his memory."

"Yes, sir," said Lace.

"Angel Dave, I want you to purchase five tickets for the big fight between Gogmagog and Corineus. Lace will see you right for the cash. Good seats mind, nothing in the gods. We'll need to be close to the action and able to move fast. Not all of us have wings, after all."

Angel Dave smiled, and his wings extended. Lace, who was standing next to him took a step back to accommodate the angel's ... excitement.

"And before you ask, you don't get a uniform, a whistle, or a warrant card – yet!" barked Judas.

30

BLOOD ON THE GROUND

Captain Blood found the Faceless Twins playing pick-up-sticks in the corner of the Chapel Royal of St Peter ad Vincula. The tourists, of which there were many, walked around and through them both, but neither child paid any attention. They were too absorbed in their game, and as ghosts they saw the living but did not feel them. The Princes had been imprisoned in the Tower long ago and to stop them from being identified as possible future threats to the Crown, their guards had been ordered to pummel their features to a messy pulp. They both wore identical white hoods, and over time they had forgotten their own names. Now, they were just called the Faceless Twins.

Captain Blood approached them and when he drew near the boys stopped playing and looked up at him.

"There you are! I have been searching the White Tower for you both. You were not in the Fusilier Museum, or the Bloody Tower. You do not normally favour this place, what brings you here at this time?"

The Faceless Twins did everything together at the same time, including speaking.

"We were bored with the White Tower, we wanted new scenery, we wanted to play," they said.

"Well then both, what if I were to tell you that a great fight is to be staged here, in our home, that there is much to arrange, and I need your help?" Captain Blood had never patronised the twins; they had seen more horror than many would see in two lifetimes. They knew the hidden halls below the Tower better than any other creature or ghost and had keys to those doors.

"A great fight? We want to know who is fighting," they said.

"The giant Gogmagog, and the giant Corineus, to the death."

"We know these two giants; it will be a savage encounter! Where do you want it to take place? We know of a hall, a huge hall. Plenty of room for violence and dark deeds, good access if you know how to unlock the gates over the underground streams. Close by."

Captain Blood turned on his heel and started to walk away.

"Come on then you two, let's go exploring. We'll need seats and benches, lamps and kindling for fires, and a ring. This is no scratched circle on the floor, last man standing and coming up to the scratch affair. We'll need hundreds of sturdy boxes all tied together with strong rope and a white canvas that will show the blood up nicely. Can you manage all of that?"

The Faceless Twins had fallen into step by his side and were busy chattering to each other in hushed tones. Their words were incomprehensible to him and to his untrained ear. Their voices sounded like silk rubbing against silk.

"We can get everything you need; we have friends and acquaintances here at the Tower, they can help us," said both.

"I knew I could rely on you boys. Get to it now and let me know when you have the ring built. Do that first; if the seating becomes an issue, we'll make them all stand. But, before you both disappear, what payment do you want?"

The twins stopped walking suddenly and the Captain did the same. They whispered to each other again and this time there was much flapping of arms and gesticulating. Finally they stopped and turned back to the Captain.

"We would like front row seats to start with, then we would like 2% of the gate, and then we would like a cruise on the River. Oh, and we want to know how much you are getting?"

"The first two demands are met but I have no idea how I can make the third work. You are captive here are you not, as I am, unable to cross the boundary and Traitor's Gate?" said the captain.

"We have a plan. We know someone that has the power to give us safe passage on the water. All we need from you is an audience with a certain person. We cannot speak with them, but you can. Do we have an accord?" The boys' voices were high and for the first time in a long, long time there was something inside those voices, and it sounded very much like hope to the captain.

"We have an agreement then," he said.

The Faceless Twins did not move. They stood stock still, waiting.

"Your end. We want to know how much you are to be paid," they said.

Captain Blood shrugged. He had thought to get away

without disclosing how much he was hoping to make, but a deal was a deal.

"Cat Tabby and Dick Whittington have arranged the fight; this is their show, and they have staked everything they own on it being a success. Because of this I was able to negotiate 15% of the gate, and 5% of the betting."

The Twins looked taken aback for a moment. They had a quick chat with each other and turned back to the captain.

"We should have gone high; we always undersell ourselves. We would like to renegotiate please."

"Oh no, my boys, you know the rules of the Tower, an agreement is an agreement."

The twins let out a dual moan and stomped away. The captain followed them, chuckling to himself but making sure that he did it out of earshot of the boys. They travelled through the unmarked tunnels below the Tower, turning left and right and then back on themselves a number of times until they came to a huge wooden door. It was three times taller than the Captain and ten times wider than the longest cannon. A bull and cart could have driven through either of the two iron rings that hung on the door. It was imposing but of no issue for the boys. They held hands and whispered to each other again. The doors swung inwards on well-oiled and silent hinges.

Captain Blood followed them inside. There was a sun trap in the far wall and down that cleverly built tunnel the daylight from far above them was sucked down into the hall. As the boys had discussed already, the hall was vast, and the captain struggled to make out the far side. It was the perfect place for the main event. The captain began to smile. Cat Tabby was going to owe him a small fortune, and this news he made sure to tell the twins because if Cat Tabby had any ideas about slipping away with the purse or playing him for a fool then he would get a nasty surprise. Captain Blood was going to make sure that there were safeguards. Cat Tabby-proof safeguards.

31

THE BREAKING OF THE BARRIER

E mily had drawn the short straw yet again, and while the rest of the maintenance team were enjoying their Pot Noodles and warming themselves by the portable heaters, here she was doing the rounds, torch in hand, in a cold and spooky tunnel underneath the Thames Barrier. The red steel safety door was open, and she could see ahead for hundreds of metres. The tunnel stretched from Silvertown all the way over to East Charlton. The design and construction of the Barrier never failed to take her breath away; it was epic and colossal. As she walked, she tapped her torch against her leg and occasionally she gave one of the steel pipes on the wall a quick tap and listened to the echo.

The Barrier could speak in its own funny way. It groaned and clanged, and the wind made thrumming noises sometimes. But tonight something was off, and Emily could hear a different set of sounds to the ones she had become used to. There was a low hum, followed by a thud. It came and went at regular intervals, almost perfect in its timing, like a metronome. Emily removed her mobile phone from her pocket and called her team leader, an experienced and level-headed lady by the name of Natalie, or Nats for short.

"Nats, there's a strange sound coming from outside, can you hear it at your end?"

The line went quiet, and Emily imagined Nats checking all of the advance warning systems to make sure there was not a surge coming up from the North Sea. She was gone longer than Emily expected, which made her feel a bit nervous and she began to tap her torch against the pipes more regularly.

"Emily! We have a surge, and we might need to raise the Barrier. Get back here. No need to panic, we have time, but you're right, the water is acting very strangely."

Emily reacted the same way everyone does when they are told not to panic and started to walk at a fast pace back to the operations room. She looked like an engineer in her hi-vis yellow jacket and hard hat but she was moving like an Olympic speed walker. When she reached the Ops room, the rest of her team were crowded around a bank of monitors. One wag had quipped that you could tell what the Thames had had for dinner that week, so complex and thorough was the technology available to them. There was no laughing now though, just a lot of head scratching from a room of very clever individuals. The water was playing up in a way that no one had ever seen or heard before, and warning bells were beginning to sound.

Emily made her way to the front and stared at one of the screens. The data on it made perfect sense but the readings and projections must be wrong.

"It says that the surge started three kilometres west of us? That's Blackfriar's Bridge, that can't be right?" said one of the technicians.

"Impossible," said another.

But the technology was infallible. The sensors were all working perfectly well. The team tested them again and again and still the origin of the surge remained the same.

"If this continues at the same rate, won't parts of London be submerged from inside the Barrier? I mean, the Barrier stops the surges from coming in through the chops of the channel and running down to the city. What sort of damage are we looking at if the surge comes from the wrong direction?" asked Emily.

The dynamic inside the room changed instantly. Nats started allocating jobs. Some of them retreated to other rooms to make contact with other organisations, giving them coded warnings and advising them to prepare for an unusual situation. Others, including Emily, were sent up to take wind readings and observe the Thames. When they got there, they trained their binoculars on the water as far away as possible in all directions. They checked the riverbanks and studied the boats. All of the vessels were either speeding with the flow of the tide like powerboats or static as they made no headway against the force of the oncoming water. Emily bit her lip and panned her binoculars from left to right. Everything was where it was supposed to be, but it wasn't acting as it should. Then one of the team called out to her and when she looked to him, he pointed back up the river, and she saw it.

Emily remembered a holiday to the States some years ago and learning to Surf in Baha. A friend that she'd made there told her to look for sets of waves. Normally you get two at a time – two good ones that is. Well, here in the UK on a fairly downcast Thursday, the waves were coming in sets of twenty-five. They were only a few feet high but there were so many of them they made the surface of the Thames look like a giant piece of corrugated cardboard. The thudding sound she'd heard in the tunnel below was the waves hitting the barrier again and again.

Nats appeared at her side. She was holding one of those oversized field telephones that were more at home in 'Nam movies from the 80s in one hand, and an iPad in the other. She could hear the sound of voices emitting from the earpiece of the phone and see graphic projections running in bright colours on the screen. Nats didn't seem too bothered; in fact she seemed downright calm and together.

"Emily, the waves and the frequency of them are diminishing but as a precaution we're raising the Barrier, just to be on the safe side. You should be able to see the waves flattening out soon. Well done for alerting us to the noise."

"Where did it come from? What caused it?" asked Emily.

"No idea, it's as if the river got angry and lost its temper and then had a bit of a toot. Bizarre, isn't it?"

"Well, whatever made it angry, it must have been pretty severe," said Emily before following her team leader back down inside the Thames Barrier.

Shortly after they returned to their stations an alarm sounded to tell the team that the Barrier was lifting into place. Once it was in the upright position, no vessels were going up or down the river and none were going out to sea.

32

THE SILVER ROADS

J udas made sure to flash his warrant card at the Harbour Master before entering the man's kingdom. The last thing he wanted was to get into some juris-dictional fracas with him. Then he made his way down to where the good ship Zennor was moored. Directly in front of the Zennor was another craft. It was listing badly to port and looked dangerously close to going all the way over. The only thing preventing that, presumed Judas, was the cat's cradle of heavy ropes that were making it fast to the dock. It was while he was looking at the half-submerged vessel that he was hailed from the Zennor.

"If you're hoping to get off tonight, or even tomorrow, you might be better off going by plane!"

The man who'd called out to him was the same height and size as Judas. He had that well-worn skin look that all mariners wore so easily. A capable man, thought Judas, unflappable and steady.

"Are you the captain of the Zennor?" asked Judas.

"I have that honour, and may I ask who you might be?"

"DCI Judas Iscariot of the Black Museum at Scotland

Yard. I have a couple of questions for one of your passengers. May I come aboard?"

The man's head disappeared. Judas heard his feet slapping on the rungs of a ladder followed by a slight thud as he dismounted. When the captain reached the gang plank, Judas put on his friendly policeman look.

"You are the Master of the Black Museum?" asked Mathey Trewells.

"I am, sir. And you are Captain Trewells?"

"I am that. Please come aboard."

Judas took the gang plank like a complete and utter lubber and wobbled in the middle before reaching out for one of the guide ropes. Trewells smiled.

"Unsteady on my feet and we're still at anchor. An old friend of mine would laugh if he could see me now."

Judas stepped onto the Zennor and the captain reached out to him and they shook hands.

"Your friend ... a sailor?"

"Another captain. A very fine sailor though and a brave man. His ship has a mind of its own, if you follow."

Mathey Trewells had a firm, dry grip, and Judas had the feeling that this man was no stranger to pulling on a rope or trimming sails.

"If you'd like to follow me, I have some coffee on the go, and we can chat about my cargo before you inspect it. That okay?"

"No problem at all," said Judas.

Trewells padded down the deck on bare feet then turned right into a very large and opulent cabin. There was a lot of polished wood, and subtle blue lighting hidden behind ergonomic units. The carpet on the floor was thick and the pictures on the walls were framed and hung in perfectly straight lines. The coffee smelled amazing, and Judas was impressed with the Le Creuset cafetiere, and the matching cups. He inhaled the aroma greedily and sat down in the chair as indicated by the captain.

Trewells poured the coffee, placed it in front of Judas, then he sat down and crossed one leg over the other. The pleasantries had been observed, and now the business end of the meeting could begin.

"She's a fine craft, Captain, very spacious. I see she's riding fairly low in the water. Your cargo must be heavy."

Captain Trewells sipped at his coffee and studied Judas through the silver wisps of steam that rose from the rim of his cup.

"Ships like these have larger cargo holds than other craft in this bracket. The reason for that is fairly straightforward. There is no subterfuge or secret holds in my ship, Inspector. We have the ability to remain at sea longer than many other vessels because our holds are structured in such a way that we can take on bulky objects and stores. She is riding low, as you noticed, but that's just a trick of the eye. These docks are funny ... if you take a look out of the window there you can see how low that unfortunate ship is riding."

Judas smiled and placed his cup back on the table. The captain's hand moved towards the pot, but Judas declined.

"It does seem to have foundered, doesn't it, right in front of the Zennor? I presume that your departure has been delayed somewhat by it?"

"Oh, I shouldn't think so. The sea has a funny way of helping an honest sailor to find his way home. Failing that, I can always rustle up a few mermaids, can't I."

Judas smiled and nodded.

"Stranger things have happened at sea. That's the saying isn't it? I often get them wrong."

"I doubt that, Inspector, you don't seem the type to get

much wrong. What is it that I can help you with?"

Judas decided to cut to the chase and show his cards.

"The Black Museum of Scotland Yard looks into crimes of an occult nature, as you well know. I am also not your run-of-the-mill policeman either. I try and do my best for the Under Folk, and if I can avoid a problem becoming a *giant-sized* problem, I will. You know why I'm here; I have your cargo's best intentions at heart and I'm here to tell you that the sabotaged vessel ten metres off your port bow is the least of your worries right now. Time is running out for him, and his whereabouts are known. If he doesn't disappear soon, he may end up disappearing forever, if you catch my drift."

Trewells returned his cup to the tabletop and stood up.

"Please follow me, Inspector, and whatever you do, don't panic him, or the good ship Zennor will have a few holes in her hull that can't be repaired."

Judas followed Trewells from the cabin. They climbed down a ladder and started to make their way to the main hold. Judas was struck by how big the Zennor actually was. He counted at least eight cabins. You couldn't describe any of them as being on the cramped side. Everything was spotlessly clean, and Judas resisted the urge to comment about it all being very ship-shape.

Trewells turned right at the end of the passageway; the door to the hold was just ahead. He motioned for Judas to wait and then stepped inside. Whatever was said between the captain and his cargo was said quickly and Trewells reappeared at the door scant moments later.

"Come in, Inspector. He is calm and he will hear you out."

Judas stepped into the main hold to find Corineus the giant, vanquisher of the all-powerful Gogmagog. Corineus was sitting with his back to the bulwark on top of a stack of king-sized mattresses. He was huge, and Judas recalled the time that the Royal De Luxe theatre performed their show of 80-feet tall puppets on the streets of Paris. Corineus was perfectly formed – his limbs were not overly large or developed, his head and his brow were not bulky in any way, he looked like a man – just a lot bigger.

"I hear that you have come to help me, Inspector, why so?" asked the giant.

"Because an old foe of yours, Gogmagog, wants to fight you, and if that happens a lot of innocent people are going to get caught up in the middle of your scrap, and I can't let that happen," said Judas.

Corineus bristled at the sound of his old enemy's name.

"And just how are you going to stop this meeting happening? What power does the Black Museum have over Gogmagog, and over me? What makes you think that you can stand between us, or save anyone?"

"I'm not going to stand between you both unless I really have to, and believe me if that happens I won't be standing there alone. There is an Archangel with a massive sword and a bad temper tasked with keeping me in one piece. Any fight with him normally comes to an end rather swiftly. But that's not what I want. I have an alternative option that I would like to share with you. Are you ready to hear it?"

Corineus leaned forwards.

"If your plan means that I can avoid a fight, and live out the remainder of my days in peace, I am all ears."

Judas nodded, then sat down on one of the upturned crates nearby. Trewells pulled up another, and Judas told them his plan.

"And you think this will work?" asked Corineus, after Judas had repeated the plan for the third time.

"I don't like it, there's too many moving parts, Inspector," said Trewells, solemnly.

Judas removed his silver coin from his pocket and began to make small circles with his thumb across it.

"I can get you there without being seen. Once there, you have to stay out of sight. Then when Gogmagog jumps into the ring and screams for your head, you can get in, and I promise you that the fight will happen, but it will end very differently to the way that Gogmagog expects."

"And this place, you can guarantee that no one will discover me there before the bell sounds for the fight, Inspector?"

"I can guarantee your safety, Corineus. The Black Museum will stand by you, whatever happens."

"What say you, Mathey? Do we trust this man and his angels?"

"It's not quite what I had expected my friend, but the inspector is right about that ship and how it got there. It didn't run aground by accident, and there's a lot of shady characters appearing in the dock. None of them know their port from their starboard, that's for sure. If I can't get you out, Corineus, I'll do whatever I can to make his plan work. Your freedom is all that matters now."

Corineus smiled and leaned back against the bulwark again. The ship groaned and started to rearrange herself in the water to accommodate the shifting cargo.

"My friend the captain thinks we should accept your plan, Inspector, and I have no interest in fighting Gogmagog on his terms, so I will do as you ask."

"Good, when can you be ready to leave?"

The giant pointed at a canvas bag; it was the size of a small yellow skip.

"All of my worldly goods are inside. I am ready when

you are."

Judas searched in his pocket for his mobile phone and dialled a number.

"Wulfric? Good, good. Did Sergeant Lace fill you in on what I need? She did? Great. Where shall I meet you? That close? You're a star. We'll be there in five minutes."

Trewells got up from his case and rested his hand on top of Corineus's thumb. There were tears in his eyes.

"Well my friend, I tried and failed. I wish that we were in the channel right now, catching the wind and putting the miles behind us. I hope to see you again after the fight."

Corineus smiled.

"How on earth could you ever fail me, my friend? I will survive this fight and I will walk upon the sand again, with you and your good lady. Fare well, Mathey."

Judas climbed up the ladder to the deck, then walked to the stern of the ship. The pontoon was empty, but not for long. Wulfric, the Warden of the Church Roads suddenly appeared and as soon as he saw Judas he pointed at his watch.

"Now, Mathey!" shouted Judas.

The Zennor shifted in her berth and Judas had to grab the taffrail to stop himself from going overboard. There was a splash and the rattling of chains. Mathey Trewells was releasing the anchor to cover the noise of Corineus's departure. The next thing Judas saw was the giant pulling himself up onto the pontoon from the water with his canvas bag slung over one shoulder. Wulfric saw him and pointed towards a hole in the air, then darted through it. Corineus turned to Judas. They acknowledged each other, then he followed the Warden and disappeared into thin air. The giant was gone. There was no going back now. Everything needed to go his way or Corineus would die.

33

ADAM

Anthony St Ledger counted the cameras and then made a mental note as to their field of vision, and the timings of each sweep. The car park was covered, so were the doors, front and back, the delivery ramp too, and lastly, the fire escape. So, he went in the old-fashioned way, from below. The manhole cover on the pavement directly behind the security portacabin was a bit stiff but yielded quickly to the searching tip of his knife and then was yanked up comfortably by his trusty leather belt. A few seconds later he was strolling casually along one of the underground passageways that housed all of the power cables that allowed one of the occupants of the building, First Garden Creations, to reach out with digital hands to strangle anyone it wanted to.

Once inside, St Ledger used the handy *void space* to move without being seen by the internal cameras, to the boardroom. The void space was described as the *inner utility core* on the fire escape diagram. Anthony smiled at that because the architect who had designed the building had used a clever name to describe the place where all of the waste pipes from the many toilets were housed. The climb up had been easy, and the smell of the disinfectant, gallons of the stuff he imagined, wasn't unpleasant. He made another mental note to find out where the architect's other constructions were, just in case he needed to break into one of them for any reason.

The boardroom was empty, and some kind soul had left a trolley with a plate of sandwiches under cellophane and a plate of croissants and pastries for the early morning meeting, no doubt. St Ledger helped himself to one of each, being careful not to make any mess. He didn't want any of the staff getting into trouble. The lock on the office door at the rear of the boardroom gave in at the mere sight of his lock-picks, and he was able to fool the digital keypad into thinking that his thumb was the right thumb.

Inside the safe he found the usual: a wrap of cocaine, a small plastic bottle of Viagra (half full) a pair of luxury time-pieces (one was the Rolex Kermit, and the other was a Rolex Hulk, so called because one had an emerald green bezel, and the other an emerald green bezel, and face) and then there were the files, the stack of polaroids of a dubious nature, and finally, a black notebook, hopefully full of all of the nasty little schemes and dark secrets that First Garden Creations would prefer that the general public remained unaware of.

The room was small and a little cramped for him, so he took the papers back into the boardroom and spread them out on the boardroom table. They made for spectacular reading. First Garden Creations had been buying up every scrap of real estate it could get its hands on. Then there were the acquisitions made by force and threat. Each one had been documented fully and padded out with photographs.

He'd expected these but he hadn't been ready for the *Red* files. This is where things started to get nasty. In these, and there were many, were the full plans and the bloody strategy for unsettling the River Gangs and their subsequent extermination. That was the only word he could find to describe it.

It was a complex strategy. A lot of time and thought had gone into it, obviously, but it was wicked, and it was cruel. First Garden Creations had formed an alliance with the Sons of Colquhoun, a secret society that St Ledger had heard of, and together they had butchered, murdered, drowned and destroyed a huge number of the Under Folk. There were images attached to the files with colour-coded paperclips. St Ledger guessed that the colour was a reference to one gang or another. At the back of each folder he found something else. The Sons thought that they were cleansing the Thames of criminal vermin, closing down and destroying the vicious Underworld elements, and doing *good works*. They'd been fooled not once but twice though because First Garden Creations had taken steps to implicate the Sons in the murders; it was amazing what an SLR camera with a long lens could do in the right hands. Here was proof of their heinous deeds in 'hi-res'.

He could not eat the remaining half of his sandwich after seeing this, and wrapped it up in a piece of a serviette and placed it inside his pocket. Then, he used the camera on his mobile phone, and made sure not to leave a single page, picture or file unrecorded.

"If only these had been around in the old days, how easy everything would have been," murmured the Thief Taker General junior.

Once he was happy that the original files were back in the same place and in the same order as they were when he started, he checked his pocket to make sure that his phone was there and pocketed the Rolex Kermit.

"This animal won't miss it," said St Ledger.

Fifteen minutes later he was climbing back out of the manhole and replacing the cover. His night so far had been a success; what he needed now was a photocopier and a lot of paper. He found both at an all-night newsagent that he knew well, and while the machine hummed and flashed behind him he called the Black Museum, and told DCI Judas Iscariot all about his findings.

When Judas heard about the sheer scale of First Garden Creation's depravities and criminal undertakings he was angry and wanted to track this *Adam* down and pull his head from his shoulders, but he knew what he needed to do, and killing him would have been a kindness. He told St Ledger to make a couple of sets of the paperwork and then to get back to the Black Museum, and stay there.

"You've done a great night's work, Anthony, Now, hopefully we can bring this whole sorry state of affairs to a close. Be safe, the front desk will know to let you up. You won't need to break into the Yard this time, okay?"

There was a chuckle from the other end of the line.

"Oh, and Anthony?"

"Yes, Inspector?"

"Breaking and entering is a crime. You're aware of that aren't you?"

There was another chuckle.

"It is, Inspector. If I hear of anyone involved in such an undertaking, I'll call the police."

Judas placed his fingertip on the red icon on his phone screen and dropped the phone into the pocket of his coat. He sat down, took a piece of A4 paper from the desk and started to write a note to the King of the Mudlarks. At the bottom of the note he made sure to ask the King to come to the Tower of London the following night. Then he folded the paper in half and then in half again, and slipped it inside an envelope. Then he looked down at his hand and groaned.

He'd given Sergeant Lace the string ring that the King had given to him, and he needed it to show the Mudlark messenger that the note had come from the Black Museum and that its contents were true. He rummaged inside his coat pocket, removed the phone and dialled Lace, but there was no answer. He had to get this message to the King; they were running out of time and the Mudlarks wouldn't remain peaceful for much longer. He dialled her number once again, and this time it rang, but the ringtone sounded odd, like it was inside a bag or something.

"Inspector! Inspector!" I could do with a hand!" shouted Lace from outside the door.

Judas crossed the office in two strides, swung the door open and stepped into the corridor. At the far end, Sergeant Lace was fighting with another woman, a woman that Judas knew well.

"Lilith! Stand down right now! If you damage my sergeant, you'll regret it!"

The struggle carried on for a second or two then the figures separated. Lilith held her hands up and Lace quickly grabbed her left wrist, and was about to secure it with a nylon cuff.

"Sergeant Lace, that won't be necessary I hope, but keep the cuffs ready, and the MACE. What brings you to my door after all this time then, Lilith?"

Lilith rubbed at her wrist and grimaced.

"You fight well, Lace, sorry about the lip."

Lace wiped the blood from her mouth with the back of her hand.

"I caught her trying to get inside the Museum, sir," said Lace.

"I was coming to turn myself in, Judas," said Lilith.

Judas shook his head.

"What for, Lilith?"

"Murder, Inspector. I killed one of your guards, the one that was protecting the Sin Eater. It was an accident though, I thought he was the Sin Eater."

"And what of Huxley Montague? Did you kill him too?"

"No, Inspector. He must have escaped during the fight with your guard."

"Well, that's something I suppose. You'd better come inside and tell me all about it. Sergeant Lace, can you keep an eye on her for me? I have to step out for a second."

Lace looked at the blood on the back of her hand again.

"With pleasure, sir, with pleasure," she said through gritted teeth.

"I'll need that ring that I gave you," he said, before diving back into the office and retrieving the envelope.

Lace followed Lilith down the corridor and into the office. She removed the ring and handed it to Judas, who placed it carefully inside the envelope and ran to the lifts. The Air Force memorial was surrounded by tourists as usual, and Judas had to manoeuvre a couple of them out of the way before he could get to the steps that led down to the mudflats. His Paul Smith shoes squelched into the mud and he steadied himself for the inevitable seeping of the foul-smelling ooze into his socks. On another day, he might get a bit miffed, but today was not that day. He scanned the shoreline and found her straightaway. She was about ten years old, dressed in Camden Town market chic: big boots, a bomber jacket and a knee-length dress made up of layers of denim and leather.

He held up the envelope so that she could see it, removed the ring from inside it, and showed it to her on the upturned palm of his right hand.

"For the King," he said.

The girl skipped across the mud. Her boots did not squelch however; Judas envied her. She took one look at the ring, snatched it from him and slipped it around her thumb, then took the envelope which disappeared into her jacket pocket.

"For the King," she said.

Judas nodded.

"As fast as you can."

She looked over his shoulder and nodded towards a Gemini Rib with a brutish looking engine attached to it.

"Fast enough?" she asked, and then leaped aboard.

The little Mudlark child hadn't left a footprint in the mud and nor did she disturb the water. Judas wasn't surprised and waved to her. She returned the compliment and then with a practised and skilled hand, she opened the throttle and swung the boat's nose out so that it faced away from the shoreline; then she was gone.

Judas breathed in the scent of the river, and it gave him hope. Hope that he would be in time; he'd placed more plates on poles than ever before and spun them as fast as he was able to. Would he be able to keep them spinning? Well, the following day would bring all the answers in the world. He looked out across the water and a flash of a memory painted a scene in his mind. A boy balanced on the centre thwart of a small, honest fishing boat, held together by rusty nails and worn out twine. Birds hovered in the air above him like daubs of white paint on a flat pink sky, hoping for a fish head or some other tasty cast-off. The sun was high, and the boy looked tired. He'd been out since dawn and his net was only half full, but he persevered and cast it out again and again. Judas was that boy and there was a part of this man that longed to go back to the simplicity of life as a fisherman; but that life was gone.

The horn from another craft sounded from further away down the Thames. It was a clear, strong sound, and it made him feel both positive and irate at once. He looked up into the sky and shouted.

"I will not break! I will not give in! I will see this out!"

There was no reply. He hadn't expected one, but he felt better for having stood in the mud and shouted at the clouds. Judas squelched back to the five-rung wooden ladder and climbed up it. When he reached the top and stepped back onto the Embankment the crowds had thinned and darkness had set in. His lovely new black shoes had turned a charming shade of low-tide sludge and his feet were like blocks of ice. Before he returned to the Yard, there was one last call he had to make.

"Anthony, I need you to do one more thing for me. I want you to call your friend Master Gander at 17:00 hours tomorrow. Give him an update on your progress so it looks like you're still working for them. Say that you think Cat Tabby is up to something, and then before you ring off, tell him that Corineus has not run away and is in fact at the Tower and looking forward to beating Gogmagog – again. Make sure you repeat the last bit about beating Gogmagog."

Anthony St Ledger replied, then Judas headed back to the Black Museum.

"I had a date tonight, and look at me, I look like I've been arresting half of Millwall!" Sergeant Lace was holding a small ice cube wrapped in a handkerchief to her lip; it was barely a scratch and Lilith told her so. If the truth be told, Lace was miffed that Lilith had got her punch in first, and she hadn't had the chance to offer a decent reply. Judas walked back into the office and sensed the mood in the room wasn't a happy one.

"Lilith, tell me everything now. Sergeant Lace and I have done so much overtime lately that we could retire to an island in the Caribbean and still have change. We're also stretched very thin and we're not in the mood to be as forgiving as we might normally be."

Lilith placed both of her palms face down on the desk and told them both everything that had transpired over the past three weeks. She told them how Lucifer the Morningstar had appeared to her one morning in Kew. How he'd told her all about Adam, the first man, and how she could find him. How Huxley Montague was a friend of Adam's, a friend that would lead her to him and allow her to get her revenge for slighting her. Lucifer's payment for the accommodation was small; he wanted the sins that Montague had eaten. They were his by right, the first of the fallen had said. Lilith told them how much this would anger the Black Museum and force God's puppet to rebel, and if Adam were to fall then *HE* would feel the loss acutely.

Judas listened and felt some of the remaining pieces of his puzzle falling into place.

"I suppose I am God's puppet, Lilith?"

The woman nodded.

"And you believed all this and sought Montague out?"

Lilith nodded again.

"And you killed one of my friends?"

Lilith bowed her head, and said nothing.

"Lucifer has done what Lucifer does. He has tricked you, Lilith, and me, come to that. Huxley Montague has never even heard of Adam. I'll put my silver coin on it, no, I'll put everything I have left on it. Lucifer wanted you to help him get the sins be believes Montague has stolen from him, and cause me as much ball-ache as possible in the process. He wants me to come over to his side to prove that redemption is a worthless pursuit."

Lilith looked up at him, and he could see that she was angry. He knew from past experience that Lilith had a temper, and it was best left alone.

"Where is Adam, Judas?"

Sergeant Lace sat up and Judas saw her hands moving for her MACE and her asp.

"Sergeant! We may not need those. What I do need right now is Angel Dave and the tickets I asked him to purchase for me."

"They're in the bottom drawer, sir. He came back with them when you stepped out just now."

"And where is that angel now, Lace?"

"No idea, sir. He was in a hurry to get away," said Lace.

Judas opened the bottom drawer and there they were: five tickets to the Tower of London for the following night. Judas handed one to Lilith.

"I want you there at 19:45. Be there and follow my orders to the letter and I will guarantee that you will have your chance with Adam. Do we have a deal, Lilith?"

Lilith looked at the ticket and then back at Judas.

"He is here? At this place? Now?"

"No, Lilith, he is not. And I won't tell you where he is either. Be at the Tower tomorrow night and you will have your revenge. Not a minute sooner, Lilith. You move when I tell you to, or we lose him."

'It will be as you say, Inspector. May I go?" Lilith stood up, closely followed by Sergeant Lace.

"You may go, Lilith. I'm sure Sergeant Lace will be delighted to show you out."

Lilith walked out of the office with Lace in close attendance. Judas was not surprised to hear the sounds of a scuffle from down the corridor, and he decided that closing the office door might be the best solution.

34

BLOOD OR NOTHING

Master Gander had taken to inventing tasks for himself because he now dreaded going into the office of his employer, the giant Gogmagog. The last few days had been torture for the goose and he found himself running his own errands in the Guildhall Under, delivering messages that he normally handed over to one of his underlings, and appearing in meetings that he had previously avoided. Gogmagog had grown increasingly restless and fractious; his frustration at not being able to challenge his true rival Corineus was eating away at him like a hungry plague. His fury was near, and Master Gander could sense it whenever he drew close to the giant. Each time that Gander had entered the office, he exited it as quickly as possible, fearing for his life.

They had not heard from the Thief Taker *yet*; his initial reports were vague although there was the last one that suggested he was getting closer to Corineus. It had not escaped Gogmagog that Gander had suggested Anthony St Ledger for the role of bloodhound and shadow to Cat Tabby.

If Ledger were to fail then the blame would land on Gander's milk bottle shaped shoulders.

Then there was the infernal Cat Tabby and his feckless partner Dick Whittington. Both had remained tight-lipped, refusing to give up the whereabouts of Corineus to Gogmagog because they were selling tickets for the fight, and laying bets with any number of bookmakers in the Underworld. News had reached Master Gander already from trusted sources about the size of the bets that the feline had made. If the cat were to lose, then he would lose big, and Master Gander, although not a friend of Cat Tabby, feared for him.

Gander honked nervously and padded over to the filing cabinets on the other side of his plush office. He was looking for yet another deed of foreclosure that Gogmagog wanted him to serve; at this rate the giant would own vast swathes of land, above and below ground. He was flipping the tabs that were affixed to the files with his beak when he heard the door to the office creak open and turned around.

"Morning, Master Gander, I hope I find you well on this day of celebration," said Cat Tabby.

Dick Whittington slipped into the room behind him and made what Gander presumed was a wave of recognition.

"Celebration? I do hope so, for your sake," said the goose.

"We have come as we promised, to invite your master to a meeting with his adversary, Corineus the giant! The location for the fight is set, the tickets have been sold, every single one of them. There is a waiting list apparently and there are reports of an increase in muggings; the Under Folk are desperate to see the spectacle. Special licences have been allocated to tavern keepers so that they may sell their wares to the masses, and there will be entertainment before the fight and something rather special at the end. All in all, a stage fit for a giant!"

Dick Whittington was excited, and Gander realised that it was not a natural high that was making the old Mayor beam and cavort around the room. Cat Tabby looked pleased with himself too.

"Master Gander, if you would announce us to your master, we would be happy to share the whereabouts of his foe."

Gander honked with relief.

Finally! Some good news! he thought to himself.

He waddled over to the internal office door and was just about to *beak* the door open when it was pulled with such force that it was ripped from its hinges. Cat Tabby and Dick Whittington skipped over to the far side of the office, and Gander honked hysterically. Gogmagog surged out of his office. He had not bathed or changed his clothes since Corineus had been spotted. His beard was wild, and he had decided that he no longer needed to dress for high office, and ripped his own shirt from his hairy back.

"At last! Take me to him now!" roared the giant.

Blobs of giant spittle spattered the walls and made large dark stains on unlucky paperwork, and the smell of his huge unwashed body made Cat Tabby want to gag.

"Now!" he roared again and Master Gander nearly fainted.

"This way, my Lord," said Cat Tabby, quickly.

Gander recovered, edged past the heaving bulk of his giant overlord and positioned himself behind his bespoke desk. He honked into one of the brass mouthpieces and waited for a reply. Mercifully, he didn't have to wait too long. A voice chattered to him, and Gander honked in the affirmative, then stared at Cat Tabby. The feline, normally so quick on the uptake stared back until Gander hissed at him.

"Where are we going?"

Cat Tabby blinked twice, and the penny dropped.

"St Catherine's Dock, pontoon number 4, the good ship Zennor," he said.

Gander nodded and then honked back into the brass mouthpiece.

"I have arranged passage through the old tunnel network, my Lord. We can be there in five minutes."

Gogmagog bellowed something in giant language and raised his mighty arms into the air, giving all of them a nasty nostril-full of his body stench again. Then he brought them back down and destroyed Gander's desk, smashing it flat.

Master Gander waddled out of range before the giant decided to flatten something else –something white with orange bits – and then made his way as fast as his webbed feet would go to the back of the office, where he pulled on a golden bell rope that hung from the ceiling with his beak. The plush navy curtains parted to reveal a large giant-shaped door. Gogmagog ripped it open. This time the hinges survived, and he stepped through it followed by a nervous Master Gander, Cat Tabby and Dick Whittington. The latter had suddenly stopped prancing about and laughing to himself.

Beyond the door was Gogmagog's private monorail. It had been specially constructed to carry his great weight, and Master Gander had moved heaven and a lot of earth to extend the length of the tracks so that his Lord and Master could travel to the far reaches of the Underworld beneath the Underground. It was a simple design. Two seats faced forwards and two faced in the opposite direction. Because it travelled underground there was no need of a roof, but it did have a glass screen mounted at the front. Most of the tunnels had been drained but there were pools and puddles and creatures living down here, and Gogmagog preferred to arrive at his destination dry.

The giant settled back into his seat. Gander tried to sit opposite him, but Cat Tabby and Dick Whittington had other ideas, and Gander had to settle for the space next to the giant. The tunnels were far from fragrant at the best of times but the stench outside the monorail was roses and violets compared to the smell inside. Gander honked twice then bent down and flipped the handbrake off and they started to move. There was no light at the end of this tunnel, but there was a fight and an opponent. Gogmagog muttered something to himself, and it sounded like thunder underground.

The small, single car they travelled in veered left and right, then left again, following some pre-determined path. It was clear to Cat Tabby and Dick there was some form of enchantment on it; or was there a gnome or a sprite driving the car from a secret compartment at the front? Whatever it was or however it was being done, the car whistled through the tunnels at great speed. At any other time it might be called enjoyable and exciting but the mood in the car was anything but. They had been travelling for no more than ten minutes when the car started to slow. Gander leaned out. He was looking for a lamp, because the lamp stood in front of the secret door they must alight at.

Gogmagog was the first to step out. He was impatient and nearly crushed Gander's wing with his hairy hand. Cat Tabby leaped out, followed by a more sedate Dick Whittington, and then the goose, having applied the handbrake to stop the car from running off, waddled across the tunnel. Gogmagog had already opened the door and Gander had to run to catch up with him. He was approaching the exit when he heard Gogmagog bellowing. All hell was breaking loose out there; loud crashes were followed by the sounds of wood splintering and canvas tearing. Gogmagog did not want to wait for the Tower of London, it seemed. Gander stuck his long white neck out of the door, and instantly wished that he hadn't.

Gogmagog had Dick Whittington in one hand and in the other he had a boat hook, which he was swinging around wildly, trying to flush Cat Tabby out from wherever the treacherous little feline was hiding.

"Where is he!" bellowed Gogmagog.

Not only was Corineus absent, but the Zennor had sailed away too. The ship that Cat Tabby had arranged to sink in front of the Zennor had been pushed to one side of the channel, leaving more than enough space for the Zennor to cruise past. There was no ship, there was no Corineus. What there was, was carnage. Gogmagog had lost his temper and when he was in this type of manic mood he did not care who saw him and who he killed. Cat Tabby was not coming out of his hiding place, so Gogmagog decided he was going to bite Whittington's head off. Cat Tabby saw his best friend's face turn white then realised what was going to happen. The giant opened his mouth, put the top half of Dick's body inside it and started to bite down.

"Wait! Wait! Please?!" Cat Tabby emerged from the hole in the pontoon decking where he had been hiding. His ears were flat against his head, and he whined between words.

"Don't kill him! Corineus was here, right here, not an hour ago. I can find him again, just let Whittington go. I promise you, I can find him!"

"It's too late, Cat Tabby! You will follow your friend into

my guts, and I will happily evacuate you both into the sewers, where you belong."

Both Cat Tabby and Dick Whittington were suddenly saved by Master Gander, the most unlikely of heroes.

"Master! Master! I have Corineus, I know where he is!"

Gogmagog's eyes narrowed as he tried to work out if this outburst was yet another ruse.

"If you're in league with these two, Gander, I'll eat you first!"

Gander honked and his wings flapped around.

"A message, my Lord! I have a message from St Ledger, received this very moment! On my portable listening device! St Ledger has Corineus at the Tower! He wants to fight you to the death! St Ledger has come good. He has tracked Corineus down and persuaded him to fight! Great news, my Lord, spectacular news!"

Gogmagog roared, threw Dick Whittington into the water, and then disappeared back down into the tunnels. Gander waddled after him, and Cat Tabby breathed a monumental sigh of relief. The ship had sailed but by some incredible stroke of luck, the giant Corineus was exactly where Cat Tabby wanted him. The fight was still on, Dick still had a head on his shoulders, and they were going to be rich, very rich before long – and Gogmagog, and the rest of them would find that things were going to change, too.

35

THE NIGHT IS SELFISH

The Faceless Twins had transformed the secret hall under the White Tower from a dark, damp hole filled with cobwebs and cold draughts into something akin to a medieval feasting hall that had been hijacked by Vikings looking for Valhalla. Every tavern in the city had sent a wagon full of ale, wine, dancing girls and boys to the event. The sides of the wagons had been cunningly designed to fold down and when a series of brightly coloured canvas screens were attached the wagons became comfortable mobile homes from home for the masses. They were all doing well, even at this early hour, and the muscle that the Twins had employed to police the event, a team of hybrid pugilists that worked the outer circuits and fayres, were nearly as busy as the tavern keepers.

Great fires had been lit in the fireplaces on each side of the hall. Oil lamps had been set on the walls at regular intervals, and candles, thousands of them, had been trimmed and set in iron hoops that hung from the ceiling. The ring had been placed on the ground at the centre of the hall. Two-hundred yards of thick cable, appropriated from

HMS Belfast's stores formed a neat, symmetrical circle. Iron spikes had been hammered into the stone to keep the cable in place, then sand and wood shavings, buckets and buckets of both, had been sprinkled evenly across the floor. Captain Blood walked the hall. He liked what he saw, and he was looking forward to seeing Cat Tabby's face.

Adam had entered the hall from Traitors' Gate. The irony wasn't wasted on him, and he smiled a cruel smile because he knew that after tonight the Tower would be his. He'd ordered the Sons of Colquhoun to pick up a device from a lock-up that he owned in Kensal Green and to bring it to the fight. It was too bulky to hide in a pocket or in a bag, so he had provided a wagon loaded with casks of ale to hide the device inside. It would pass unchecked from the riverside and be parked along with the rest of the supplies. No one would question an extra wagon; the arrangements for the fight had been made at such speed that there were sure to be extras – Adam was counting on this.

So was Cat Tabby. He had chosen to arrive early and find somewhere safe from which he could observe the festivities. Adam had told him which symbol to look for. Find the mark, find the device. Cat Tabby had found it already and chosen to sit as far away from it as possible, just in case something untoward happened and he and Dick were killed along with the rest of the Under Folk in attendance. They had agreed with Adam, in one of their many clandestine meetings, to kill three birds with one stone. The fight would rid everyone of Gogmagog one way or another; the River Gangs would arrive, and the Mudlarks would tear them all to pieces; and then, all of them would be destroyed and the waterfront, the real estate that went with it and the future of London Under, would be theirs. It was a perfect plan, years in the making, and carried out with skill and verve. And as an added bonus the Black Museum would perish along with the giants. Tonight was going to be the night of all nights and Cat Tabby started to purr.

The Faceless Twins were worn out and they had decided to find somewhere to hide away and play some pick-up-sticks. They had found a small wagon that no one seemed to be all that interested in, crawled underneath it and started to play their game. It was as they were drawing the results of the game in the dirt under the wagon that it creaked and rocked. Then they heard voices, and names like Mr. Deck, and Mr. Sail, discussing something called a *device* and how dangerous it was. Then the men with the nautical names finished their business and dropped down from the wagon and walked away. The Twins were puzzled by what they had just heard and decided to investigate. As they were ghosts they chose whether they wanted to be seen or not, and because they'd done such a bloody good job in such a short time, and suspected that someone might be trying to ruin it all, they chose invisibility and started to check the wagon's contents.

36

BLOOD AND EARTH

A large man dressed in a leather apron was collecting tickets at Traitors' Gate. His arms, muscular and hairy, were abnormally long and if he extended his fingers, he would have been able to reach the ground without leaning over. Resting against the wall to one side of him was a wicked-looking axe. On the other side was a hogshead barrel, and on top of the barrel were five ravens. Judas and Lace approached the giant.

"Tickets!" said one of the ravens.

Judas removed his from his jacket pocket.

"Do I give it to you or the bird?" asked Judas.

"You give the ticket to one of us," said a different raven.

"Charlton is here for gate crashers. You're not trying to get in using a fake ticket, are you? Charlton doesn't like people who try to con their way inside," said the raven at the back of the barrel.

"This ticket is kosher," said Judas and passed it over to the raven in the front.

"Caw! Caw! Caw!" exclaimed the raven as he passed his jet-black eye over Judas's ticket.

"All in order, you may go in," it said.

Lace presented her ticket and watched in fascination as it was scrutinised by the bird. She was also allowed to enter. They joined the back of a longish queue; every single race of the Under Folk appeared to be well represented here. The line moved quickly, and they were shown to a doorway which opened out onto a passage. They followed the creatures in front of them to the far end of the passageway and then they were directed to take the stone steps down to the hall where the festivities were to be held. When they entered the hall, Judas saw someone of interest and nudged Lace. Queen Boudica of the Iceni and her bodyguards were occupying a large, wooden circular table. They were drinking and eating, and the Queen caught his eye and nodded to him; the Black Museum had come to her aid recently and she owed Judas a debt.

Judas noticed that Lace was looking but trying not to look like she was looking.

"Meeting someone?" he asked.

"Me? No, sir. Just taking it all in."

They walked around the hall; the fires had been built up and it was getting very warm. It was an old Inn Keeper's trick: get the punters in, make them comfortable, get them hot and make a big noise about how cold your ale is. Worked every time. There were already some unsteady legs and soaked beards.

They found a table at the back of the hall and ordered some drinks. The fight wouldn't start for a while and Judas wanted to observe some of the Under Folk more closely. On the way to the Tower, Judas had told Sergeant Lace about his plan. It was intricate, and there were lots of moving parts. The first thing they needed to resolve concerned Captain Blood, and they found him holding court with some of the heavy-hitters in the Underworld. Judas did not intrude; he stood casually away to one side, and waited patiently for Blood to finish whatever tale of derring-do he was embellishing. The captain finished his story and his guests roared with laughter, then he made his excuses and walked away from the table, heading towards a door set in the wall.

Judas and Lace followed, at a distance. Captain Blood had a reputation to uphold and fraternising with the police would not work any wonders for him, so Judas waited for him to unlock the door and disappear inside before taking his time and then following. The room was small. There was barely room for the three of them, so Judas asked Lace to stand watch outside.

"Well, what's this all about, Inspector? I did as you asked and made sure that Cat Tabby was accommodated, which as you can see, he has been, and then more so."

"You've done exactly as I asked, and I'm very grateful, but things have changed, and I will need to ask you another favour," said Judas.

"It will cost you, Inspector."

"I have something that might be of interest to you, Captain. Will you hear my proposition?"

The captain nodded, and Judas started to tell him what he wanted him to do. The captain's face went from concern to wonder very quickly, and then he burst out laughing and offered Judas his hand.

The Sons of Colquhoun had entered the hall unobserved and were sitting near one of the fires. They were one fewer in number tonight and the death of their brother was hanging heavy over them. They had wooden tankards in front of them, but all were still full to the brim with ale; they had no appetite for merry making, it seemed. A man approached their table and without asking permission, sat on the stool normally occupied by one of the Sons. He was dressed in a sharp, dark-blue suit. His cuff-links were mother of pearl and the size of starlings' eggs. He smiled and his eyes twinkled. His face was relaxed, and his scent was filthy rich.

Adam clicked his fingers, and waited for service. When it didn't arrive in the regulation half a nano-second he bellowed at one of the boys that were running between tables and when the boy trotted over to him, he slipped a golden coin into his palm and gave the lad his instructions. Seconds later the boy returned and set the fresh tankard on the table in front of him. He drank from it and then wiped his freshly shaved and pomaded chin with the back of his hand.

"Did you place the device as I instructed?" Adam asked.

Mr. Sail answered.

"Yes, sir. Would you like to know where, or doesn't it matter?"

"Don't spoil the surprise for me. I won't be here when it activates," Adam replied.

"Neither will we," said Mr. Deck.

"Our payment?" enquired Mr. Sail.

"I have a small leather pouch containing five diamonds in my pocket. They are of incredible clarity and when you agree a price with whichever specialist you choose to patronise, you will have more than enough cash to do whatever you wish."

"And, what of the land we discussed?" asked Mr. Deck.

"That will only be available after tonight. I'll need to see what lots are up for sale in the morning, or which ones have suddenly become *vacant*."

"If you were to try and renege on our agreement, Adam,"

said Mr. Sail solemnly, "First Garden Creations would be no more, understand?"

"Gentlemen, please. I would never go back on a deal, especially not with men of your calibre. Here, take the pouch. More drinks?" Adam asked.

The Sons accepted the fresh beers and started to drink; their moods improved further when they each sneaked a look at the stones.

Outside, at Traitors' Gate, Charlton, the hired muscle, was hefting his axe and trying to look menacing. The ravens were all talking at once and hopping about, clearly agitated. They had good reason to be: a flotilla of boats had suddenly appeared out of the fog and a small army had landed. The Mudlarks had come to the Tower, and they had come in force. The chamberlain approached the ravens and produced a stack of tickets, tied together with string.

"There are enough tickets for my people there. Tell your man to stand aside or he'll be nailed to the prow of one of our boats," he demanded.

The ravens spluttered and flapped some more, but they knew when to caw and when to remain silent. The Mudlarks did not look in the mood to be kept waiting, so the ravens ordered Charlton to stand down. He did so, in as manly a fashion as he could muster, and the Mudlarks trooped inside.

Half an hour later, Charlton was repeating his actions and getting well and truly fed up with the ravens. The River Gangs had arrived in much the same fashion as the Mudlarks, in great numbers and without humour. It looked like there were going to be a few unscheduled fights to watch this evening.

Cat Tabby purred like a German refrigerator. He liked what he was seeing. They'd made a small fortune already from the ticket sales alone. When they got around to taking their cut from the innkeepers and the other performers, the pickpockets and the touts, they would be back in the game. Cat Tabby decided to take a quick look around the hall. He dropped down from his position on the ledge and padded through legs and under tables. He was feeling incredibly chipper right up until the moment he nearly rubbed up against DCI Judas Iscariot's leg! He took evasive action and slinked away as fast as his furry little legs would carry him. When he was absolutely sure that he had not been seen by old scar neck, he watched the Black Museum closely. He hadn't factored in the Black Museum, had he? A basic mistake; he was getting old, and his tail swished around erratically.

Angel Dave sat at the back of the hall. The Cunning Man and his granite-fisted sidekick had crawled out from under their rocks, just as the Inspector had said they would. The big fight was the hottest ticket in town, and they had taken the bait. The Cunning Man looked to be enjoying himself; you couldn't tell with Golems. They had few facial expressions and chose not to use them very often. Angel Dave sipped at his beer and observed the Gilded Goat's killers searching the crowd for their next victim.

"They'll be calling you the Captive Man after tonight, Mr. Murrell," said Angel Dave to himself.

Anthony St Ledger did not look like Anthony St Ledger tonight. He was wearing his 'apprehending' suit. His uniform consisted of a long coat, with lots of hidden pockets, a flat sweep's cap, and a dark-blue neckerchief at his throat. The coat pockets were full of weapons and rope; the cap was slightly too big so that he could cover most of his face if he needed to pull it down; and the neckerchief disguised a thick leather stock he wore around his neck to protect himself against stranglers or cheese wires. He had only just arrived, choosing to wait until the crowds were dense and unruly. After elbowing his way to a table that was miraculously empty, he took a breather and had a well-deserved tot of rum. It was while he was contemplating another that he saw Cat Tabby slinking around. The feline had been darting here and there but suddenly stopped and froze. Anthony could see why: DCI Judas Iscariot was only a few tables away.

Sergeant Lace saw her new *friend* arrive along with the rest of the Mudlarks and she tapped a finger on the table and nodded towards them. Judas followed her gaze and saw the King. He also noticed the other captains and when the Mudlarks chose to occupy the tables directly in front and behind them, he groaned. This was going to get messy.

He was just making a mental note of their numbers and where the exits were when there was a savage roar and Gogmagog, in full gladiator mode carrying a spiked mace the size of a telegraph pole, surged through the crowds and stepped into the ring.

"I'll break his bones, I'll eat his organs, I'll paint the walls with his blood! Come one, come all, and watch the mighty Gogmagog make Corineus fall!"

As an opening line it wasn't half bad, and the crowds enjoyed it and started to chant his name. Judas looked at his sergeant, and hoped that Corineus would do the right thing.

37

THE COWARD

Corineus heard the roar, and clenched his fists. He was ready and focused. Then he heard the screech of the train's wheels as it sought purchase on the steel tracks, and the carriage juddered as if it were being rocked by a playful hurricane. The driver in the cabin ahead opened another valve and the engine roared once again.

In the first class carriage, halfway down the train, the witch sat very still, her eyes trained on his face. She had not left his side since the Warden of the Church Roads had handed him over and into her keeping. The letter the Warden had given her was from Judas. She had scanned it quickly, folded it up and slipped it inside her robe. Then she had conjured up a spell that had made the carriage swell in size but appear normal to anyone who passed it.

He'd been here all along, drinking fine wines, resting and sleeping, hidden away from the prying eyes of the enemy and the Under Folk. The Master of the Black Museum had been true to his word. He was escaping again; the Zennor was sailing away and Mathey, his dear friend, was free of him. Corineus had been upset that he had put his old friend in danger. It would not happen again. He was about to say, 'for as long as I live', but that would not be very long, all things considered. The Ley Line Express pulled away from the platform smoothly and soon it was gliding through the city, heading into the West.

Meanwhile, only a short distance away as the raven flies, Gogmagog was shouting for his opponent to come forth.

"Coward!" he bellowed.

"Come and fight!" he roared.

But the silence from the hall would not be broken by Corineus.

Judas took a deep breath, and walked into the ring.

38

THE FALLING OF THE SCALES

When Gogmagog looked down at him, Judas could see all the way up his nose. It wasn't a pretty sight; huge bogeys were wrapped around nasal hair the size of javelins, and his breath was enough to take the paint off a submarine – when it was underwater. The crowds had been silenced and now only the flickering of the torches could be heard.

"Where is he?"

Gogmagog's eyes looked as though they were about to burst.

Judas held both of his arms aloft, palms facing outwards. He was trying to get the giant to calm down.

"I am here in my professional capacity as the keeper of the peace for the Under Folk," said Judas.

He was trying to channel Winston Churchill, but he had the feeling that he was coming across as the Churchill that advertised insurance on television instead. The masses started to boo and heckle him, and the odd bit of half-eaten sausage started to head his way. Sergeant Lace stepped into the ring and stood beside him. She was knee-high to a grasshopper, but she almost filled their side of the ring with her bravery alone. The sausage missiles came to a halt and the crowd went quiet. Judas nodded to her. They were a good team, and he was proud to be standing with her.

"I couldn't care less if you were the Ghost of Christmas Past! Give me the yellow, lying piece of offal Corineus! He said he was here to fight me!"

"And what are you hoping to achieve, Gogmagog, the all-powerful?" Judas had rehearsed this speech a few times; he only hoped that Gogmagog would allow him to finish it.

"Achieve? I want him dead, you fool! He has been walking this earth wearing the mantle of the King of the Giants! He did not best me! I tripped and fell! I was not beaten, merely stunned, and what did I discover on my waking? Corineus had disappeared, he had left Albion with my crown, and all about me I heard the songs and the stories celebrating his victory. You could not move among the Under Folk without hearing his name. I heard my name too, always accompanied by another word – *loser.* That will end now. Here!"

Judas listened carefully to the giant's words. He'd hoped for an opening like this, and when it appeared, he ran through it.

"You want to kill him? You want everyone to know that you could have won, that you are the strongest and the best? Well, Gogmagog, you can't kill him here, because you already killed him that day on the cliffs. The wounds he suffered at your hand have eaten away at him. The damage you did to him could never be healed or set right. He was dead the second you fell. All these years, you've wanted to break your cudgel over his skull because you believed that he had tricked you. Now you know that he was defeated and will never fight again. You destroyed Corineus, and rather than searching for the truth, you fed your anger with the perception that others thought you second best."

Gogmagog did not drop to his knees and scream to the heavens, acknowledging his frailties and his weaknesses, but Judas could see that something had changed in him. The giant dropped his weapon. It rolled off the platform and nearly flattened the occupants of three tables.

"What proof do you have that what you say is true?" asked the giant.

"You have my word that it is true, and if that is not good enough for you, just think it through. What honour is there in beating a half-dead giant to a pulp? If you believe that your reputation is suspect now, what will it be like after the Under Folk witness you stomping all over Corineus? He has months left to live; he won't see out the year."

"Do you hear the Master of the Black Museum?" shouted Gogmagog.

"Corineus is dying – at my hand – I killed him! Me! Gogmagog, King of the Giants!"

"We heard him!" shouted someone at the back of the crowd.

"So did we!" shouted someone else.

Around and around it went; voices called out that they had heard the truth. Gogmagog stared out at the crowds, searching faces for signs that they were lying to him. But it soon became apparent that no one had the stomach for a one-sided fight or to see a crippled giant be crippled some more.

"I am satisfied!" bellowed Gogmagog.

Judas breathed out a sigh of relief.

Gogmagog left the ring and the crowds parted for him. Then he marched away, followed by a six-foot tall goose that honked with every step.

At first, the huge crowd just milled about, then pockets of conversation started to blossom. The crowd started to find its voice once again. Judas had worried that after the bombshell had dropped that there would be no big fight after all, the crowd would get ugly and there would be more than one other fight taking place. His fears were being realised and much quicker than he had anticipated.

Adam looked around him, and decided that it was perhaps time to make himself scarce. He started to push his way towards the nearest exit but there were hundreds all around him with the same idea; he had to move fast, or he would be trapped inside with the rest of the scum. Then he remembered the device.

Angel Dave unfurled his wings and leaped into the air. He did not have far to go, and landed next to Sergeant Lace in the ring. He used his wings to create a barrier over them and the missiles being thrown from the crowd reduced dramatically. Judas looked for the captain, who was where he should be, and shouted as loudly as he could over the noise of the crowd.

"Seal the hall, Captain! Do it now!"

Captain Blood disappeared into the crowd and seconds later, there was a loud bang, followed by another and then another. The gates had been closed and the crowd had grown quiet again. There was no way out, and they looked at each other with silent suspicion.

"Before you all decide to go on your merry way, there is something that I need to talk to you about. So stay your weapons, and give me five minutes of your time," said Judas.

There was a rumble of agreement from around the hall; the more intelligent of them were trying to work out why they had all been trapped inside. Judas continued.

"The Gilded Goat, known to many if not all of you, was

butchered recently. It was thought that his murder had been committed by one of the gangs that work the fayres. That is what we were meant to believe, isn't it, Angel Dave?"

The angel flapped his wings once and it lifted him above the crowd, where he hovered and looked for the Golem. There was a scuffle at the edge of the hall and then a grunt. The crowd parted and formed a rough circle. Inside it was Charles Murrell, also known as the Cunning Man, accompanied by his minder, the Golem.

"These are the ones responsible for the Gilded Goat's heinous murder!" shouted Angel Dave.

Murrell's eyes were on the Golem; it was his only means of escape now, and he sidled around it, putting the stone man between himself and harm's way. Judas read all of this in the blink of an eye, and laughed.

"There's no way out for you, Murrell. The only place you're going is the Black Museum –and your Golem, too."

"Who's going to stand against him?" sneered Murrell.

"Aside, stand, me," growled the Golem.

"Will be punished. Is okay," it continued.

Murrell squeaked and tried to make a run for it, but the Golem spun around and caught the Cunning Man by the wrist. He was going nowhere. Fast.

"Part two complete," said Judas under his breath. Sergeant Lace smiled.

"The King of the Mudlarks has lost two of his children. The Heavy Horse, the Night Plunderers, the Light Horsemen, the Game Lightermen and the Lumpers have all been implicated. But they are not the killers. Anthony, if you would be so kind?"

Anthony St Ledger removed his large flat cap, did away with his neckerchief and leather stock, and stepped into the ring. He held up a manilla file and showed it to all four corners of the room.

"What my good friend has in his hand," said Judas, "are plans, paperwork, and other undeniable evidence. The paperwork tells a story of horror and of greed, but fortunately, the person responsible for setting this enterprise in motion is here with us tonight. This man ordered the killing of the Mudlark children, so as to pit the River Gangs against each other in a bloody civil war. When the killings and the bloodshed were finally over he was going to sweep in and relieve the remaining wounded of their territories."

A murmur of discontent swept through the crowd, and Judas saw the Mudlarks begin to push their way towards the ring. Scuffles began to break out and Judas realised he had misjudged how long he could hold the floor for.

"Who is he?!" roared the King of the Mudlarks.

"He has to face justice, my Lord, I can't just hand him over to you."

Judas felt the first stirrings of panic.

"Identify him and we shall go. If you refuse to give him up then we will take one of yours. Sergeant Lace will be our hostage," said the King.

Judas hadn't factored that in and he reacted without thinking.

"Touch one hair on my sergeant's head and you will regret it," he growled.

The King nodded. The look on his face was set.

"I expected you to do the right thing, Master of the Black Museum, but this creature will die today; it is inevitable. I cannot – and will not – allow him to walk free."

Adam had been trying to get further away from the ring ever since Judas had started to address the crowd. Initially, he had just wanted to put a lot of distance between himself and the device; now he had something else to worry about. He had managed to reach the gate and he fancied that he could slip through it unnoticed, but just as he thought he was through a hand with a grip of steel grabbed him by the scruff the neck. He was lifted off the ground and turned around.

"Lilith! he squeaked. "I've been searching for you, my love!"

Lilith raised one hand and slapped him across the face.

"Searching for me, Adam? I don't think so. You left me to die. Now it's your turn."

Lilith carried the whimpering Adam back to the ring and threw him down at Judas's feet.

"As requested, Judas," she said.

The King of the Mudlarks looked down at Adam.

"Is this the man?" he hissed.

Judas stepped between Adam and the King of the Mudlarks.

"Give me a minute, please, my Lord?" Judas pleaded.

The King performed the slightest of nods. Judas had a minute and that was all.

"This man is the head of a company called First Garden Creations. He's been murdering, bullying and extorting money and land from you all. He wants to take over the Under Folk, all of you. He wants a piece of everything you earn. He's been helped by the Sons of Colquhoun, who just so happen to be here tonight as well! Just over there!" he shouted.

The Sons were outnumbered and encircled. They knew their time was up and marched to the ring, where St Ledger and Sergeant Lace cuffed them quietly and quickly.

"So, here we have the master and servants, and the killers of the Gilded Goat. But there are two more that deserve justice here. Cat Tabby and Dick Whittington. They set up the fight, and they were heavily involved in First Garden Creations. The blood of many of the Under Folk is on their hands (and paws). Come forward, Cat Tabby, I know you're here!" said Judas.

But Cat Tabby was not there. He and Dick Whittington could not be found; neither could the gate money. The slippery feline must have guessed what was about to happen and run for it.

That was one problem that Judas could deal with in time; he didn't have that luxury with the Mudlarks, Adam, the Sons and First Garden Creations. His minute was up, and he had to make a choice between Sergeant Lace and Adam the first man.

"You may take him, my Lord. Do with him what you will."

The King raised a hand. The Sons were snatched from the ring, and Adam was dragged away. As he was pulled to his doom, Judas heard Adam laughing. It chilled him to the bone.

"Open the gates, Captain, it's all over now," said Judas.

He'd done a deal with the captain before the fight. The captain would use his powers to secure the Tower, and stop any of the culprits from escaping. His reward was a nice juicy piece of First Garden Creations' stock, just down the river from the Tower. The captain was thinking about relocating. But the captain did not reply, and the gates were not opened. Panic started to spread throughout the crowd. A stampede was near, and many would die if the gates were not opened. That was why Adam was laughing.

"Find the captain now!" he shouted.

Angel Dave and Sergeant Lace had been relieved of their prisoners by the Mudlarks, so they ran into the crowd to search for Blood but returned quickly, empty handed. Without the captain the gates would remain locked tight, and things were starting to turn ugly. The innkeepers had their wagons in the hall and the horses that pulled them were whinnying and neighing; they could sense the change in mood.

Some of the more opportunistic criminals had decided that a riot might be helpful and had started to topple some of the braziers over to help the stampede along. Valuables would be left behind in the rush and if they were in the right place at the right time, they'd make a fortune. Judas could smell the smoke now and he heard more and more screaming and crying. Fire had taken hold of the eastern side of the hall and the crowd had shifted to get away from it. Judas was starting to get very worried indeed when he felt hands pawing at him. He looked down, and was shocked to see two small figures wearing white silk hoods. Smoke had started to turn them grey, and their clothes were covered in soot.

"Come and see!" they shouted in unison.

"Now is not a good time my friends, look around you," he replied.

"Come and see, or you will die," they insisted, solemnly.

Judas allowed himself to be pulled through the crowd to a small unattended wagon. The two little people climbed up onto the tail gate and lifted a heavy tarpaulin to reveal a large wooden chest with its lid removed.

"What the!" Judas exclaimed.

"All dead very soon," said the little people.

"Dark magic device, very powerful, needs containing," they continued.

"Can you find the captain for me? Can you get him to unlock the gates?"

The two figures in what used to be white hoods nodded then disappeared, leaving Judas to gaze down at the brass bomb with glass tubes of purple liquid sticking out of it like a well-used hairbrush. God had given him the ability to heal and repair himself but there were thousands here that could not. And what of the White Tower above? That would all come tumbling down around their ears too.

"Blown to pieces and then crushed. Wonderful!" he said to himself as the hall descended into chaos.

The hall was full of black smoke now. Many of the crowd had already succumbed to the fumes and were laying where they fell. Fighting had broken out, and there was blood on the walls. Angel Dave and Sergeant Lace had returned, both showing the signs of combat, and St Ledger was unconscious. One of the thieves he had taken care of in the past had paid him back with a wooden chair over the head. It all looked very grim indeed. But then, the smoke began to clear, and a strong, cold breeze pushed it away. Judas looked ahead and saw that people and creatures were moving; one of the gates had been opened.

Captain Blood reappeared with the two little grey people in tow. They had found him bound and gagged inside a barrel. His imprisonment had made him a little tetchy.

"Sons of Colquhoun! They'll be the Dead Sons when I get my hands on them!"

Judas told him what had happened to the Sons and Captain Blood decided that his quarry was in good hands. Then he showed the captain what was in the chest.

"Captain, can you and the munchkins here get everybody out safe through the tunnels?"

The captain replied, "Of course, the gates are there for show really, we'll have everybody out in a trice."

And with that he raced away into the crowds with the

Faceless Twins, shouting orders and guiding all they found to secret doors and hatches.

Judas turned to Sergeant Lace and Angel Dave.

"Get that Golem and Murrell back to the Black Museum. I'll deal with this."

Angel Dave shook his head. He looked confused, and Judas thought it might be the smoke clouding his mind. But it wasn't. Angel Dave had made a decision. He could fly the bomb out of the hall through the light shaft in the ceiling and drop it into the Thames. In his mind it was easy, and it would work, so he flicked the inspector to one side with his wing, scooped up the device and took to the air.

"No!" shouted Judas.

But Angel Dave was already heading up the shaft, clutching the brass bomb to his chest. He shot out and into a black night sky alive with moonlight and stars. He angled his wings and made for the centre of the river. He wanted to drop it into the deepest part, just to be safe. He felt wonderful, and strong emotions and thoughts he had forgotten since the Second Fall coursed through him. It was good to be alive.

And then the device activated, and Angel Dave was no more.

39

THE LAST STOP

The Ley Line Express powered its way through the countryside. Onboard, Corineus had started to feel unwell. At first he thought it might be travel sickness, but he had covered half the globe this last month, and never suffered from more than hiccups. At the back of his mind a voice called out to him, telling him he knew what it was, but he ignored the voice and pretended to feel okay. The witch appeared again. She had been keeping an eye on him. Once, he had woken to find her sitting opposite him. He'd been taken by surprise and felt like asking her what she thought she was doing, but her presence was soothing.

She handed him an apple. It was green and had a small red flower where the stalk should be. She told him to eat it, that it would help him in the next few days. So he did, and fell back to sleep. He dreamed of Gogmagog and that fateful day, but there was not the usual revulsion and anger. It was like he was watching the fight from above, seeing the blows land but not feeling them.

When he opened his eyes again, the rushing world outside his window had calmed itself and was still. He could see green hills, shot through with white, seagulls coasting over them riding the breeze. Then he saw Mathey Trewells standing at the station with a huge smile on his weather-beaten face. The witch slid open the glass doors to the cabin and motioned with her head that he was to alight. He had no baggage save for his sack, so he stepped off the train and onto the platform. The witch handed him a small cloth bag, pulled the door closed, then the Ley Line Express pulled away.

"Still in one piece then, Corineus?" asked Mathey.

"Thanks to you and the Black Museum I am," he replied.

They walked up the hill together, slowly. The giant took in great gulps of the sea air and he smiled for the first time in a long time. When they reached the top of the hill, Corineus stopped for a second. He wanted to take it all in and hold it in his heart forever.

"There she is," said Mathey, pointing at the Zennor, which was moored up in the cove below.

"And there *she* is," said Corineus.

A figure could be seen swimming in the crystal clear water below. Half woman, half fish.

Corineus walked down the hill and when he reached the beach he removed his great boots and socks, and scrunched his toes in the sand. It felt incredible, and a tear came to his eye.

"There is your new home, my friend," said Mathey, pointing towards a cave opening.

Corineus followed him inside and for the second time in as many minutes a tear ran down his cheek. The cave had been transformed into a home. A vast bed sat in a stone alcove, and a table and chair fit for a giant rested in front of a fire that crackled and popped.

"This is a wonderful place to die in," said Corineus.

His friend kicked him in the ankle, hurting himself in the process.

"A good place to *live* my friend, for as long as that is. We will make it a good place to *live*. Now, cheer up and let's go swimming with my wife! She's been badgering me about you for days."

40

GOGMAGOG'S PRICE

ngel Dave's flat, halfway up Upper Street in the borough of Islington, was very neat and tidy. Judas sat in the angel's lounge with his head in his hands. He'd known what was going to happen but had been powerless to stop it. Angel Dave was gone, and it was his duty to see that any of the angel's belongings were given into the keeping and care of those that had loved him. Judas had been through his wardrobes, checked his post, and searched for anything that shouldn't be there. He'd discovered a couple of pieces of contraband, nothing serious, and removed them. Judas had packed the keepsakes and the objects of value, and sealed them away inside a carboard box. He'd spoken to Angel Dave's landlord and paid any fees outstanding. It was the least he could do. Now, all he had to do was wait for the leader of Angel Dave's order. He dreaded having the conversation. Dreaded telling the angel how one of his kin had died. He would place the box in his hands and apologise, knowing that the angel despised him.

When Judas returned to the Black Museum, he found Sergeant Lace and Anthony St Ledger waiting for him. They had performed well under pressure and together they had solved the murder of the Mudlarks. They also had Charles Murrell waiting in the Time Fields for his cell to be created for him. His Golem was walking the long path back to the East; it should get there in the next hundred years or so.

"Sergeant Lace, how would you like to be Detective Sergeant Lace?" asked Judas.

"I'd like that very much, sir. Thank you, sir," she replied.

"You've earned it, Lace, I'm lucky to have you. Now, you'll need to drop HR a line to accept the offer. Once you've done that, take the rest of the day off. Rest, see a bit of life."

The newly promoted Detective Sergeant Lace fired up her computer and started tapping the keys on her keyboard like she was possessed. It was good to see her smile.

"Anthony, I've spoken to Master Gander and he's agreed, reluctantly, to pay you for the job he employed you for. I managed to get him to increase your day rate a bit so don't look too surprised when he hands it over to you."

"That's very generous of you, sir. I thank you," said St Ledger.

"You've earned it, and as far as I'm concerned, we're straight, you don't owe me anything anymore. Gogmagog has put a price on Cat Tabby's head for stealing the money from the fight. He'll need someone to track him down, big reward. I'd volunteer if I were you."

Judas shook St Ledger's hand and the Thief Taker departed. When he turned to speak to Lace, her seat was empty.

Judas embraced the silence, took his silver coin from his pocket and used it to make the world go quiet. There was a ceremony to attend and some long overdue housekeeping to take care of.

41

SANS SINS

uxley Montague had turned into a curtain twitcher. Anyone that approached his mobile home on the Isle of Sheppey was subjected to a severe analysis. Judas however, had been welcomed with open arms, and after a rancid cup of tea, he'd escorted Huxley Montague to St. Mary's church in Battersea. In the grounds of this lovely old church is a tree, and under the tree, deep down in the earth is a stone table in a room the size of a monk's cell. The table used to stand in the gardens of another holy place, long since gone. It is here that Huxley Montague comes when he needs to release the sins he has consumed.

Judas has promised to stand guard at the door as Montague begins the ceremony, and sits with his back to the stone wall in the churchyard directly above them. The sun is shining, and the wall is warm. The grass is lush and Judas decides not to take his coin out but instead, just breathe and watch the world go by.

Montague appears some hours later. He looks happier,

brighter, and possibly even a bit lighter, but that might just be Judas's imagination.

"So, Huxley Montague, Sin Eater and caravan enthusiast. What's it to be?"

"I have many more sins to take on, Inspector. There is always a backlog, and my enforced holiday has not helped to reduce it. My thanks to you, Inspector, and I mourn Junior, he was a good man. I'm sorry he died because of me."

"I'll take care of Junior, don't worry about that. I must get on, do call into the Museum when you're about, and take care of yourself."

"Thank you once again, Inspector. Goodbye."

Judas watched Huxley walk away and turned back to the river. There was one last thing that needed attending to.

42

RIVER'S END

Henry and Constance had been laid to rest according to Mudlark tradition. No outsiders were allowed to attend the ceremony, so Judas had sent a letter to the King, offering his condolences and his sincere apologies that he had not been able to bring the murderers to justice more quickly. The fates of Adam and the Sons were as yet unknown. That they had suffered and could quite possibly still be suffering did not bother Judas in the slightest. He would not lose any sleep over them. Inside the letter were also the deeds to much of the land that First Garden Creations had stolen. This was to be used in any way the Mudlarks saw fit. The land would not bring the children back, but Judas hoped that it would in some way repair any damage between the Mudlarks and the Black Museum.

The River Gangs were also given a smaller share of the spoils; they had after all been implicated and had suffered the ignominy of association. Of Cat Tabby there was no news, but he was a bad penny, and he would turn up again, and when he did, Judas would make sure he was apprehended.

Judas sat in his chair and listened to the familiar creak as he leaned backwards. It had been a long, fraught few weeks, and he was exhausted. He looked up at the big map for the tenth time that day and tried counting the blue pins again, but gave up after twenty-eight. He was just about to put his coat on and leave for the weekend when he heard a tap at the window. He turned to find an angel dressed in the uniform of a well-known delivery company hanging in the air outside. In one hand was a letter, in the other was one of those digital pads that you're supposed to sign your name on, but succeed only in leaving a squiggle and the image of a badly drawn seagull instead.

Judas opened the window and received the letter. He signed his name, then watched the angel tap the pad to prove to head office that he had delivered it to the right person, and more importantly, on time. The angel flew off to complete his mail run and Judas took the letter back to his chair. He opened it. Inside was a ticket, a first class train ticket on the Ley Line Express. A slip of paper fell from the envelope and landed on his desk while he was studying it. Judas placed the ticket down on the desk and looked at the slip. On it was drawn the shape of a half moon.

The Witch was waiting, and instead of heading home, Judas headed to King's Cross Under instead.

43

THE END OF JUDAS

S imon, the Zealot, glided through the Black Museum on a cloud of his own self-importance and self-righteousness. He was the King of the Castle now, the Lord of the Manor, and any other titles he could bestow upon himself. His smile was broad, and there was a spring in his step. Judas, his hated overseer and relentless watchdog, was gone. Now was the moment. Simon had been hiding inside the Time Fields, learning its secrets and mapping its topography. Whatever anyone said about Simon, they could not deny that he was meticulous and as bent as a £9 note.

The Key Room was silent, even the annoying flicker and tink of the neon lighting tube on the ceiling was holding its breath, and the very fabric of the Black Museum felt tense. Simon had wandered its grand halls and journeyed as deep as he dared into its darkest regions in the short space of time that he had been imprisoned, and he had found the ideal place from which to plot his revenge on Judas.

The small piece of driftwood with its rusty red nail looked like a young child's attempt at making a sailboat. It floated, immobile, in the shadow of a vicious looking hack-saw. Simon had felt its pull as he scrutinised the objects that acted as keys to the private hells of the murderers and the inmates of the Black Museum. As soon as he had touched it, he had spied upon Judas many times and learned how to transport himself to these nightmarish holes; he felt the customary pull and experienced the familiar sensation of travelling.

When he reopened his eyes, he was back on a grey gravel beach. In the distance, he could see the young lady who liked to drown children. On this bleak and cold shore, she had taken her unholy death tally to 27. Those poor little souls had been held under the water here until the life had seeped away from them with the inevitable turn of the tide.

Now, the murderess was forced to walk along the beach with her head turned to the water. If she tried to look away, the beach just reappeared in front of her; whichever way she turned, there was the beach. She tried closing her eyes, but that did not work because as soon as she did, a fierce wind blew in from the ocean, and the salt it brought with it stung her body and caused her to scream.

Her only option was to look at the bloated white corpses of the children she had put to death. These were not the souls of the actual children, they were mere copies, and they screamed under the water and stared at her with such hatred that she had lost her mind – long ago.

Simon paid her no notice and walked past her, he was heading further down the beach, around the headland, and in the space, between two great rocks, there was a cave. It smelt of dead seaweed and bird waste, and this was his destination. Once inside, Simon searched behind a rock at the back of the cave and found the crude torch he had made from brittle sticks and discarded feathers. He removed a lighter from his pocket and flicked it twice. On the second attempt, the torch flared into life and cast a crooked shadow against the wall—his shadow.

Simon thrust the torch out in front of him and searched for the opening of the passage he had discovered weeks before, it was not a vast cave, and he found it quickly. The air was fetid, and it stung his nostrils, but he pressed on, and after 20 paces, he found the boxes he had stashed there.

In one box was a small folding table, which he set up first, then he removed the storm lantern that he had liberated from the office. It would not be missed; he had seen to that. He pumped the tiny gas pump set into the metal canister at the lamp's base, and once he was satisfied that there was enough pressure, he opened the valve, heard the hiss of the gas, and then flicked the lighter more.

The flame cuddled the wick, and then there was light. Simon extinguished the torch he carried in the wet sand beneath his feet; he would make sure to take it back to its hiding place when he left. The space he had chosen for his own Key Room was small, windowless, and very hard to find – precisely what he was looking for. If Judas ever found this place, Simon deserved to fail.

At the bottom of the second box was a camp chair, he unfolded it and set it beside the table, and then he sat down. In his pocket, wrapped in a rag he had found, was the silver cufflink that he had stolen from the place where the Women of the Chapel had taken their revenge against Jack the Ripper. He had felt the surge of energy as soon as he had touched it, he'd almost dropped it straight away, and the shock of the cold and negativity that coursed through it had surprised him.

But Simon knew that if he had any chance of destroying Judas and escaping from this awful place, he needed an ally, and the only entity he deemed capable of helping him succeed was Jack the Ripper. Simon unwrapped the cufflink and set it down on the centre of the table. He saw his twisted face reflected in the silver and recoiled. There was something odd about how the light rippled across the cufflink; it slithered and made him feel nervous.

Simon reached out to touch it but held his hand just above the object. He had committed to bringing about the fall of The Betrayer, and if his plan went the way he hoped, then maybe, John the Baptist could be rescued? With Jack the Ripper on one side and John on the other, maybe, just maybe, it would work.

Simon bit his lip, took a deep breath, and then picked up the cufflink and closed his hand around it. From far away, he heard a scream, followed by laughter.

AFTERWORD

If you've enjoyed this book, please consider leaving a brief review of it on the Amazon website. Even a few positive words make a huge difference to independent authors like me, so I'd be both delighted and grateful if you were to share your appreciation.

Many thanks, Martin

ABOUT THE AUTHOR

Martin Davey is the author of the Black Museum series of novels featuring the world's most unlikely and misunderstood hero – DCI Judas Iscariot. The Murder of the Mudlarks is the 5th full-length novel in the series.

Martin studied at the prestigious Central St. Martins School of Art in London. After graduating, he worked in advertising agencies in London, New York, Barcelona, and Amsterdam. He has also worked on a speedboat on the Costa Del Crime. These days he can be found in Tunbridge Wells with his wife and two children. He is a proud member of the James Bond Fan Club with his own 'oo' number and is a serial collector of unusual experiences.

Please find out more at judasthehero.me

facebook.com/martindaveyauthor

instagram.com/martdaveyauthor

ALSO BY MARTIN DAVEY

Judas the Hero

The Children of the Lightning

Oliver Twisted

The Blind Beak of Bow Street

The Curious Case of Cat Tabby

The Death of the Black Museum

Printed in Great Britain
by Amazon

23969689R00169